PATRICIA WENTWORTH
WILL O' THE WISP

PATRICIA WENTWORTH was born Dora Amy Elles in India in 1877 (not 1878 as has sometimes been stated). She was first educated privately in India, and later at Blackheath School for Girls. Her first husband was George Dillon, with whom she had her only child, a daughter. She also had two stepsons from her first marriage, one of whom died in the Somme during World War I.

Her first novel was published in 1910, but it wasn't until the 1920's that she embarked on her long career as a writer of mysteries. Her most famous creation was Miss Maud Silver, who appeared in 32 novels, though there were a further 33 full-length mysteries not featuring Miss Silver—the entire run of these is now reissued by Dean Street Press.

Patricia Wentworth died in 1961. She is recognized today as one of the pre-eminent exponents of the classic British golden age mystery novel.

By Patricia Wentworth

The Benbow Smith Mysteries
Fool Errant
Danger Calling
Walk with Care
Down Under

The Frank Garrett Mysteries
Dead or Alive
Rolling Stone

The Ernest Lamb Mysteries
The Blind Side
Who Pays the Piper?
Pursuit of a Parcel

Standalones
The Astonishing Adventure of Jane Smith
The Red Lacquer Case
The Annam Jewel
The Black Cabinet
The Dower House Mystery
The Amazing Chance
Hue and Cry
Anne Belinda
Will-o'-the-Wisp
Beggar's Choice
The Coldstone
Kingdom Lost
Nothing Venture
Red Shadow
Outrageous Fortune
Touch and Go
Fear by Night
Red Stefan
Blindfold
Hole and Corner
Mr. Zero
Run!
Weekend with Death
Silence in Court

PATRICIA WENTWORTH

WILL O' THE WISP

With an introduction by
Curtis Evans

DEAN STREET PRESS

Introduction

BRITISH AUTHOR Patricia Wentworth published her first novel, a gripping tale of desperate love during the French Revolution entitled *A Marriage under the Terror*, a little over a century ago, in 1910. The book won first prize in the Melrose Novel Competition and was a popular success in both the United States and the United Kingdom. Over the next five years Wentworth published five additional novels, the majority of them historical fiction, the best-known of which today is *The Devil's Wind* (1912), another sweeping period romance, this one set during the Sepoy Mutiny (1857-58) in India, a region with which the author, as we shall see, had extensive familiarity. Like *A Marriage under the Terror*, *The Devil's Wind* received much praise from reviewers for its sheer storytelling élan. One notice, for example, pronounced the novel "an achievement of some magnitude" on account of "the extraordinary vividness...the reality of the atmosphere...the scenes that shift and move with the swiftness of a moving picture...." (*The Bookman*, August 1912) With her knack for spinning a yarn, it perhaps should come as no surprise that Patricia Wentworth during the early years of the Golden Age of mystery fiction (roughly from 1920 into the 1940s) launched upon her own mystery-writing career, a course charted most successfully for nearly four decades by the prolific author, right up to the year of her death in 1961.

Considering that Patricia Wentworth belongs to the select company of Golden Age mystery writers with books which have remained in print in every decade for nearly a century now (the centenary of Agatha Christie's first mystery, *The Mysterious Affair at Styles*, is in 2020; the centenary of Wentworth's first mystery, *The Astonishing Adventure of Jane Smith*, follows merely three years later, in 2023), relatively little is known about the author herself. It appears, for example, that even the widely given year of Wentworth's birth, 1878, is incorrect. Yet it is sufficiently clear that Wentworth lived a varied and intriguing life that provided her ample inspiration for a writing career devoted to imaginative fiction.

It is usually stated that Patricia Wentworth was born Dora Amy Elles on 10 November 1878 in Mussoorie, India, during the heyday of the British Raj; however, her Indian birth and baptismal record states that she in fact was born on 15 October 1877 and was baptized on 26 November of that same year in Gwalior. Whatever doubts surround her actual birth year, however, unquestionably the future author came from a prominent Anglo-Indian military family. Her father, Edmond Roche Elles, a son of Malcolm Jamieson Elles, a Porto, Portugal wine merchant originally from Ardrossan, Scotland, entered the British Royal Artillery in 1867, a decade before Wentworth's birth, and first saw service in India during the Lushai Expedition of 1871-72. The next year Elles in India wed Clara Gertrude Rothney, daughter of Brigadier-General Octavius Edward Rothney, commander of the Gwalior District, and Maria (Dempster) Rothney, daughter of a surgeon in the Bengal Medical Service. Four children were born of the union of Edmond and Clara Elles, Wentworth being the only daughter.

Before his retirement from the army in 1908, Edmond Elles rose to the rank of lieutenant-general and was awarded the KCB (Knight Commander of the Order of Bath), as was the case with his elder brother, Wentworth's uncle, Lieutenant-General Sir William Kidston Elles, of the Bengal Command. Edmond Elles also served as Military Member to the Council of the Governor-General of India from 1901 to 1905. Two of Wentworth's brothers, Malcolm Rothney Elles and Edmond Claude Elles, served in the Indian Army as well, though both of them died young (Malcolm in 1906 drowned in the Ganges Canal while attempting to rescue his orderly, who had fallen into the water), while her youngest brother, Hugh Jamieson Elles, achieved great distinction in the British Army. During the First World War he catapulted, at the relatively youthful age of 37, to the rank of brigadier-general and the command of the British Tank Corps, at the Battle of Cambrai personally leading the advance of more than 350 tanks against the German line. Years later Hugh Elles also played a major role in British civil defense during the Second World War. In the event of a German invasion of Great Britain, something which seemed all too possible in 1940, he was tasked with leading the defense of southwestern England. Like Sir Edmond and Sir William,

Hugh Elles attained the rank of lieutenant-general and was awarded the KCB.

Although she was born in India, Patricia Wentworth spent much of her childhood in England. In 1881 she with her mother and two younger brothers was at Tunbridge Wells, Kent, on what appears to have been a rather extended visit in her ancestral country; while a decade later the same family group resided at Blackheath, London at Lennox House, domicile of Wentworth's widowed maternal grandmother, Maria Rothney. (Her eldest brother, Malcolm, was in Bristol attending Clifton College.) During her years at Lennox House, Wentworth attended Blackheath High School for Girls, then only recently founded as "one of the first schools in the country to give girls a proper education" (*The London Encyclopaedia*, 3rd ed., p. 74). Lennox House was an ample Victorian villa with a great glassed-in conservatory running all along the back and a substantial garden--most happily, one presumes, for Wentworth, who resided there not only with her grandmother, mother and two brothers, but also five aunts (Maria Rothney's unmarried daughters, aged 26 to 42), one adult first cousin once removed and nine first cousins, adolescents like Wentworth herself, from no less than three different families (one Barrow, three Masons and five Dempsters); their parents, like Wentworth's father, presumably were living many miles away in various far-flung British dominions. Three servants--a cook, parlourmaid and housemaid--were tasked with serving this full score of individuals.

Sometime after graduating from Blackheath High School in the mid-1890s, Wentworth returned to India, where in a local British newspaper she is said to have published her first fiction. In 1901 the 23-year-old Wentworth married widower George Fredrick Horace Dillon, a 41-year-old lieutenant-colonel in the Indian Army with three sons from his prior marriage. Two years later Wentworth gave birth to her only child, a daughter named Clare Roche Dillon. (In some sources it is erroneously stated that Clare was the offspring of Wentworth's second marriage.) However in 1906, after just five years of marriage, George Dillon died suddenly on a sea voyage, leaving Wentworth with sole responsibility for her three teenaged stepsons and baby daughter. A very short span of years, 1904 to 1907, saw the deaths of Wentworth's husband, mother, grandmother and brothers Malcolm and Edmond, removing much of her support network. In 1908, however, her father, who was now sixty years old, retired from the army and returned to England, settling at Guildford, Surrey with an older unmarried sister named Dora (for whom his daughter presumably had been named). Wentworth joined this household as well, along with her daughter and her youngest stepson. Here in Surrey Wentworth, presumably with the goal of making herself financially independent for the first time in her life (she was now in her early thirties), wrote the novel that changed the course of her life, *A Marriage under the Terror*, for the first time we know of utilizing her famous *nom de plume*.

The burst of creative energy that resulted in Wentworth's publication of six novels in six years suddenly halted after the appearance of *Queen Anne Is Dead* in 1915. It seems not unlikely that the Great War impinged in various ways on her writing. One tragic episode was the death on the western front of one of her stepsons, George Charles Tracey Dillon. Mining in Colorado when war was declared, young Dillon worked his passage from Galveston, Texas to Bristol, England as a shipboard muleteer (mule-tender) and joined the Gloucestershire Regiment. In 1916 he died at the Somme at the age of 29 (about the age of Wentworth's two brothers when they had passed away in India).

A couple of years after the conflict's cessation in 1918, a happy event occurred in Wentworth's life when at Frimley, Surrey she wed George Oliver Turnbull, up to this time a lifelong bachelor who like the author's first husband was a lieutenant-colonel in the Indian Army. Like his bride now forty-two years old, George Turnbull as a younger man had distinguished himself for his athletic prowess, playing forward for eight years for the Scottish rugby team and while a student at the Royal Military Academy winning the medal awarded the best athlete of his term. It seems not unlikely that Turnbull played a role in his wife's turn toward writing mystery fiction, for he is said to have strongly supported Wentworth's career, even assisting her in preparing manuscripts for publication. In 1936 the couple in Camberley, Surrey built Heatherglade House, a large two-story structure on substantial grounds, where they resided until Wentworth's death a quarter of a century later. (George Turnbull survived his wife by nearly a decade, passing away in 1970 at the age of 92.) This highly successful middle-aged companionate marriage contrasts sharply with the more youthful yet rocky union of Agatha and Archie Christie, which was three years away from sundering when Wentworth published *The Astonishing Adventure of Jane Smith* (1923), the first of her sixty-five mystery novels.

Although Patricia Wentworth became best-known for her cozy tales of the criminal investigations of consulting detective Miss Maud Silver, one of the mystery genre's most prominent spinster sleuths, in truth the Miss Silver tales account for just under half of Wentworth's 65 mystery novels. Miss Silver did not make her debut until 1928 and she did not come to predominate in Wentworth's fictional criminous output until the 1940s. Between 1923 and 1945 Wentworth published 33 mystery novels without Miss Silver, a handsome and substantial legacy in and of itself to vintage crime fiction fans. Many of these books are standalone tales of mystery, but nine of them have series characters. Debuting in the novel *Fool Errant* in 1929, a year after Miss Silver first appeared in print, was the enigmatic, nautically-named *eminence grise* Benbow Collingwood Horatio Smith, owner of a most expressively opinionated parrot named Ananias (and quite a colorful character in his own right). Benbow Smith went on to appear in three additional Wentworth mysteries: *Danger Calling* (1931), *Walk with Care* (1933) and *Down Under* (1937). Working in tandem with Smith in the investigation of sinister affairs threatening the security of Great Britain in *Danger Calling* and *Walk with Care* is Frank Garrett, Head of Intelligence for the Foreign Office, who also appears solo in *Dead or Alive* (1936) and *Rolling Stone* (1940) and collaborates with additional series characters, Scotland Yard's Inspector Ernest Lamb and Sergeant Frank Abbott, in *Pursuit of a Parcel* (1942). Inspector Lamb and Sergeant Abbott headlined a further pair of mysteries, *The Blind Side* (1939) and *Who Pays the Piper?* (1940), before they became absorbed, beginning with *Miss Silver Deals with Death* (1943), into the burgeoning Miss Silver canon. Lamb would make his farewell appearance in 1955 in *The Listening Eye*, while Abbott would take his final bow in mystery fiction with Wentworth's last published novel, *The Girl in the Cellar* (1961), which went into print the year of the author's death at the age of 83.

The remaining two dozen Wentworth mysteries, from the fantastical *The Astonishing Adventure of Jane Smith* in 1923 to the intense legal drama *Silence in Court* in 1945, are, like the author's series novels, highly imaginative and entertaining tales of mystery and adventure, told by a writer gifted with a consummate flair for storytelling. As one confirmed Patricia Wentworth mystery fiction addict, American Golden Age mystery writer Todd Downing, admiringly declared in the 1930s, "There's something about Miss Wentworth's yarns that is contagious." This attractive new series of Patricia Wentworth reissues by Dean Street Press provides modern fans of vintage mystery a splendid opportunity to catch the Wentworth fever.

Curtis Evans

Chapter One

THE TELEPHONE BELL rang again. David Fordyce looked up from the plan of an Elizabethan manor-house into which Mrs. Homer-Halliday insisted that a minimum of four bathrooms should be intruded. He frowned a black frown, said a sharp word, and put the receiver to his ear.

A cough came to him along the line, the deprecatory cough which was part of Miss Editha St. Kern's social equipment.

"Is Mr. David—is Mr. Fordyce—is this Mr. David Fordyce's office?"

"David speaking. Good-morning, Aunt Editha."

"Oh, David, dear boy, how nice to get you at once! Clerks are so stupid. I suppose they can't hear me, can they? Did you say 'No'?"

"I said 'No.' Did you want anything, Aunt Editha?"

"I always wondered if they could hear. It's so nice to feel that they can't, and that our little conversations are quite private. It gives one such a different feeling—doesn't it?"

David jabbed the pencil that he was holding into an unoffending piece of blotting-paper. The point of the pencil broke. He scowled.

"Anything I can do for you, Aunt Editha?"

"For me? No, dear boy. I shouldn't *dream*. In office hours, too, when we all know that time is money!"

"Well, I am rather busy. So if there isn't anything—"

"Nothing. No, no, nothing at all—that is, nothing for me. I only rang up to make sure that you remembered—not, of course, that you *would* forget, but just to make sure."

"Yes?"

"By the way, you received my little greeting? No, no, it's nothing at all—just the veriest trifle, just to show you that you are remembered. And of course I ought to have begun by wishing you many, many happy returns of the day."

David jabbed with the broken pencil. This time the wood splintered.

"Thank you, Aunt Editha." The voice was not a thankful one.

"No, no, dear boy, it's nothing—really nothing. And I only rang up just to say how I am looking forward to seeing you this afternoon."

"This afternoon?"

"Dear Grandmamma's little gathering—so delightful! She's looking forward to it so much. Fancy, she has had twenty-five presents, and fifty-three cards and letters, which makes *several* more than last year. Delightful—isn't it? I've been helping to lay out the presents for this afternoon—quite like a wedding. But I mustn't keep you. We shall meet anon, and I mustn't be tempted to tell you beforehand of a delightful *surprise. Good*-bye."

David jammed the receiver back on its hook, flung the broken pencil across the room, and picked up another. He became absorbed in bathrooms. His dark face relaxed.

The telephone bell rang.

When he had snatched the receiver, his sister Betty's voice, its slightly plaintive quality enhanced by the telephone, came faintly to his ear. Betty was always maddeningly indistinct.

"David, is that you? Oh, thank goodness! I've had three wrong numbers. I *am* speaking up."

"You're not—you never do. What do you want?"

"Just to remind you—" Her voice trailed away and was not.

"Look here," said David viciously, "if you're reminding me that Grandmamma and I have our joint birthday to-day, and that there's the usual damnable show on, you're a bit late with it."

Betty's voice came on again, suddenly loud:

"Am I? David, are you there?"

"Yes—I wish I wasn't."

"You *are* coming, aren't you? Why did you say I was late?"

"Because Grandmamma's maid rang me up whilst I was having my bath, and Milly had been trying to get on for half an hour before I got to office, and then I had Aunt Mary for a quarter of an hour, and Aunt Editha for about twenty minutes. I'm now going to smash the telephone."

"David!"

David rang off.

In about half a minute the bell was clattering again.

"What is it?" said David ferociously.

Betty's faint accents wavered on the wire:

"David—I thought you'd better know beforehand—"

"What is it? You know I've got some work to do. Millionairesses who are clamouring for bathrooms don't like being kept waiting."

"No. David, I won't keep you; but I really do think you ought to know—" Something inaudible just tickled his ear, but conveyed no meaning. Then he distinguished the word "coming."

"For the Lord's sake speak up!"

"I am. I thought you ought to know she was coming."

"Who is coming?"

"I told you."

"I keep telling you I can't hear a word you say."

"Eleanor," said Betty on a sudden burst of sound. "She crossed yesterday, and the Aunts collected her and got her to promise to come this afternoon. And I thought you'd rather know beforehand, and not have them all thinking you were turning red, or turning pale, or something, when you weren't."

David burst into a roar of laughter.

"I shall turn puce and writhe on the carpet. Aunt Mary can pour coffee all over my front, and Aunt Editha can put hot scones on the back of my neck."

"David!" said Betty Lester.

David rang off.

So this was Aunt Editha's "delightful surprise." He pictured her romantic mind dwelling fondly upon his meeting with Eleanor. The whole Family was doubtless in a state of pleasurable anticipation.

Seven years ago Eleanor Rayne had been Eleanor Fordyce. A convenient cousinship had thrown together two handsome and impressionable creatures. Result, an engagement so imprudent as to bring the Family about their ears, and to some purpose. David, then two-and-twenty, was sent to America to complete his training as an architect, whilst Eleanor sailed in the opposite direction to visit a convenient uncle in India.

In India she met and married Cosmo Rayne, who after six bitter years had left her widowed. She and David had not met since that final interview when heart-broken youth had taken what it most certainly believed to be a final farewell of happiness.

David looked back curiously across the seven years. It seemed so extraordinarily far away—all that passionate emotion; Eleanor's dark beauty frozen into dumb white misery; the tears through which he had last beheld her. It was all distinct in his memory; but it was like a photograph—lifeless, flat, and devoid of colour or interest. Betty's warning had been well meant but quite unnecessary. Betty always meant well—and she was very often unnecessary.

David felt himself capable of meeting Eleanor with the utmost cheerfulness and detachment. As they were cousins, he thought he would probably kiss her. He felt that to kiss Eleanor under the eyes of the assembled Family would add zest to Grandmamma's birthday party; it would make it go; it would give the Family something to talk about for months.

He laughed, and returned to the Elizabethan manor-house.

Chapter Two

MRS. FORDYCE'S BIRTHDAY was an Event. Six months in the year led up to it. During those months Miss Editha St. Kern, her sister, Miss Mary Fordyce, her daughter, and, in a lesser degree, the rest of the Family, were engaged in preparing for Grandmamma's birthday. For the remainder of the year it provided them with a topic of conversation and matter either for congratulation or regret. They dated other events by it. Queen Victoria, for instance, died "just after Grandmamma's birthday." There was a dreadful year when Grandmamma could not have her birthday party because she was not well. And there was another year spoken of in hushed tones as "the time when David forgot."

David's aunts would certainly never let him forget again. "And his own birthday too! How *could* he!" they murmured to one another.

Not one in the Family had any idea of how much David had always resented this communal birthday. Other little boys had birthdays of their own, but David had only the leavings of Grandmamma's birthday, and the birthday party was most indisputably not David's at all; it was a mere clutter of aunts, uncles, cousins, and adoring friends, grouped about Grandmamma. David's portion, of best clothes, scrubbed hands, and company behaviour, was one which he found extremely little to his taste.

Mrs. Fordyce lived very comfortably in an old-fashioned house in an old-fashioned London square. The drawing-room in which she was receiving her guests was a good-sized L-shaped room with windows on both sides of it. Curtains of olive-green plush had been drawn across these windows, and two chandeliers, each containing five unshaded lights, flared brightly down upon the faded Brussels carpet and the rather startling new chair-covers which were Miss Editha's birthday present. The covers, made by Miss Editha herself, displayed portions of an enormous pattern of blue, crimson, and purple peonies upon a green background. "So bright, dear," as Miss Editha said when she presented them.

Mrs. Fordyce sat in an upright padded chair by the fire. She had the large nose and very bright blue eyes of some famous military commanders; her mouth was set in firm though not unpleasant lines; and she was inordinately proud of the fact that her teeth were all her own. She wore, upon a stiffly upright frame, a dress of handsome black brocade surmounted by a purple silk sports coat. Her bony fingers supported an extraordinary number of aged, valuable, and very dirty rings. And her own white hair was completely hidden by a coal-black transformation of most forbidding aspect.

Her sister Editha and her daughter Mary remained standing. Miss Editha plump, untidy, in grey silk, with floating wisps of snow-white hair and trailing scarves of blue and pink chiffon. And Miss Mary very little, timid, and thin in the snuffy sagging black which she wore year in, year out, and which never seemed to vary in age or date. She was just twenty years younger than her mother, and so nearly of an age with Miss Editha that she had never called her Aunt. Both ladies habitually spoke of Mrs. Fordyce as Grandmamma.

The first guest to arrive was the Family's latest recruit, Julie, Frank Alderey's newly acquired wife—Julie, rather nervously aware of being the first to arrive and of having to explain to Frank's great-aunts that Frank would certainly be late.

Miss Editha enveloped her in billowy arms and flowing bits of chiffon.

"Dear Julie! But where is Frank? But no, I mustn't keep you from Grandmamma. Tell her, and I shall hear."

Julie was handed on to Miss Mary, who touched her hand with small cold fingers.

"Grandmamma is waiting," she murmured; and Julie turned to Mrs. Fordyce.

Did she kiss Frank's great-aunt, or did she not? She paused for a lead, her hand extended, her pretty little head just tilted so as to be ready if an embrace were offered.

Mrs. Fordyce kept her hands folded in her lap and gazed intently at Julie's knees. Julie's skirt cleared them by half an inch. They were quite pretty knees. But Mrs. Fordyce did not look at them with admiration; she just looked at them until Julie, crimson, burst into speech:

"How do you do, Aunt Anna? And—many happy returns of the day—and—Frank is so dreadfully sorry not to—I mean he's been kept—I mean he's so dreadfully sorry—I mean he was coming with me, only just as I was starting, he telephoned to say someone had come in to see him on some very important business, and he asked me to tell you how sorry he was, and to say he'd come as quickly as he possibly could, and to wish you many happy returns from him."

Julie had a pretty, eager way of talking. She looked a good deal like a little girl who has been put up to say her piece. All the time she was saying it, and for a long half-minute afterwards, Mrs. Fordyce continued to look fixedly at the pretty knees, which, in their flesh-coloured stockings, might almost have been bare. At the end of half a minute she said, "Thank you," in a deep, dry voice, and Milly March came in, hot in spite of the January cold, panting from the stairs, full of voluble conversation and loud cheery laughter, with her hat on the back of her head and a rustling paper parcel in her outstretched hands.

Julie faded thankfully into a corner and watched the Family arrive. What a frightful lot of relations Frank had! They were all nice, of course—Julie was a friendly little soul—but there were such a lot of them, and it was so confusing to have them all calling Mrs. Fordyce "Grandmamma." She wondered whether she ought to have said "Grandmamma" instead of "Aunt Anna." Milly March, who was exactly the same relation as Frank, was saying "Grandmamma"; and so was Miss Fordyce, though she was really her daughter; and so was old Mr. St. Clair St. Kern, though he was her brother. It was really dreadful of Frank to have made her come by herself; she was quite sure to do the wrong thing.

She told David so when he had greeted Grandmamma and drifted into her corner.

"Where's that blighter Frank? Don't tell me he's shirked!"

"No—he's coming. No, David, he really is. No, he really couldn't help it. Oh, David, that's too bad! He really *couldn't*."

David's sister Betty came in as Julie spoke. Her high voice with its plaintive note could be heard quite easily above all the other voices.

Betty Lester was older than her brother. She was neither like David nor like her own name. Betty suited her as little as Elizabeth; she had not the smooth curves of the one, or the massive dignity of the other. She was thin with the modern thinness, and pale with the modern pallor, the lack of bloom accentuated by the carmine which she had freely applied to her lips; her spine sagged in the mannequin bend; her fleshless legs were revealed to the knee. She looked so immature in the distance that the nearer view was apt to come as a shock.

Julie watched her embrace Mrs. Fordyce, and turned indignantly to David.

"Her skirt's as short as mine!"

"Is it?"

"I mean she—Aunt Anna—she looked—no, really *glared* at my knees. Why didn't she look at Betty's?"

"I don't know," said David, laughing. "Perhaps she liked yours better."

"She didn't! I tell you she *glared*. Frank oughtn't to have made me come here alone. Or do you think it wasn't the knees? I called her Aunt Anna. Do you think it was because of that? Ought I to have said Grandmamma? Everybody seems to. But she *is* Frank's great-aunt. David, I don't think you need laugh at me like that."

"I like laughing at you," said David, who thought Frank a very lucky fellow. He liked to see Julie all pink and breathless. He liked

Julie herself, with her eager voice and the quick movements which the Aunts considered a little too quick. "Dear Julie is rather unformed—a trifle gauche," had been Aunt Editha's verdict.

"They make me so nervous," said Julie in a whisper. "And when I'm nervous I do the wrong thing."

She looked up at David's teasing eyes and then down again. And quite suddenly David was reminded of Erica. He thought of her so seldom now that his thoughts of her were dim and unfamiliar, just stirring in the deeply shadowed places of memory. This was a different thought; it was so sharp and vivid that it hurt.

It was Julie who reminded him. She was slipping off her gloves, and for a moment she stopped to look sideways at her left hand with Frank's ring on it. It was this look that brought Erica back—Erica looking at her ring, her new wedding ring—Erica looking sideways— Erica, not Julie. It was only just for an instant; but it hurt, because Erica had been so young and she had never had any happy times; it hurt, because he had meant to make her happy.

"Hullo, David!" said Betty.

The Charles Aldereys had taken her place by Grandmamma's chair. Mrs. Charles stout and beaming, and the three Alderey girls, pretty, gushing, and arrayed in remnants snatched from the sales and boasted of as tokens of prowess.

Betty looked down her long nose at them and said plaintively:

"It's the first birthday Dick has missed. I do think schools are inconsiderate. I did think they'd let me have him up for the afternoon. But they simply wouldn't; they said he'd only just gone back—as if that had anything to do with it! I do think they might have some consideration for Grandmamma, if not for me!"

"Too bad!" said Julie.

Betty just trailed on.

"They simply make one's life a burden to one with their rules. You wait till you've got boys, and then you'll know what it is. I believe they do it on purpose, just to show parents that they don't mean to take any notice of them."

Julie put up her hand to screen a foolish hot cheek.

"Who's that?" she said.

The room had been filling fast; one could hardly see Miss Editha's bright new chair-covers for relations. The St. Clair St. Kerns, Grandmamma's contemporaries, with a stout unmarried son and a thin unmarried daughter, Marches, Aldereys, and more St. Kerns, sat, stood, or moved in a space that became every moment more crowded. One by one they greeted Grandmamma and passed on, telling one another how wonderful she was.

At the moment that Julie said "Who's that?" there was a lull in the buzz of talk because, like Julie, everyone was looking at the door, which had just opened.

Julie saw a tall woman in black stand for a moment on the threshold. With a quick, warm admiration she forgot Betty's chatter and said:

"Who's that?"

David looked across the crowd and saw Eleanor Rayne. To his surprise his heart beat a little faster. She was thinner; she looked taller. She wore black, but it did not look like mourning. India, or grief, had robbed her of her lovely bloom, but without it she was more beautiful than he remembered. There was something proud and sweet about the way she looked; there was a sad enchantment in her smile, which outweighed the loss of curve and colour.

She met David's eyes. The smile deepened in her own. She stepped into the room, and David saw that she was wearing violets, the large pale double violets which smell so sweet.

Miss Editha's embrace engulfed her.

"Dear Eleanor!"—three rapid kisses—"My dearest girl, how delightful to see you again! But I mustn't keep you—no, not a moment—Grandmamma first. And—yes, just one word with Aunt Mary. Mary, dearest, isn't this delightful? But we mustn't keep her."

"I'll come back."

David caught the deep, grave tone. Eleanor's voice at least had not altered. It gave him an odd sensation.

"Grandmamma"—this was Miss Editha again—"isn't this too delightful? Here's Eleanor."

"H'm," said Mrs. Fordyce.

Her hands, with the rings all crooked, were lying on the arms of her padded chair. It was upholstered in dark maroon; the deep colour made her hands look very white, the veins on them dark and knotted. She lifted the right hand now, touched Eleanor's glove with it, and gave her a little push.

"Scent!" she said. "Out!"

She withdrew the hand, covered her mouth with it, and coughed.

"Mary—" She coughed again.

Eleanor stood before her, still smiling but a little bewildered.

"It's my flowers, Grandmamma—my violets. Don't you like violets?"

"Grandmamma doesn't care for flowers," murmured Miss Mary.

"Scent!" said Grandmamma, and coughed again.

A shocked Miss Editha took Eleanor by the arm.

"My dearest girl! Had you forgotten? Grandmamma can't endure flowers—not scented ones. We *never* have them. Are they fastened with a pin?" Her fingers moved about the bunch. "My dear, perhaps if you—I don't seem to—oh, my dear, take them off *quickly*!"

Eleanor unfastened the diamond arrow which held her violets. With the bunch in her hand, she looked at David. There was a little colour in her cheeks, and a hint of laughter in her eyes.

He came out of his corner.

"How d'you do, Eleanor?" he said; and Grandmamma stopped coughing.

An interested Family gave them its whole attention.

"I'm so sorry," said Eleanor. "I'd forgotten." She spoke to Mrs. Fordyce. "David will take them away. I'm so sorry I forgot—it was stupid of me."

She put the violets into David's hand. He touched her glove, and violet leaves, and stalks just faintly damp. And then she was kissing Grandmamma, and Miss Editha was sighing with relief.

The violets smelt very sweet.

Chapter Three

A LITTLE GILT CHAIR, very upright in the back and rather narrow in the seat, stood in the corner between Grandmamma's chair and the fire. When Mrs. Fordyce singled out one of the Family for conversation, Miss Mary would indicate this fragile seat. When Mrs. Fordyce had had enough of anyone's society, she had only to glance at her daughter, and Miss Mary would murmur in her little mousey voice: "I think, dear, if you don't mind, perhaps Grandmamma has talked enough."

Eleanor was sitting on the little gilt chair when David came back into the room after leaving the violets in the hall. He came across to his old corner and stood there propped against the wall. He could see Mrs. Fordyce in profile, and he could see Eleanor.

She was much more graceful than Eleanor Fordyce had been. Her black was black velvet—a coat and skirt; the coat open to show something white and the sparkle of a diamond brooch. She leaned forward a little and spoke low. But, low as she spoke, David found himself hearing what she said. Grandmamma was putting her through a catechism.

"I thought he died in the spring. I believe Editha told me that your husband died in the spring."

Then Eleanor's answer:

"No, it was December—December last year."

Mrs. Fordyce looked with intention at the little twinkling diamond brooch.

"I'm sure Editha told me it was the spring, and that you didn't come home at once on account of the heat."

"No, Grandmamma, it was December."

"Then why didn't you come home?" Mrs. Fordyce's fingers tapped impatiently on the padded arm of her chair.

"I stayed to settle things up, and then to pay some visits. And then I went into Kashmir with a friend. I had always wanted to go."

Mrs. Fordyce coughed dryly.

"Mourning used to be a time for seclusion," she said. "Times change." She coughed again, "Weeds for a year, and black for a year, and half-mourning for another year, was the least that was expected of a widow—the very least. I remember very well that I decided to drop Marion Craddock's acquaintance when I saw her wearing jet wheat-ears in her bonnet eighteen months after George Craddock's death." She looked again at the twinkling brooch.

"Mourning is just a fashion. Don't you think so, Grandmamma? One does what other people do, but it doesn't make any difference to what one feels."

"Ah!" said Mrs. Fordyce. "That's the modern way of talking. It's very convenient, my dear—h'm—no doubt." She put up her hand and coughed again. "You've all got such deep feelings that you don't require what used to be considered decent observance. H'm—no—that's not required. But there's this to be said for the old way: all the world can see a black dress. They can't see your thoughts, and I'd be very greatly surprised if you'd want them to."

Eleanor's colour rose in the bright carnation of her girlhood, and Mrs. Fordyce gave an odd short laugh.

"So you went into Kashmir? I used to read 'Lalla Rookh.' And your father—yes, it was your father—he had a nice tenor voice when he was a young man, and your mother played his accompaniments. He was very fond of that song about Kashmir in the days when everyone spelt it with a C, and we called our shawls Cashmeres, even when they came from Paris. The Empress Eugénie set the fashion—no, it was Queen Victoria who always gave one as a wedding present." She drummed with her fingers and hummed in a deep, cracked whisper: "'I'll sing thee songs of Araby, and tales of fair Cashmere.' And now, I suppose, you're going to settle down. How many years were you in India?"

"Six years." The words fell as something falls from a tired hand.

"It's a long time to be out of your own country. You weren't in a hurry to get back. You've been staying in Paris, haven't you?"

"In Florence first, with Amy Barton, and then with an old schoolfellow in Paris. She's an artist."

"You'd better settle down. You're not left badly off?"

Eleanor's colour ebbed.

"No."

"That's something. You must settle down. You will find some changes. Perhaps you'll like them. Most people seem to like change nowadays. I can't say I care for it myself." She paused, and added dryly: "Frank Alderey's married."

"Yes, I want to meet her."

"H'm! There's not so very much of her to meet. Her clothes oughtn't to cost Frank much; hut it seems the less stuff there is in a thing, the more you pay for it. H'm!" Her tone became drier still. "David isn't married. It's time he was thinking about it. The longer people wait, the worse fools they make of themselves as a rule. Of course, he has his affairs"—there was a little scornful glitter in the hard blue eyes—"but they don't come to anything. Two years ago, now, there was a friend of Betty's—a good-looking girl, rather like you, my dear, before you lost your colour. H'm! I can't say India's improved you." She gave the little short laugh which was so like a cough, and flicked at her nose with six inches of *point-de-Venise* set round a bit of lawn the size of a half-crown. "Well, it didn't come to anything—it never seems to come to anything with David. And there was a girl with red hair before that—red hair and a temper, if I'm not very much mistaken. That didn't come to anything either. I suppose there's some entanglement."

Eleanor refused the challenge. She sat with her gloved hands upon her knees; they clasped one another lightly. Mrs. Fordyce looked at them. She always looked at a victim's hands. She had, before now, found them betray what eyes and mouth kept hidden. Eleanor's hands told her nothing; Eleanor's face, quiet, smiling, and a little sad, told her nothing either. She put up her hand with the crowded, crooked rings and yawned.

Miss Mary was at Eleanor's side in a moment.

"I think, my dear, if you don't mind, perhaps Grandmamma has talked enough."

Eleanor stood up thankfully. That scorching fire at her back, and Grandmamma's relentless eyes on her face—she couldn't have stood a great deal more. As she moved to speak to Milly March, she heard Miss Mary summoned in a voice which held no hint of fatigue:

"Mary! Where's David? I want to speak to David."

David looked at the gimcrack gilt chair.

"What happens if I break it?"

"You won't—it's stronger than it looks. Sit down." Mrs. Fordyce used a sharp, commanding undertone.

David sat down. He was wondering why no one had ever told Grandmamma what a rude old woman she was. It would have given him the greatest pleasure to tell her, in a perfectly frank heart-to-heart conversation, just what he thought about the way in which she had been talking to Eleanor. It was the limit, the absolute outside limit.

At this point he became aware that he was providing Grandmamma with amusement. She smiled a wintry smile that showed the famous teeth.

"I've been talking to Eleanor," she said.

"Yes. I saw you."

"Perhaps you heard me." There was a little icy sparkle in the pale blue eyes. "Perhaps you heard me, David. H'm! Listeners never hear any good of themselves. I was saying it was high time you were married."

David's frown vanished. Grandmamma generally enraged him; but occasionally she amused him too. The fact that she persisted in regarding him as a Lothario generally amused him.

"That's what Betty says. Whom shall I marry?"

Mrs. Fordyce sniffed. A counter-attack always disconcerted her. She had hoped to see David in a black fury, but obliged to be polite because she was Grandmamma and this was her eighty-ninth birthday. She lifted her left hand from its dark maroon background and tapped David on the knee.

"I was serious."

David's look was gay and challenging.

"Of course. Match-making is a very serious business. Who is it to be?"

Mrs. Fordyce knew when she held losing cards. She leaned back in her chair and just closed her eyes for a moment. If David had been six years old, she would have slapped him as hard as she could. A grandson of twenty-eight cannot be slapped; but he can be presented with a touching picture of an old lady of eighty-nine whose affectionate solicitude he has rebuffed. She closed her eyes, sighed, put the *point-de-Venise* to her lips for a moment, and then said, with an effect of vagueness:

"Ah—yes—what were we talking about? Dear Eleanor, I think."

David said nothing. He was trying not to feel a brute.

"Yes—Eleanor," said Grandmamma, a little more briskly this time. "H'm—yes—she's back. Looks shocking. Have you seen her?"

"Just for a moment."

"Looks shocking—doesn't she? Quite lost her complexion—India, I suppose, or Cosmo Rayne. He's no great loss, according to all accounts, but I suppose she was in love with him. Someone said he beat her. H'm—well, there are worse things than beating. Pity she's lost her looks so! H'm—what do you think?"

"I don't think out of office hours. Hullo! Who's that?"

Mrs. Fordyce turned slowly. A red-faced man had just come in, and behind him a slip of a girl.

"George March," said Mrs. Fordyce impatiently. "Yes, just retired. He's been Commissioner at one of those places that end in 'bad—Mirabad—Morabad—h'm—I can't remember. His wife ran away. The daughter's a handful, I should say. Her name's Flora, and they call her Folly—*Folly!*"

She laughed on a sharp, satirical note, and a moment later just touched George March's hand and said, "How d'ye do, George?" in her least interested voice.

"Glad to see you looking so well," said George March heartily.

Folly stood behind him, waiting for her turn. A high-crowned vagabond hat with a wavy brim hid every vestige of hair. Under it her little round head was black and sleek as a seal's, hair cropped close as could be. The hat was red—not the dark, serious red smiled upon by fashion, but a full, bright scarlet. Jumper and skirt were the same colour, and she carried a scarlet leather bag that was nearly as large as herself.

When she tilted her head and looked at David, he saw a little round face whose skin had been creamed and powdered to an ivory tint unbroken except by the vivid scarlet of lips that were painted to match the scarlet bag. She tilted her head a little more, and David saw that her eyes were green and impudent. If she had suddenly put out her tongue at him, he would not have been in the least surprised—a little, pointed scarlet tongue—a little serpent's tongue. He concluded that his Cousin Folly was likely to make the Family sit up.

"Very glad indeed to see you looking so well," said George March.

"Thank you, George," said Mrs. Fordyce. "How do you do, Flora?"

"How do you do, Aunt Anna?" said Miss Folly March. She had a little, soft, purring voice. She put her hand into Grandmamma's with the prettiest grace in the world.

Grandmamma dropped the hand without further speech. Miss Folly followed her father across the room.

Mrs. Fordyce gave her dry cough.

"Her mother ran away with an Australian. I dare say he deserved it. George was well rid of her. None of you young people seem to have much luck with your marriages. H'm! Do you? George—Betty—Eleanor. H'm! No, not much luck! We managed these things better in my generation—h'm—a great deal better!"

For one cold moment David had wondered if his name was going to follow Eleanor's; there had been just the ghost of a pause whilst Grandmamma's malicious eyes had raked him. He didn't think she had got much for her pains. But with Grandmamma one could never be sure.

"Eleanor's better off than Betty," pursued Mrs. Fordyce. "George and Eleanor are both better off. George has divorced his mistake, and Eleanor's buried hers. You—"

David wasn't sure whether he jumped or not. There was an imperceptible pause and a little rattling laugh.

"You haven't made yours yet. Betty's the worst off of the lot of you. I never did like Francis Lester. But of course Betty would have him. And what's she got out of it? A clumping boy to bring up, and a husband whom she won't divorce, and who hasn't the common decency to leave her a widow."

David had heard all this so many times before that he allowed his attention to wander. Mrs. Fordyce had a pointed prickle ready for him:

"I've kept you long enough. I've talked long enough too. Go and make it up with Eleanor if you want to. I dare say she'll be very pleased." She dabbed at her chin with the yellow lace hand-kerchief and leaned back.

Miss Mary stole from behind her chair.

"What is it, dear?"

"I've talked enough."

"Yes, yes."

She came to David with her little mouse-like run.

"David, I think Grandmamma is just a little tired—if you don't mind."

David went across to where Folly March was standing listening to the three Alderey girls, who were all talking at once. They greeted David with little shrieks of "Make him guess!"; "No, I can't!"; "Yes, do!"; and "Oh, nonsense!"

"What am I to guess?" said David.

"Winnie—" said the youngest Alderey girl.

"Pobbles, you're not to! It wasn't me; it was Minnie."

"David, don't listen to them!"

David felt reasonably bored. He frowned, and saw a green glint between Folly's eyelashes. They were very black eyelashes. An imp—a whole impery of imps—undoubtedly lived behind them; and all the time the creature had a little round ivory face and a painted scarlet mouth as expressionless as one of those little ivory faces on a painted China fan.

"Make him guess! David, guess how much—"

"Pobbles, you're not to!"

"I *shall*!"

"Minnie, stop her!"

"Winnie, don't let her!"

"David, guess how much Minnie paid—"

"I'm rotten at guessing." David had no use for the Alderey girls. "I'm absolutely rotten. And I think clothes are a bore, and sales immoral. And now, please, I'd like to be introduced to my cousin Flora. It is Flora, isn't it?"

The scarlet painted mouth opened and said, "No—Folly."

All three Alderey girls spoke together, giggling.

"Oh, Folly!"

"Who is he?" said the little purring voice. Another imp, a different one this time, beckoned to David.

He responded with alacrity.

"Let me introduce David Fordyce. I'm either a third cousin twice removed, or a second cousin three times removed. Are you any good at the Family tree? I'm rotten at it myself."

"I want some tea," said Folly.

She turned her back on the Alderey girls and edged towards the door. David followed her.

Later on, in the hall, he gave Eleanor back her violets. It seemed quite natural to both of them that he should put the bunch into her hand with no more than a casual "Here are your flowers."

"Oh, thank you," said Eleanor. They might have been meeting every day.

She stood on the bottom step of the stair with her left hand on the newel-post; her right hand held the violets between them. She looked down on David because they were nearly of a height and the step made her the taller for the moment.

"They're faded." David's voice was a little different to the voice he had for the Family.

"Yes." Eleanor's voice was different too.

David was remembering that at their last meeting he had knelt and hidden his face against her dress; and Eleanor remembered the sound of the sobbing breath with which she had tried at the last to say his name. She said now, quickly:

"David, come and see me."

"Where are you?"

"Milly March found me a flat—just a furnished one, whilst I look round."

She stepped down into the hall and laid the violets back on the oak chest from which David had taken them.

"I'll give you a card with the address. When will you come?"

"When *may* I come?"

"To-morrow. Can you get away at tea-time?"

"Yes, I can get away."

She wrote on her card with a little violet pencil.

"There—that's the address, and the telephone number. If you can't come, call me up."

"I shall come."

He held her coat for her and watched her take the flowers again. Then Milly March came heavy-footed down the stairs, a little out of breath.

"Grandmamma kept me!" she panted. Then she saw David, and had an access of tact: "Are you sure you've got room for me, Eleanor? Because if you haven't—I mean if you're taking David—"

"I'm not taking David," said Eleanor Rayne.

Chapter Four

A GRANDFATHER CLOCK struck the half-hour as David crossed the hall of Eleanor Rayne's temporary flat. A piercing silver chime sounded from what he took to be the dining-room.

The maid who had let him in threw open a door on the right and announced him to an empty drawing-room. As she murmured "I'll tell Mrs. Rayne," and withdrew, a gilt clock with a painted face struck two deep whirring notes from the mantelpiece, where it stood amongst a medley of china cups, Chelsea figures, ivory elephants, wooden bears, and silver peacocks. The room had a great many chairs in it. There were two walnut bureaux, three china cabinets, a tea-table set with tea things, a marble table supported by monstrously fat gilts Cupids, an Empire card-table with brass claw feet, and a frankly Victorian walnut pedestal table upon which stood a large group of stuffed birds under a glass dome.

David wrinkled his nose at the room and disliked it a good deal. The carpet had once displayed magenta roses wreathed with blue ribbon on a pearl-grey ground. The magenta was now just a wine-coloured smear, and the pearl had darkened to smoke. The walls were covered with satin stripes that had once been white. From three of the walls a gloomy ancestor stared from his or her discoloured frame. Two of the ancestors were male, and one, the least attractive of the three, a female with an elderly simper.

David disliked the ancestors even more than he disliked the room. He was frowning ferociously when the door opened and Eleanor came in. She wore a short grey skirt and a white jumper, and she was holding a smoke-coloured Persian kitten in both her hands. It had orange eyes, and it mewed fiercely and unremittingly because it wished to sit on Eleanor's shoulder.

Eleanor did not shake hands with David; she held the kitten, and she smiled, and said:

"You got here."

David said: "What a beastly room!"

And then Eleanor laughed.

"Thank you, David!"

"Nonsense! It's not your room. How does the same person manage to have wooden bears, and ivory and apes and peacocks, and poisonous ancestors, and ormolu tables?"

"It's quite easy, really. The flat belongs to an old Miss Johnson. She left a much bigger house to come here; but she wouldn't leave any of her furniture. Some of the things are inherited, and some were given to her—a brother in Burma sent her the peacocks long ago when she was young. And she simply loves the bears because she bought them herself in Berne."

"How do you know?"

"Milly told me. Milly knows her. She got me the flat by guaranteeing that I should be careful of the ancestors and kind to the bears."

Eleanor sat down beside the tea-table and put the kitten in her lap with a little pat.

"Timothy, be good. Isn't he a lamb, David?"

"Where did you raise him?"

"Milly raised him. She *is* a good sort—she thought I'd be lonely. Oh, *Timmy!*"

After being patted, Timothy had crouched; his eyes glowed, his two inches of furry tail twitched. The moment that Eleanor looked away from him to David he leapt, took a clawing hold of the white jumper, kicked himself upwards, and landed, growling in a fierce whisper, in the hollow between Eleanor's neck and Eleanor's shoulder.

Eleanor rubbed her cheek against him.

"Timmy, you're the worst kitten in the world!"

Timmy stopped growling and began to purr. Just for a moment that soft triumphant purr was the only sound in the room. Then the door opened and the maid brought in tea.

After a moment's frowning consideration David pushed a chair up to the table and sat down with his back to the female ancestor.

"They're all bad, but she's the worst," he explained. "I should think her name was Sophronisba. If I've got to look at one of 'em, I prefer the old buster whose top has faded into the general gloom. I say, mustn't those tight white breeks have been the limit?"

Eleanor laughed and gave him some tea. There was another little pause. Then he said, without looking at her:

"I expect you're glad to get home. Where are you going to live?"

"I don't know. I used to think I'd like London, but now I'm sure I shouldn't."

"Why?"

"I don't know. It's a lonely place—there are such a lot of people, and they're all so busy. And oh, David, I do *hate* the crossings. I think I'll just stay here till the country warms up, and then I'll get a little car and run round till I find a house that I really love."

"Let me build you one," said David.

"Would it be all bathrooms? Aunt Editha seemed quite worried about the number of bathrooms you put into houses. She said that Grandmamma said it was just a modern craze, and in her young days nobody ever had bathrooms at all. She said Grandmamma thought such a lot of washing was most unwholesome, and that everybody would feel much warmer if they didn't wash so much."

"I've made three new bathrooms at Ford," said David. "They're topping. Come and see them. When will you come? I told Betty I'd find out. And she says, would you like a party, or just us?"

Eleanor did not answer him at once.

"It seems funny to think of Ford belonging to you."

"Why?"

"I don't know—it does. Your father was so strict; we all had to do exactly as we were told, and nobody was allowed to be a moment late for meals. Oh, it just seems odd."

"I've got used to it."

"Betty keeps house for you?"

"More or less."

"What does that mean?"

"It means she's rotten at it. But she *will* do it."

"Poor Betty! She told me Dick had just gone to school. I thought she was going to cry. She must miss him dreadfully."

"She spoils him dreadfully. It's a jolly good thing for Master Dick that he's a boy and bound to go to school."

"What's he like?"

"Not a bad little ruffian. Quite good stuff—a stocky little chap— wants licking."

Eleanor put out her hand and took his cup.

"Do you still take three lumps of sugar? I put them in without thinking the first time. Help yourself to cake, and give me a bit." She gave him back his cup. "David, what's happened about Betty's husband?"

"Nothing."

"How do you mean—nothing?"

"Well, just that."

"Aunt Editha said—"

David laughed.

"Grandmamma and the Aunts probably know a lot more about it than Betty and I do. The plain fact is that Francis went off into the blue just after I got back to England five years ago. As far as I know, nobody's heard of him since. It leaves Betty rather high and dry; but, honestly, she was well rid of him at any price. If ever there was an out-and-out rotter—and how on earth he got round my father I can't imagine. Poor old Betty had an absolutely poisonous time of it, and she took it very hard. It's bad luck, that sort of thing. I mean with any number of good fellows about, it's hard lines when a girl gets let down by an out-and-out rotter."

"Yes," said Eleanor. Her lips felt a little stiff, but she wanted to say something quickly.

And then all of a sudden the dark colour ran up into David's face. To Eleanor's horror, the tears rushed scalding to her eyes. She clenched her hands and leaned back, struggling for composure. After all that she had been through, to break down at a chance word!

Timothy nuzzled softly against her ear; his orange eyes peeped at David between the curls of Eleanor's hair.

She got up quickly and went over to the hearth. As she stooped and pushed a log down on to the red embers, the two burning tears fell.

David's voice sounded from behind her:

"Eleanor—my dear—I didn't mean—"

"No, of course you didn't."

He got up.

"Look here, we can be friends—can't we? We always were friends. We wanted to be something more, and it didn't come off. And one way and another we've both had a pretty thin time of it. We needn't talk about it; but it's not the sort of thing you forget. I'd like to start square on that basis. If we try and ignore it, we shall just feel uncomfortable. You see what I mean?"

Eleanor turned. Her eyes were still wet, but it didn't really matter. Tact and the social conventions seemed to have vanished. David had always been a singularly direct person. There was a sort of comfort about it. She said:

"Yes, I see."

"Then, when will you come down to Ford?"

"I don't know. Do you go up and down every day?"

"I do in summer, and when I'm not too busy. It's only thirty miles. When will you come?"

"Well—I've got Folly March coming to me."

David stared.

"What for?"

"To stay."

"My dear girl!"

Eleanor laughed, sat down on the fender-stool, and removed a shrieking Timmy from her shoulder.

"Timothy, you're not to bite my hair! Oh, you little horror!"

The kitten spat, scratched, and fled. After glaring defiance from the middle of the floor, he backed sideways to the marble table with its gilded supports and lurked behind a bulging Cupid's foot.

"George is going to pay visits—bachelor visits; so I said I'd have Folly. We came home on the same boat, you know. I expect George will be away for about a month."

"What are you going to do with her? You'd better bring her to Ford. She can't get into mischief there, anyhow."

Eleanor looked resigned. The corners of her mouth twitched and something danced in her dark eyes.

"Folly March can get into mischief anywhere," she said.

Chapter Five

IT WAS OVER a hundred years since the Fordyces had crossed the Tweed. David's great-grandfather bought the estate, to which he gave the name of Ford, and began to build the house, which was finished by his son.

To Ford Anna St. Kern came as a bride; and at Ford she presently developed into Grandmamma. David's father being a widower at the time of his succession, her rule endured until his death, after which, greatly to David's relief, she announced a preference for London. With a masterly grasp of the situation she installed herself in the very middle of the Family web. She very seldom went out; but the Family came to her, and she directed its affairs with merciless decision.

The house at Ford was a comfortable square Georgian building of modest size. It stood on a grassy spur which ran down gently into woodland on two sides, and on the third dropped sharply from an artificial terrace to a fair-sized sheet of water. The terrace was bounded by a low stone wall, and a long grey flight of steps led down to the water's edge.

Eleanor Rayne came down to Ford and brought Folly March with her.

"And remember, Folly, you've promised to be good."

"I'm bored when I'm good—and I can't be good when I'm bored."

"You can if you like," said Eleanor, laughing.

Folly was good for two days. She rode with David; she played golf with Eleanor; and she let Betty teach her a double patience in the evenings.

Eleanor found it very pleasant to be at Ford again, and very pleasant to be with David. After a cold spell, January was playing at spring, with soft fresh winds, April showers, and exquisite pale turquoise skies.

On the third evening Folly looked askance at Betty's patience board. They were sitting in the drawing-room, "to air it," as Betty said. She was one of the people whose rooms have no middle stage between stiffness and disorder; and the drawing-room, which David hated, was as coldly angular as a problem in geometry.

Eleanor amused herself by thinking of how different it could be made. The cold, faded brocade curtains would go, of course. The room wanted bright chintzes; it wanted colour and life, more flowers, and a few dark rugs, instead of half an acre of prehistoric Brussels.

Folly also had ideas of her own—the room was large; it had a parquet floor smothered by a frightful carpet. She came up to David with her hands behind her back, tilted her chin at him, and said:

"*Do* get married and give a dance."

"An expensive dance!"

"Not *very.*"

"It would be if I had to get married as a preliminary—rather like burning down the house to cook the bacon."

"*Do!*" said Folly.

"Burn the house down?"

"That would be fun too! But I'd rather have a dance. I do dance well."

"Aren't you going to play patience to-night?" Betty's voice was fretful and disapproving.

"No, I'm going to dance."

She set her arms akimbo, whistled shrilly, and began to Charleston. She wore a singularly brief sleeveless garment that ended at the knee. It was black, and it was hemmed with monkey fur. There was a little string of bright beads round her neck, just the sort of thing that she might have worn with socks and sash when she was six years old. The socks had given way to very thin flesh-coloured stockings kept up by scarlet garters which showed every time she kicked. Her dancing had a sort of furious abandonment that was just on the edge of grace, but never overstepped it.

All of a sudden she stopped quite close to David.

"*Do* give a dance! Will you?"

"No, I won't."

"I'm bored with the Charleston—really. I want to learn the Black Bottom. It's perfectly hideous, and no one knows how to do it properly yet. I do like being ahead of the crowd. Don't you?"

"Not specially."

Folly took him by the lapels of his coat and shook them.

"You're as dull as ditch-water!" Then she looked at him full out of her green eyes for just the merest fraction of a second. "I play the piano almost as well as I dance," she said in her soft purring voice. "I'll play you things you'll simply adore."

She began to whistle again and danced backwards to the piano, a big lugubrious grand in an ebony case. After pushing at the lid with an ineffective little hand, she raised it half an inch and let it down with a bang.

"David—come and open it, David."

Betty said, "What's that?" and then went on telling Eleanor everything that Dick had done and said for the last six years.

David went across to the piano, opened it, and then stood there, a little curious as to what Miss Folly's taste in music might be. She settled herself demurely and began to play Mendelssohn's "Gondellied" in a manner as softly sentimental as if she had been a Victorian miss in a crinoline.

David glanced at the little sleek black head with the hair cut a good deal shorter than Dicky Lester's. Then he looked across to where Betty and Eleanor sat under a tall electric lamp.

Eleanor had on a black dress with long floating sleeves. She was working at a piece of embroidery stretched on a frame, and her lap was full of the brilliant coloured silks—the blue and green of a peacock's neck and breast; the rose of last year's roses; the bright sapphire of the little ring he had given her long ago (perhaps she had lost it—or perhaps she had it still). The colours made a shimmering beauty under the lamp. It had a pale blue shade which made Betty look ghastly. He wondered idly whether she knew how unbecoming it was.

Eleanor, in the same pale light, was beautiful enough. She had the very white skin which sometimes goes with black hair. The line of neck and shoulder was a free and noble one. She looked sometimes at Betty, and sometimes at her rainbow silks. She had cut her hair, but it had its old crisp wave; there were little dark curls that hid her ears.

Folly March rocked the singing notes and said:

"David—*David!*"

He turned his head.

"Do you think Eleanor is beautiful?"

"Do you?"

"Yes."

David looked back at Eleanor and agreed in silence.

"David—*David!*"

"What is it?"

"Shall I grow my hair?"

David frowned and said "Yes" rather impatiently.

"You don't like it short?"

"No."

"David."

"Well?"

"Shall I stop putting stuff on my face?"

She went on playing with her left hand, drew a finger down one smooth cheek, and held it out covered with ivory powder.

David made a face of disgust.

"Shall I leave it off?"

"Yes."

"And not paint my lips?"

The gondola was rocking steadily again. Folly's black lashes were cast down; the scarlet mouth trembled a little.

"*Yes,*" said David impatiently.

Then his heart smote him. Suppose she began to cry. Girls did.

Folly went on playing very softly. Suddenly she looked up at him, her eyes alive with green malice.

"Why don't you marry, David?"

"You'd better ask Grandmamma."

"I'd rather ask you. Why, David?"

"You can have three guesses."

Something a good deal older than Folly peeped at him. David received rather a shock. Folly was what? Nineteen? Where did she get that look—hard, knowing?

She said quite softly, watching him:

"She won't marry you—*or* you won't marry her—*or* you're married already."

She had the satisfaction of seeing his look of black anger. Then he turned his back on her and went over to the fire.

Folly hit the keyboard with both hands and produced a medley of screaming notes. Then, to a series of discords, she sang in a husky, penetrating whisper:

"My baby's a scream,
My baby's a dream,
She's a hula mula wula girl,
She's a crazy daisy nightmare—ula
My baby's a scream."

Chapter Six

ELEANOR CAME into Folly's room that night after they had all gone upstairs. She found three electric lights on and Miss Folly in her shift practising barefoot dancing. Her black frock lay in a heap on the floor. There was one stocking by the washstand and another at the foot of the bed. The high-heeled black shoes were in opposite corners of the room. One scarlet garter decorated the bedpost.

Folly went on dancing without taking any notice of Eleanor, who said, "Untidy little wretch!" and then watched her indulgently. In the end Folly turned her head over her shoulder and inquired laconically:

"Pie-jaw?"

"Do you deserve one?"

"Prob." She rose on her bare toes, clasped her hands above her head, and yawned.

"Folly, what did you say to David? He hardly spoke for the rest of the evening. What on earth did you say to him?"

Folly looked sleepy and innocent. Then she laughed. The laugh was not so innocent.

"I ran a pin into him—I ran three pins, and one of them pricked him. I wish I knew which pin it was."

A look of distress crossed Eleanor's face.

"I wanted David to like you—but you're such a little fool."

"They should have called me Flora. I should have been perfectly good if I'd been called Flora—I get no end of moral uplift every time Grandmamma does it. But when I'm Folly—ooh! Eleanor, I'm going to tea with a nice young man the day after to-morrow. I met him this morning, and he asked me. I think he's a farmer."

"Nonsense!"

"His name is Matthew Brown. You can't say that isn't respectable, and you can't say I didn't tell you. He's got a sister called Gladys Ann—she lives with him. And if I can't go to a night club with Stingo to-morrow, I do think I might be allowed to go and have a respectably chaperoned tea with Matthew Brown."

"Rubbish!" said Eleanor. "Look here, Folly."

Folly was leaning out of the open window, the chintz curtain held aside.

"I think I shall go for a moonlight ramble. Perhaps I should pick up something more exciting than Matthew Brown."

"Folly—it's icy! Do shut that window."

"Stuffy old thing!" The words came just above a whisper in a little child's voice. Then the window banged and the curtains fell. "It must be frightfully odd to be a widow. I expect it adds years to one's natural stuffiness. I'm going to grow my hair and do it in curls. David would like me to."

"Did he say so?" Eleanor's tone was dry.

"'M—he *did*. He thinks you're beautiful."

Eleanor laughed.

"I suppose he told you that too?"

"'M—I said, 'Do you think Eleanor is beautiful?' And he said—no, I shan't tell you what he said—and then I thought I'd grow my hair and have it in curls like you, and not put any stuff on my face, or do my lips, and always be *good*. You and David were engaged, weren't you?"

"Folly, what a little idiot you are!"

"You *were* engaged, weren't you?"

"Ancient history," said Eleanor.

"Why didn't you get married?"

"We were infants—there was nothing in it."

Folly looked through half-closed eyelids; and something in the look set a spark to Eleanor's temper.

"Perhaps if I'm very good, and let my hair grow, and wash my face with yellow soap—Do you wash your face with yellow soap, Eleanor darling?"

"Do I look as if I did?"

"Sometimes. No—not really. What a temper you've got! It jumped out of your eyes like red-hot knives. Does David like people with tempers? I could grow one whilst I was growing my hair if he does."

She stood on one foot and caught the heel of the other in her left hand. With the fingers of the right she blew Eleanor a kiss.

"I haven't quite made up my mind whether I'll have David," she said. "I might get bored with him."

Eleanor was conscious of colour in her cheeks.

"It's time you stopped talking nonsense and went to bed."

"Of course, if *you* want him," said Folly, twirling on one bare foot.

Eleanor went out of the room; the door shut sharply.

By the time she reached her own room she was wondering why she had so nearly lost her temper. Folly had scored instead of being coolly snubbed as she deserved. She moved about the room for a little without undressing. There was a pleasant fire. A fire-lit room and a still house. There was something about Ford that felt like home. She sat down by the fire and let the stillness and the firelight and that home feeling have their way.

It might have been half an hour later that she heard the sound and raised her head to listen. It was quite a little sound, faint and distant.

As she listened, she heard another sound, fainter still. Someone had opened one of the long windows in the room below; she had heard the bolt move and the catch slip. She sprang up and went to the window.

The shadow of the house lay black upon a flagged path and a stretch of turf. She pushed the window open and leaned out, listening. In the shadow someone was moving. She could not see the movement, but she could hear it. The sound grew fainter.

The shadow lay twenty feet wide. Eleanor's window looked upon the path and a steep grassy slope that fell away to woodland. The terrace lay on the right, and the moon shone on it. The edge of the shadow was very sharp and black. It crossed the flagged path at an angle.

Eleanor leaned out, and heard the footsteps pass; someone was going in the direction of the terrace. She watched the edge of the shadow and held her breath.

Quite suddenly a black-cloaked figure crossed the line between shadow and moonlight. Eleanor saw blackness—movement—a cloak that covered everything. And then the figure was gone. Just short of the terrace the path descended by a dozen steps; the wall of the terrace shadowed them.

The figure that had come out of the darkness dropped down the steps and was lost in the dark again.

Eleanor shut her window and snatched a fur-lined cloak from the tall mahogany wardrobe. That little idiot Folly! Who could have imagined that she really meant to go out? Of course, it might be one of the maids. No, that wasn't likely. She slipped out of the room and felt her way noiselessly down the stairs and through the hall.

The room immediately below her bedroom was Betty Lester's sitting-room. Eleanor felt her way across it until her hands touched the chintz curtains. They were cold and shiny, and as she pulled them back, the draught that came from behind them was colder still. The window was a French window, opening to the ground, and it stood a hand's breadth ajar.

"Little idiot!" said Eleanor to herself. Then she pulled her cloak round her and ran to the corner of the house.

The steps were at her foot, very black; they went down to a path which wound back along the slope and then lost itself in the darkness of the woods. Eleanor stood on the top step and called softly:

"Folly—Folly!"

She waited a moment, and then called again:

"Folly! *Folly!* Are you there?"

An owl hooted in the wood. Eleanor hated owls. She shivered a little; and the owl cried again, on an unearthly, floating note that sounded nearer. She decided that it would be ridiculous for her to follow the little wretch; besides, she might quite easily miss her in the wood. The sensible thing to do was to go back into Betty's room and wait for her there.

She drew back from the steps and walked to the edge of the terrace. It was such a lovely night—so still, so clear, with the moon coming up over the edge of the little hill away on the left—a golden moon very nearly full. It was just clear of the tree-tops, and half the lake below the terrace shone in a light between gold and silver; the other half lay black in the shadow of the wooded hill.

Eleanor looked at the water and moved along the terrace until she came to the head of the stone steps which led down to it. They were bathed in the soft light. She went down a little way, and then stood for a while letting the beauty in upon her troubled thought.

Folly—what had possessed her? How lovely the tracery of bare boughs against the moon-flushed sky! Why had Folly kept to the dark path instead of coming this way?

Her hand moved on the wall that followed the steps. There were little dry stalks and withered leaves on it. In a month or two there would be arabis, and aubretia, and alyssum, in sheets of white, and lilac, and violet, and yellow.

"Perhaps I ought to have gone after Folly. The wood's so dark—and I do hate owls. Why did she go into the wood? It's dark. I ought to have gone after her. Why on *earth* did she go into the wood? I'm a coward. I ought to have gone after her."

She took her hand off the wall, and, as she turned, something moved where the wood ran down to the lake.

It wasn't Folly; it was a man.

Eleanor's heart thumped, and then quieted. It was David. It was only David. She ran down the steps to meet him; her "Have you seen her?" was a little breathless.

"Her?"

"Folly—have you seen Folly?"

"No—why should I? It's a topping night—isn't it?"

She nodded.

"Yes. Folly—Folly's gone for a walk."

"Nonsense!"

"But she has. She said something about it, and I thought she was joking. But I heard the morning-room window open, and I saw someone go down the steps."

"These steps?"

"No."

"How do you know it was Folly?"

"Well, I can't think of anyone else who'd be so idiotic."

David laughed unexpectedly.

"Well, I'm out, and you're out. As a matter of fact, I often go for a walk before I turn in. I shouldn't bother about that little image if I were you."

"David, she oughtn't to."

He laughed again.

"Do you think you or anyone else'll ever stop her doing the things she oughtn't to? Don't you worry about her—she'll come back all right. Naught comes to naught."

"Don't!" said Eleanor quickly. "David, I did want you to like her."

"Did you?" His voice was dry. "Look here, we'd better be getting up on to the terrace."

"Oh yes—I mustn't be locked out!"

"Don't run—I've got a key."

They had reached the topmost step when David asked:

"Why do you want me to like her?"

"She wants friends. She's picked up with a perfectly rotten crowd."

"I'm afraid I can't compete."

Eleanor slipped her hand into his arm.

"No, David, listen! She *does* want friends. She—you know her mother ran away?"

"Vaguely. I shouldn't be surprised at anyone running away from George. Oh, he's a bore!"

Eleanor shook the arm she was holding.

"Don't!"

"My dear girl, that George is an unqualified and undisputed bore is the sort of thing you can't argue about—it's simply a bed-rock fact, and every time I meet George I stub my toe on it."

"Well, you can't say Folly's a bore, anyhow."

"No—she's not a bore—I'll give her that. Is she like her mother?"

"No, she isn't. Why must people be like someone? She's herself."

"She's a little devil. What was the mother?"

"Big—fat—fair—sleepy—looked at you sideways—fat white hands. I loathed her."

"So I see. Folly looks at you sideways."

"She doesn't—not like that. David, she doesn't really. Don't you see how rotten it is for a girl when everyone—*everyone*—expects her to go off the rails because her mother did? And she's not like her— she's *not*. She's naughty and she's provoking; but she's not in the least like her mother. David, do you know the woman carried on with that child in the house and didn't care whether she knew about it or not?" She dropped his arm and stepped back with an angry stamp of the foot. "It makes me wild!"

"How old was she?"

"Folly? Fourteen. Can you imagine it? The child hasn't had a chance. George doesn't pretend to care a rap for her. And, David, she's only nineteen now. Do make friends with her."

David looked at Eleanor in the moonlight. He felt an extreme disinclination to talk about Folly March. Eleanor did not look at him; her eyes were on the bright lake and the dark woods; her thoughts were far away.

"How bright and cold!" she said at last, only just above her breath.

"It's too cold for you. Come in."

"I didn't mean that." Then, after a pause: "It's like Indian moonlight frozen." On the last word her voice fell lower still.

David said, "Did you like India? Do you want to go back?" He had not meant to say it, but the words came.

"No," said Eleanor quickly. "No!"

He was sorry he had spoken, because she shivered; and yet, having spoken, something pricked him on.

"Eleanor—how has it been—all these years?"

Eleanor winced.

"It's over."

"My dear, I—was it as bad as that?" He laid a hand on her shoulder and felt it rigid.

"It's over," she said again.

Someone was coming up the dark steps on their right, softly and with great caution. Just for a moment this someone stood in the shadow looking at the lighted terrace and the two figures standing so close together that they made one figure in the moonlight. Then, quickly and silently, a woman in a black cloak crossed from shadow to shadow and was gone.

David and Eleanor were aware of one another and of the past; they neither saw nor heard. David's hand tightened on Eleanor's shoulder, and he said:

"Why did you do it?"

"I don't know—you were so far away—I don't know—" Then quite suddenly: "That's not true. I do know. I was a fool—girls don't understand very much—he fascinated me—it was like a fever—I didn't think—I just did it. And then—when it was too late—I woke up."

She shivered and drew away from him, holding her cloak with cold, clenched fingers.

"David—" She choked on the word and began again. "Why did you ask? No—I suppose you've a right to ask."

"No," said David. "No."

She controlled her voice.

"I don't know why I should mind. Everyone knew. There'd been someone else for years. I would have cared for him if it had been possible. It wasn't—and everybody knew."

David knew something too. Cosmo Rayne had had a reputation; amongst other things, he drank. It was not hard to believe that Eleanor had not found it possible to care. Gay, unscrupulous, a drunkard, trusted even less by men than by women. He felt a pity, which had no words, for Eleanor.

With an effort she turned her eyes from the glittering water.

"Betty and I—we both made rather a mess of things—didn't we?" She paused; something tragic looked out of her eyes. "Betty's got Dick. I lost my baby. Did you know?"

"Yes," said David.

Eleanor walked away towards the house. She wanted to reach the black shadow, to pass through it to her own dark room, and to cry her heart out. The old mournful pain which never quite left her heart had risen in sudden flood; it overwhelmed her, and she could only just hold back the tears.

She came to the window of Betty's room, groped for the pane, and pushed. The window was shut.

David came up behind her.

"What is it? Are you faint?"

Her hand was on the glass; she leaned against the jamb.

"David, it's shut!"

"You came out this way?"

"Yes."

"You're sure?"

"Quite sure."

"Then she's slipped in and done us down. It doesn't matter—I've got a key."

He took her arm in an easy, brotherly fashion, and they came together to the door which led into the garden-room.

David switched on the light.

"Run up and see if you can catch her. She deserves a wigging."

In the light Eleanor was very pale, but her composure had come back. David's friendly clasp, the bare room full of familiar shabby things, the light—all helped to restore her to her everyday self. There was the old battered croquet set, the fishing rods, the old garden chairs. She said, "Yes, she does," and ran across the hall and up the stairs to Folly's room.

She did not knock, but opened the door quickly and stood listening. Darkness and silence. Her hand went up and pulled down the switch; the bulb in the ceiling sprang into brilliance. The light shone on one stocking by the washstand and another by the dressing-table; on a pair of shoes in opposite corners of the room; on a scarlet garter hanging from the bedpost; on Folly's scattered garments; and on Folly March in bed, with a pale blue eiderdown snuggled tightly up to her chin.

Eleanor crossed over to the bed and stood there looking down. Folly's black lashes lay smoothly upon Folly's pale smooth cheek; Folly's little red mouth, washed clean of lipstick, was firmly closed; one little ear showed pink against the sleek black hair. She looked very young.

Eleanor put a hand on the blue eiderdown; and all of a sudden Folly cried out and turned, her eyes wide open and an arm flung out. Her cry was the unintelligible murmur of a dream. The wide green eyes were as empty and blank as water; there was no imp in them; there was nothing but sleep.

Eleanor said, "Folly!" and Folly said, "O—oh!" She flung out her other arm and blinked at the light.

"Folly!"

Folly woke up.

"What is it? Is the house on fire? O—oh!" Her yawn was natural enough.

"Folly—have you been out?"

The imps woke up; one peeped rather sleepily at Eleanor.

"Out?"

"Yes—out."

"Out where?"

"Folly, someone went out of the house and down into the woods. Was it you?"

"'M—" She sat up and locked her arms about her knees. "I said I should like a walk—didn't I?"

"Folly! Was it you?"

"'M—" said Folly again. Her pink diaphanous nightgown slipped from her shoulder. Her eyes were very wicked; she looked sideways at

Eleanor. "Perhaps *David* went for a walk. Did he? It's quite proper to go for a walk with one's cousin. Now, if it had been Stingo—"

"Folly! You didn't go to meet that horrible man?"

"David?"

Eleanor shook her.

"Mr. St. Inigo."

"No one calls him that—he's always Stingo."

"Did you go to meet him?"

Folly unlocked her hands and kissed all ten fingers to Eleanor.

"Darling Mrs. Grundy!" she said. "I *do* love you!"

"Did you?"

"Pahssionately!"

As she spoke, she whisked down into the bed and pulled the eiderdown over her head. Her muffled voice reached Eleanor:

"Don't you ask no questions, and you won't be told no lies!"

Chapter Seven

FOLLY WAS AS GOOD as gold next day. David went off early to town. Betty and Eleanor drove into Guildford, taking Folly with them. They lunched with Mrs. Norris, a cousin so distant that even the Fordyces might have considered the kinship negligible if she had not been Eleanor's godmother.

Folly, on her best behaviour and prepared to suffer boredom meekly, was a good deal cheered by the discovery that Mrs. Norris had a son living at home. He was a very personable youth, just down from Oxford, and casting about him for a job. He wore a brilliant red tie, and political opinions of an even more ferocious shade. He considered Lenin the greatest man of the century, and discoursed to Folly upon the Soviet system.

Folly listened beautifully. The imps were under lock and key; an innocent yearning for information looked out of her limpid green eyes. Aubrey Norris's admiration for the late M. Lenin became pleasantly merged in admiration for Miss Folly March. Altogether a successful lunch-party.

On the way home Folly asked to stop at a hairdresser's, where she kept the car, a patient Eleanor, and an impatient Betty for about twenty minutes. To Betty's outraged "What *have* you been doing?" she returned a flighty nod and a "Wait and see!"

David got back just in time to dress for dinner. He came into the drawing-room to find Eleanor and Betty there. A moment later Folly skipped down the stairs, whisked into the room, banged the door, and stood just inside it with modestly cast-down eyes. She wore a slip of a pale pink frock; her face was washed quite clean, her mouth had only its natural red; her little black head was bound with a silver fillet; from under the fillet, on either side, hung a cluster of shining black curls.

Betty said, "Good gracious!" and Eleanor said, "Oh Folly, how pretty! I do like it!" David said nothing at all. But something tugged at his heart—perhaps it was one of Folly's imps. He was frowning when she lifted her eyes and looked at him with a little clear colour in her cheeks.

"'M—d'you like it? Aren't I clever to grow them so quickly?" She put up a finger and just touched the curls. "Don't you like them?"

"They're not bad."

Folly broke at the knees in a charity bob.

"Thank you, David," she said meekly.

After dinner she sat curled in a chair with a book. Eleanor, passing behind her, caught the title and leant over her shoulder.

"Folly, where *did* you get that? It's a beast of a book. Why do you read it?" The low indignant whisper was pitched for Folly's ear.

Folly smiled at the page she was reading.

"Why *do* you?"

"To please Mrs. Grundy," said Folly in a voice that was meant to carry across the room. She gazed artlessly at David, who was standing with his back to the fire reading the paper. "*And* Mr. Grundy," she added.

Eleanor went back to her own chair. She was still picking up the stray threads of her embroidery when Folly ran across the room to David.

"David—"

David looked over the paper frowning.

"What is it?"

"David, Eleanor says this isn't a proper book for me to read."

She held it out, and the frown became a scowl.

"Where did you pick that up?"

"George had it," said Folly with downcast eyes.

"George?"

"'M—George March."

A scandalized Betty cut into the conversation:

"You don't call your *father* George?"

"Always," said Folly firmly.

Then she turned back to David.

"Is it as bad as all that? I'm glad I took it away from him. I have to be very careful about George's morals."

David was torn between a desire to burst out laughing and a most raging desire to pick Folly up and give her a good shaking. He did neither. Instead, he dropped one side of the paper he was holding, took the book out of Folly's hand, and pitched it behind him on to the blazing logs.

"O-oh!" said Folly. "What will George say?"

"I haven't the slightest idea," said David, and went back to his paper.

Folly made a face at the advertisement sheet of *The Times*, a little ugly, malicious face. Then she ran to Eleanor.

"Darling, give me a nice book to read—the sort I'd read if I was Flora, all about a strong, silent hero and a *fearfully* good heroine who simply adores him and licks his boots."

Presently, as she sat on a cushion at Eleanor's feet snuggled up over the "nice" book, one of the little bunches of black curls fell off and obscured the page. Folly came out with a monosyllable which the "fearfully good heroine" would not have used.

Betty dropped a card, looked down her nose, and said: "Oh, Folly!"

Eleanor patted the little shorn head, and Folly sighed with ostentation. Then she picked up the curls, sat them up very stiffly on the thin wire mount, tickled Eleanor's hand with them, and finally stuck them bolt upright in the silver ribbon on the top of her head, where they waved like elfish court feathers gone black. Perhaps they were in mourning for Folly's good behaviour.

David did not take the least notice of them or of Folly. When he had finished *The Times*, he plunged into a book. When he said good-night to Folly, he looked over her head at Eleanor.

Folly went upstairs with a little scarlet patch on either cheek. An hour later, Eleanor, coming late from Betty's room, stopped at her door, opened it, and stood there listening. There was such a stillness that she felt her way to the bed and switched on the shaded light beside it.

Folly lay crumpled up with her clenched fists under her chin like a baby; her little face was stained with tears, the black lashes all stuck together by threes and fours in little points; her lips were parted. She seemed to be sunk in the soundest depths of sleep.

Eleanor put out the light and went away troubled.

David came down to his early breakfast next morning to find that Miss Folly March intended to breakfast with him; and not only to breakfast with him, but to accompany him to town.

"What on earth do you want to go to town for?"

"'M—" said Folly. "I like driving up. And, of course"—very sweetly—"I like going with you."

David surveyed her with disapproval. The scarlet hat and suit he had seen before, but the black patent leather shoes with scarlet heels were a new horror.

"My good girl, you can't go up to town in those shoes!"

"I don't think I'm anybody's good girl. Am I?"

She did a dance step to display the shoes, kicked up the little red heels with a flourish, and announced that they were dinky.

David turned away and picked up the paper. His conviction that Folly wanted slapping passed into a strong desire to administer some of the arrears which he considered were a good deal overdue.

"Of course, if you don't mind being followed in the street," he observed coldly. He shook out the paper. "You will be, to a dead cert."

"I get followed anyhow," said Folly in a little whispering voice.

David was not at all surprised to hear it. What did surprise him was his own furious anger. If the door had not opened, he might have spoken. A moment later he was blessing Carter's timely entrance with haddock and coffee.

Folly pounced on the coffee-pot and began to pour out. David, erecting *The Times* between them, replied as shortly as possible to inquiries about milk, sugar, toast, butter, and marmalade.

They had finished breakfast, and Folly was slipping into a dark fur coat, when David, folding the paper over, found his eye caught and held. He had just said to Folly: "I suppose you know I'm staying the night with Frank and Julie. You'll have to come down by train." But he did not hear her answer; he had not, in fact, the very slightest idea whether she answered or not. He stared at the Agony Column, and then, rising with a jerk, he walked across to the window and stood there with his back to the room, looking at his own initials.

It was the third advertisement in the column; if it had been a little lower down, he might easily have missed it. "D. A. St. K. F."—David Alderey St. Kern Fordyce. The letters seemed blacker than the surrounding print; the whole message seemed to detach itself and to float a little above the paper upon which it was printed:

"D. A. St. K. F.—Your wife is alive."

Chapter Eight

DAVID DROPPED Folly in Knightsbridge. She had sat by his side for thirty miles like the little image he had called her, and neither of them had said a word. Folly could see David's face in the glass screen; its expression certainly did not invite conversation. She could see her own face too powdered and whitened as if yesterday had never been; the vermilion-red lips matched the hat that hid every vestige of hair.

When the car drew up, she jumped nimbly out, fished out a suitcase which David did not remember to have seen before, nodded quite gravely, and was gone. He saw the twinkle of the scarlet heels, and he saw one or two people look at them. Then Miss Folly dived into a shop, and he forgot her and her suitcase for eight or nine hours.

It was in the middle of the Aldereys' dinner that Eleanor rang him up. Frank answered the telephone and spoke over his shoulder:

"It's Eleanor—she wants you."

David got up, wondering if the house were on fire. He wondered still more when he realized that Eleanor was trying to steady her voice and not succeeding very well.

"David—can you hear me?"

"Yes. What's the matter?"

"Folly hasn't come back."

"Is that all?"

"David, you don't understand."

David remembered the suitcase.

Eleanor went on speaking.

"I rang up my flat, and she was there."

"Then that's all right."

"No, it *isn't*—it's frightfully wrong. Do you know a man called St. Inigo?"

David whistled.

"I don't know him. As a matter of fact I wouldn't touch him with a barge pole. I know *of* him."

"David, that little idiot's gone up to meet him. She's been having a silly flirtation with him just out of sheer contradictoriness and because George for once in his life said 'No.' That's why I was so anxious to get her down here."

"Well, I don't quite see what we can do about it," said David. "I expect she's pretty well able to look after herself, you know."

"She *isn't*. Girls aren't—they think they know everything, and they don't—Yes, another three minutes, please."

"All the same, my dear girl—"

"No, David—*listen*. I want to tell you. I got on to the little wretch. And she's dining with him, and then they're going to a revue, and then on to a night-club to dance. That's all bad enough; but she's proposing to sleep at my flat."

"Well?"

"She *mustn't*."

"Why not?"

"There's nobody there. That's what I wanted to tell you. The cook's mother's ill, and I said she could sleep at home; and the other girl's having a holiday. She simply mustn't come home with that man to an empty flat."

David whistled again.

"Perhaps the cook will have stayed."

"No—she'd just gone. Folly told me so and rang off before I could say anything. I couldn't get on again. If the last train hadn't gone, I'd come up myself. Of course I could get a car and come. Only then Betty would have to know, and I don't want her to. She'd tell one of the Aunts, and they'd tell Grandmamma, and the Family'd go on talking about it for the next hundred years or so."

"No," said David. "You can't come up. What do you want me to do?"

"Well, if you could be there when they get back. The little wretch has got my key. It was in my bag, and she simply helped herself to it. What did you say?"

"Never mind."

"No, don't cut us off—I want three minutes more. David, are you there?"

"Yes—go on. What am I to do with her?"

"I thought perhaps Julie—she's such a little dear, she won't talk—I don't want the Family to know."

"Good Lord—no! Look here, Eleanor, don't worry. And don't dream of coming up. I'll fix something. Julie's only got one spare room; but I can sleep at the office—I do sometimes. Now, is that all?"

"Yes. David—don't be very angry with her."

David fairly snorted.

"She wants a good leathering!"

He hung up the receiver and came back to the table.

"Who are we taking in instead of you?" said Frank with a laugh. "Is it Eleanor?"

"No—Folly March. She's got herself stuck in town, and Eleanor's fussed."

"I like Folly," said Julie.

David was surprised to find himself liking Julie the better for it. He couldn't imagine why. He finished a rather tepid helping of beefsteak pie, and as soon as the maid had left the room, he told Julie pretty nearly everything that Eleanor had told him.

Julie was deeply interested.

"Of course I'll have her. But how are you going to get hold of her? Oh! I've got a *lovely* plan! Let's go to all the night-clubs."

"Us!" said Frank with vehemence.

"You and me and David, Franko. I think it would be tremendous fun."

"Nothing doing," said Frank. "Look here, David, Julie's not on in this. We'll take Folly in, though, if you can collect her. What did you say the man's name was?"

"I didn't say—but it's St. Inigo."

Frank's eyebrows went up, and he exclaimed sharply:

"St. Inigo! She's rather going the limit, isn't she?"

"She's a little fool."

"St. Inigo's a member of The Soupçon. You'll probably find them there—if the committee hasn't kicked him out yet. I happen to know they're going to, because Mordaunt told me so—can't hold his tongue to save his life, and he said St. Inigo had been making the place too hot to hold him. What on earth's George March about to let the girl pick up with a fellow like that?"

"I gather that she picked up with him because George said she wasn't to."

"George is a damned fool," said Frank Alderey with contempt.

Julie sat with her elbows on the table and her chin in her hands. She wore a pale blue velvet wrap with fur on it. Her cheeks were pink, and her eyes bright with excitement as she looked from Frank to David.

"Look here," said Frank. "I'll get on to Mordaunt and say you want to look in at The Soupçon. That'll make it all right for you. When you get there—"

David laughed a little harshly.

"When I get there! Well, what do I do then? As a matter of fact I can't do anything."

"Oh, but you'll *go*?" said Julie eagerly.

David laughed again.

"Oh yes, I'll go."

Chapter Nine

WHEN DAVID CAME into the room with the crowded dancing-floor and the little tables set close to the wall all round it, the first person that he saw was Tommy Wingate, plump and rosy. His large round eyeglass—Tommy's monocle always looked larger and shinier than anyone else's—winked joyously at the many lights. His hair had gone a trifle farther back in the three years since David had seen him last. Otherwise the same Tommy.

David was very glad to see him now. He smote him on the shoulder, hauled him to a table, and ordered drinks.

"You with anyone?"

"Meeting a man. He's late, or I'm early. Man called Devlin. Said he'd introduce me. I'm a pilgrim, I'm a stranger. Oh, David, it's good to get home! Anyone"—he leaned forward and struck David painfully on the knee—"*anyone*—"

"Tommy, I'll break your head if you do that again!"

"Then you'll get chucked out. They were raided a month ago, and we don't break heads any more. What I was going to say when you interrupted me was that any blooming fellow can have the whole blooming East as far as I'm concerned."

He began to warble:

"I ain't going back no more, no more,
Oh, I ain't going back no more,
Tarara!"

The last word was so startlingly loud that it achieved an audience. Tommy was in admirable form.

"What are you doing? Leave?"

"Just a spot. I'm for the Staff College and the midnight oil—not this sort, worse luck. I failed till they got tired of failing me and gave me a nomination. Er—" Tommy's voice dropped from its loud and cheerful note. "Er—how's everything?"

"Oh, all right."

Tommy let his eyeglass fall, picked it up, squinted through it with his other eye, and remarked absently:

"Er—Eleanor's home."

"Yes, she's home."

"She all right?"

"Going strong. She's down at Ford staying with Betty. Better come and look us up."

Tommy dropped his eyeglass again.

"Well," he said, "I'll come—but I don't suppose it's any earthly." He screwed up his jolly face and looked deprecatingly at David. "I've always been an ass about her, and I always shall be, and it's never been any earthly. There you are—I don't think she minds me when I don't make too big an ass of myself." He brightened a little. "When shall I come along?"

"What about to-morrow? I'm driving down."

The prospect of the *tête-à-tête* drive with Folly was one of the things which was making David monosyllabic. He positively grabbed at Tommy Wingate. But Tommy shook his head.

"To-morrow I lunch with an aunt and take three flapper cousins to the Zoo, or a cinema, or some other low haunt. And when that's over I dine with a great-uncle who has the worst cook in London. He lives on nuts—give you my word he does—weighs 'em out on a little thingummy-jig that sits on the table in front of him. Last time I went there he ate half a walnut too much and was dreadfully fussed. It'll be a roaring sort of evening, my lad, and no mistake. I'll totter down to you next day—what? Hullo, there's Devlin!"

Tommy precipitated himself into a crowd which had just stopped dancing and was now moving in every direction at once. David saw him accost a tall, thin red-haired man and a party which included no less than three extremely personable young things, with one of whom Tommy presently took the floor.

David cast his eyes about the room in search of Folly March. The place was crowded with an odd medley of people—young men and old in dinner jackets and long coats; girls in hats, and girls in evening frocks; women with the minimum of clothing and the maximum number of pearls that it is possible to crowd upon the human frame. At the table on his right there sat a woman huddled in cloth of gold to the ears. She had a dead face and pale, square-cut hair as lank as tow. She held a cigarette in a very long amber holder, but never put it to her mouth, and during all the time that David was in the room she neither moved nor spoke to her companion. Just opposite, by a table near the door, a very tall woman was talking to half a dozen men at once. She wore a little black cap that hid her hair, and long emerald earrings that fell below her shoulder; her dress was a glittering black sheath that ended above the knee. She might have been Pierrot from the zeal with which she had whitened her face. The magenta lips appeared to emit a steady flow of bad language.

David glanced at his wrist-watch. All the theatres must be out by now. If Folly did not turn up in five minutes, he would just have to go to the flat and wait for her there.

As he looked up again he saw her coming into the room with St. Inigo. She was looking all round her like a pleased child, and she wore the new little black curls tied on with a pale blue ribbon which ended in an artless bow over one ear. Her frock might very properly have appeared at a breaking-up party of the most decorous of schools— little white frills and a pale blue girdle. She wore a coral necklace—not coral beads, but a necklace of the real old-fashioned spiky red coral which all little girls possess and break.

Something pricked David sharply at the sight of the coral necklace. He was being got at. And knowing that he was being got at, he said to himself, "Little devil!" and then was pulled up sharply by the very patent fact that St. Inigo was drunk.

Folly slipped her hand into St. Inigo's arm and they made a half circuit of the room. They came to a standstill a yard or two from David.

Without any plan he got up and walked over to them. St. Inigo was certainly drunk—steady enough on his feet and steady enough with his tongue, but drunk for all that, his very handsome features pale and expressionless, his light eyes fixed and glittering.

David said, "Hullo, Folly!" and just for an instant the little devil in its schoolgirl dress made a movement towards him. It was so slight a movement, and so quickly checked, that he wondered why he had imagined that Folly was glad to see him. She stood there looking down and tapping with her foot. A complete absence of make-up allowed him to see that her colour had risen. St. Inigo stared.

David's temper began to rise.

"Can you spare me a moment? I've got a message for you—from Eleanor."

Folly shot him a glance, but he made nothing of it. Suspicion—appeal—no, he couldn't place it.

He began, "I won't keep you"; and then Folly said in her little purring voice:

"Do you know Stingo? You ought to. Stingo, I'm sure you're pleased to meet David. He's my deputy chaperon." Then she looked at David with little dancing green sparks in her eyes. "That's what you're here for, aren't you? I suppose Eleanor sent you. Did she?"

"Well, I've got a message from her." He turned to St. Inigo. "Will you excuse Miss March for a moment? Mrs. Rayne asked me to give her a message."

The bright, glittering eyes shifted a point. Folly went on quickly:

"How did you know I was here?" The purr was an angry one. "Did Eleanor tell you to come after me? Did she? Did she tell you to follow me round and—and make a laughing-stock of me? I suppose she told you she'd forbidden me to come, and so she sent you to fetch me home as if I was five years old!"

"Perhaps you'd better go," said St. Inigo with a sneer.

Folly sparkled at him.

"Shall I?"

"Oh yes—much better go with him. Always go home with your chaperon. Let him take you home and tuck you up in bye-bye." Mr. St. Inigo's look and voice were even more offensive than Mr. St. Inigo's words.

David controlled his fury and addressed himself to Miss Folly March:

"Folly, Julie's expecting you, and I think—"

Folly had turned quite white; she was so angry that she could hardly speak. But her anger was with David. It shook her from head to foot. She was not often angry, and she did not know why she was angry now. She felt that she would kill David if he looked at her. She was one blazing flame of fury, and she did not know why. She caught St. Inigo by the arm and whirled him round.

"Stingo, I want to dance! We came here to dance—didn't we?"

David watched them plunge into the crowd of dancers. Over Folly's shoulder St. Inigo looked at him, a long, cold, insolent look.

He came out of the club in a black rage. Short of making a public scene he could do no more. For Eleanor's sake he would wait at the flat until Folly came in. If St. Inigo were with her, he might possibly have the pleasure of knocking St. Inigo down.

The air was very cold. He walked quickly. By the time he reached the entrance to the block of flats his anger had passed into disgust. If it were not for Eleanor, Folly might go her own way. What could you do with a girl who took up with a swab like St. Inigo? Disgust sharpened into contempt, and then, quick and vivid, came the picture of a child in a white frock and a coral necklace, with bobbing black curls put on to please him. The something that had tugged at his heart in the drawing-room at Ford plucked at him now, and the more shrewdly because he winced away from it.

Chapter Ten

DAVID STOOD by the entrance to the block of flats and considered gloomily that he might have to keep his eye on it for hours. He began to walk up and down Chieveley Street. Fifty yards one way with the wind in his face, and hundred yards back with the wind behind him.

After half an hour it occurred to him that he had mentioned to Folly that Julie was expecting her. It was unlikely that she would have a spasm of sanity and go straight to the Aldereys', but it was possible; in which case David would be walking up and down Chieveley Street till daylight overtook him.

When he had walked for another half hour he began to wonder how long one could walk up and down the same street without attracting the attention of the police. He also wondered what he would say if he were asked what he was doing. The plain truth would hardly have convinced a child of five. "My cousin, Mrs. Rayne, has a flat up there. She's away, and my other cousin, Miss March, who has a key, is coming there. And I'm waiting to tell her she can't stay there alone, and to take her to yet another cousin, Mrs. Frank Alderey." A simple tale and one likely to leave Robert cold. With a shrug of the shoulders he put Folly and her affairs away, and let his mind swing back to the problem which had burdened him all day.

The words of the advertisement stood out in a garish dazzle, senseless and bewildering. His thoughts beat against it like moths, only to fall back in confusion. If it was a practical joke, it was both cruel and pointless; and who was there who knew enough of his private affairs to jest with them? If it was serious, from whom did it come? From Erica herself? He couldn't believe it. If by some extraordinary chance she had survived, she would have written to him—she *must* have written to him.

As he paced up and down, he saw, not Chieveley Street and the lamps shining in a frosty air, but the tilted deck of the *Bomongo*; his ears were filled again with the sounds of wreck and disaster; he saw, as he had not seen it for years, Erica's ghastly face against his shoulder, and felt the rigid terror of her clasp.

David went on walking, sometimes on one side of the road and sometimes on the other. He looked at his watch and made it half-past two. A perfectly fresh access of anger came to him and he quickened his pace a little. At his usual turning place he paused, looked up and down the street, and walked on to the corner. There was a lamppost there. He stood under it looking into the dark side street; and as he did so, he saw something move.

He had hardly taken more than half a dozen steps away from the lamp when the moving something came out of the shadows at a stumbling run and caught at him with two little icy hands. The light showed him Folly March in a dark fur coat with her curls all crooked.

She looked dreadfully white, and the hands that clutched his arm were shaking.

He exclaimed sharply: "Folly, what on earth!"

"Take me home," said Folly in a ghost of a voice. "I want to go home at once."

"You're just there."

He was walking her along, his anger gone, and a fear that had no words in its place. What had happened?

Eleanor's flat was on the second floor. They reached the door without a spoken word on either side. Folly put the key, a cold key in a little cold hand, into David's palm and the door swung open. He switched on the light and took her into the room where he and Eleanor had had tea.

"Folly, what's the matter? Can't you tell me?"

"It's so cold," said Folly on a caught breath.

David put his arm round her.

"My dear, what's the matter?"

"Nothing," said Folly.

She leaned hard against his arm for a moment, then went and sat down in the corner of the sofa, holding her fur coat about her.

"It's so cold! Do light the fire."

At his wits' end, David knelt on the hearth and put a match to the neatly laid fire. As the flame went up and the sticks caught, Folly gave a little sigh and leaned towards it holding out her hands. With his back to her David fed the blaze with coal. He kept his eyes away from the little shaking hands. After a while she sighed again and said in a childish whisper:

"Stingo was rude."

David turned, still on his knees.

"Folly, for the Lord's sake tell me what's happened! The swine was drunk. Has he hurt you?"

Folly caught her breath.

"N-no—he frightened me."

"What happened?"

"He was bringing me home in a taxi—he was rude—I got out."

"He let you?"

"I b-bit him."

"What!"

"I b-bit him hard. He wouldn't let go, and I bit him as hard as I could. I wish I could bite twice as hard. I wish you'd been there. You would—wouldn't you?"

David's relief broke from him in sudden laughter.

"I would what?"

"B-bite," said Folly viciously.

"I should probably have pushed his face in. Go on. What happened?"

"I b-bit—and he swore—and I got the door open—and I got out on to the step—and he grabbed at me—and I jumped. And there was a policeman at the corner, so he didn't follow me, and I walked home— and it was miles. Ooh! What a lovely fire!"

"You've got to come away from it. Julie's expecting you."

David got up as he spoke. Folly looked at him sideways. Her hands were still shaking a little, but her colour was coming back.

"Why can't I stay here? You can stay and look after me. You can have the sofa and Eleanor's eiderdown."

"Don't talk nonsense!" said David.

"I call it nonsense to go out and be frozen to death just when I'm getting nice and warm."

"Well, you've got to."

"Why have I got to?"

"Because Eleanor says so."

Folly pursed her lips and looked into the fire. After a moment she said in a meek little voice:

"Does Mr. Grundy always do what Mrs. Grundy tells him?"

David looked at his watch.

"You can have another five minutes. I'm afraid you'll have to walk—there isn't an earthly chance of getting a taxi at this hour."

"We could telephone for one."

"We could; but I don't think we will."

"Why not?"

"Well—I don't think we want to advertise this show, you know. Anyhow it's no distance. Now you'd better go and pack your bag."

She got up and stood for a moment looking into the glass that hung above the mantelpiece.

"My curls won't stay straight," she murmured. "They look awfully drunk when they're crooked—don't they?" She straightened them, whisked round, and dropped him a curtsy. "You do like them though—don't you?"

"Go and pack!"

"How impatient you are! David, do say you like them."

She came quite close to him, her fur coat slipping from her shoulders.

"Where's your necklace?" said David, speaking quickly and saying what he hadn't meant to say.

Folly went back a step. She put her hand to her throat, and the quick, bright colour flamed in her cheeks; her eyes looked away from him.

"It—broke."

There was just a moment's strained silence, and then, with one of the quick movements which reminded him of a kitten, she ran out of the room.

Left alone, David felt a wave of nausea sweep over him; the words had brought Folly's danger just too near. He flung round to the hearth with a jerk and began to rake out the fire.

Folly found him on his knees there when she came back with her suitcase.

"Ooh! My nice fire!" she said. But she handed over her case and followed him out of the flat without any further protest, a good deal to his relief, for it had occurred to him more than once that if she really insisted on staying at the flat, he would just have to let her stay.

They came out into the dark street and the nip of the wind. Folly slipped a hand inside his arm, and when they had gone half a dozen steps she pulled on it.

"Is my case heavy?"

"You know it isn't."

"Do you mind carrying it?"

"No."

They passed a lamp-post as he said, "No," and he looked down at her, frowning. The collar of her fur coat stood up about her ears; the curls were lost in it; the ribbon showed like a pale streak. Her eyes were like pools of sad green water. She pulled at his arm again.

"David—"

"What is it?"

"David—" in a very small voice indeed.

"Well?"

"Did you come to that place to look for me?"

"You seemed pretty sure of it at the time."

"'M—I was angry. Did you come there to look for me?"

"Yes, I did."

"Because Eleanor told you to?"

"Eleanor didn't know where you were. Frank Alderey said St. Inigo was a member of The Soupçon, so I just dropped in on the chance of finding you."

Folly pulled her hand away.

"What's the matter now?"

"Didn't any more relations send you? Didn't *Grandmamma* tell you to come?"

"Don't be a little idiot!"

After a moment she snuggled up to him again.

"Would you have come of your very own self if Eleanor hadn't sent you?" Her cheek just brushed his sleeve.

"Eleanor didn't send me, I tell you."

"'M—would you have come just of your very own self?"

David stiffened.

"I don't know," said Folly. "Would you?"

"I haven't the slightest idea."

Folly pulled her hand away again. This time she did not put it back. Halfway down the next street she was visibly lagging. David took her by the elbow and felt her quiver.

"We're nearly there," he said in a kind voice. With Julie's door only half a dozen houses away, it was safe to be kind.

"I wanted to stay at that flat," said Folly.

"Well, you couldn't. This is the house. Wait till I find the key. There's a gas-fire in your room, so you'll be warm—the first to the left at the top of the stairs."

"Aren't you coming in?"

He produced the key and opened the door before he said: "No, I'm going to the office."

"Oh! Have I got your room?"

David pushed the door open. There was a light in the hall. He set the suitcase down and went out on to the step again.

"In with you! Good-night," he said, and ran down the steps.

Folly pulled the door to within half an inch of closing and ran after him.

He heard "David!" in a breathless voice and turned.

"Folly, go in!"

"I'm going. I wasn't going to say good-night. But you did walk about for hours and wait for me. Eleanor didn't tell you to do that, did she?"

"Look here," said David, "if you think I'm going to flirt with you on Julie's doorstep at three o'clock in the morning, I'm not. Go in at once!"

"I'm going," said Folly, in a sort of mournful whisper. "You're a b-beast, and I'm going."

She went up two steps, and then came down them with a little jump. Before David had the slightest idea of what was going to happen, she was putting up her face to be kissed, and he was kissing her. She stood in front of him like a child and put up her face, and he kissed her. Her mouth was very soft and cold.

She gave him just the one half-careless kiss and ran up the steps and into the house. The door shut.

Chapter Eleven

At breakfast next morning Frank Alderey encountered a white-faced child whose lashes moistened when he looked at her and whose mouth quivered painfully. He administered a very bowdlerized edition of the lecture previously rehearsed to a protesting Julie, and departed to the office feeling that he had been a brute.

As the day advanced, Folly revived, made friends with Julie, and confided the whole adventure from start to finish. The finish, however, came when David lighted the fire at the flat.

"I'm a little bit afraid of David," said Julie.

"'M—I'm not."

"Was he very angry?"

Folly made a face.

"Did he scold you? I should hate to be scolded by David. But then, I'm very bad about being scolded at all—I cry. Frank says it's awfully silly of me."

"'M—I shouldn't cry if David scolded me."

"What would you do?"

"I don't know," said Folly, looking down. "He hasn't done it yet."

David called for her at three o'clock. He had made an effort to detach Tommy Wingate from his engagement to eat nuts with the valetudinarian great-uncle, but in vain. He arrived armed with a frown of the first magnitude. His manner was one of detached politeness.

Folly sat beside him with downcast eyes and folded hands. She said that it was cold; she said that it was kind of him to drive her down to Ford; and she said that she liked Julie. As David did not answer any of these remarks, the conversation languished.

They drove along wet, thawing roads. There were brown hedgerows and brown fields. Here and there the alders were flushing into purple. A thin bluish mist crept in from the horizon upon every side; the full grey clouds hung low; there was a dampness in the air that presently blurred the wind-screen with tiny drops.

They reached Ford in time for tea. Folly stood on the step for a moment. She was reluctant to go in. Tea was nice—but was everyone going to make an awful fuss? She watched David drive round to the garage, and then went in with a lagging step.

Eleanor ran into the hall to find her slipping out of her fur coat and gloves. As the coat dropped, Folly shivered ostentatiously. She looked at Eleanor with a wary eye.

"Is there a row on?" she inquired.

"Ssh—no—Betty doesn't know anything."

"As if I cared for Betty!" Folly pranced across the hall with her chin in the air. "Are you *frightfully* angry?"

"I wasn't angry; I was frightened. Folly, what happened?"

Folly stood on tiptoe and put soft arms round Eleanor's neck.

"Silly Mrs. Grundy!"

"Little wretch! What happened?"

Folly warmed a very cold nose against Eleanor's cheek.

"You're pussy-warm," she murmured. "Ooh! There's David! Didn't he tell you what happened?"

"No—only that he'd collected you."

"Pouf!" said Folly. "I collected myself. I b-bit Stingo."

"Folly!"

"I b-bit him. And David's going to push his face in." She sprang back as David came into the hall. "Ooh! I do want my tea!" she cried, and ran into the drawing-room.

In the middle of tea she remarked suddenly: "I nearly brought Timmy down."

Betty's eyebrows went up. They were pale and thin like Betty herself. They made rather fretful marks of interrogation.

"Timothy Catkins," said Folly. "He's Eleanor's kitten—and he's an absolutely dinky lamb. Only the cook takes him home to sleep with her, and she said she wouldn't stay there all day if she didn't have him for company; so I didn't bring him. I thought Eleanor'd be peeved if the cook ran away."

"Doesn't the cook sleep at the flat?" said Betty in a puzzled voice. Then sharply: "Folly, you didn't stay there alone?"

Folly's eyes opened wide.

"Of *course* I didn't—it wouldn't have been *proper*. I stayed with Julie."

Eleanor bit her lip.

A little later David put down his cup and got up. On his way to the door he stopped for a moment by Eleanor's chair and said in a low voice:

"Can you spare me half an hour in the study?"

She said, "Of course"; and they went out together.

Folly finished her tea and escaped. She came down an hour later in a little blue frock with long sleeves, and the most discreet neck in the world.

In the drawing-room Betty sat over the fire with a book. Folly fetched a stool with a needle-work top, set it down in the middle of the hearthrug, and planted herself upon it, two neat feet on the fender and a fluff of blue skirts spread out all around her. She gazed first at the fire and then at Betty.

Betty had a book, but she wasn't reading. She went on looking at the same place on the same page; sometimes her eyebrows went up, and sometimes the corners of her mouth went down. She had on an ugly petunia dress and a string of large pearl beads that fitted her thin neck closely.

Folly cocked her head a little on one side and said, "Are they *still* talking?"

"Who? What d'you mean?" Betty's voice was very cross.

"Eleanor and David. She hasn't come upstairs. They must have a lot to say to each other."

"Nonsense!" Betty flicked over two pages at once and held the book a little higher.

"I expect they have. They were engaged, weren't they?"

Betty stared.

"What are you talking about?"

"About Eleanor and David. They were engaged, weren't they, before Eleanor was married?"

"Who told you that?"

"Pouf! Everyone knows! I've known for years. I think it's frightfully interesting. Don't you?"

Betty turned another page.

"I think they'd both be very much annoyed if they thought you were discussing them like this."

"Yes—*wouldn't* they?" Folly locked her hands about her knees and gazed in a rapt manner at Betty. "They'd be simply frightfully angry, I expect. That's what makes it so thrilling."

"I do wish you wouldn't talk such nonsense!"

Folly transferred her gaze to the fire. A fascinating procession of blazing sparks was flying up from the end of a half-burnt log. She watched the sparks for about a minute, and then she said:

"Perhaps they'll get engaged all over again now Eleanor's a widow."

Betty dropped her book. There was a dry, angry colour in her face.

"Folly, you're too old to say things like that."

Folly stared.

"Wouldn't you be pleased? I'm only saying it to you. I should think you'd love to have Eleanor for a sister. I think it's *too* exciting. Perhaps he's asking her this very minute. I think it's simply dinkily romantic."

Betty lost her temper. She stood up with a jerk, letting her book fall on the floor.

"Considering the absolutely shameless way you've been trying to get David to flirt with you—"

"Oh, your poor book!" said Folly. She made a dive for it without getting up, and offered it with a meek upward gaze.

"I suppose you imagine that men like that sort of thing."

"'M—" said Folly, "they *do*!"

Betty stared hard at her, swallowed angrily once or twice, and walked to the door. Just before she reached it she stopped.

"Men flirt with girls like you, but they don't marry them," she said. Then she went out of the room and banged the door.

Chapter Twelve

IN THE STUDY David switched on his reading-lamp and turned out the other lights. He put Eleanor in the big armchair and sat down at his writing-table. The lamp with its green shade threw a steady light over the books and papers on the table; it left Eleanor in the shadow.

"I wanted to talk to you," said David.

"About Folly? David, what happened?"

"Nothing. She'll tell you herself. It's not that at all—it's about myself. It's—well, it's something I want to talk to you about. You don't mind?"

Eleanor wasn't sure. She knew David well enough to discern an unaccustomed emotion, and she shrank very much from any suggestion of an emotional contact between them. Two nights ago her guard had been pierced for a moment; she still shrank a little at remembering how much it had hurt. She said, "What is it, David?" and her voice was slow and rather frightened.

David was too much absorbed to notice anything unusual in her manner. He leaned his right elbow on the table and with his left hand pulled upon one of the drawers on that side.

"I wanted to talk to you about it. I—it was a bit of a shock, and I want to talk to you."

"David, what is it?" She was puzzled as well as nervous now.

"It's this," said David.

He took from the drawer a newspaper cutting and held it under the lamp for a moment.

"From yesterday's *Times*," he said, and laid it on Eleanor's knee.

She took it, and then had to lean forward to get the light on the small print. The arm of the chair was between her and David. She leaned on it with the strip of paper in her hand and read what he had read in the Agony Column of yesterday's *Times*:

"D. A. St. K. F.—Your wife is alive."

David saw her eyes travel along the line and go back to the beginning again. She read to the end, coloured deeply, and lifted her eyes to his. They were dark and clear, with a trouble in them.

"What does it mean?"

"I don't know."

He still had his elbow on the table; his face, turned towards her, showed two deep lines between the eyes; his hand hid his mouth.

"Why did you show it to me? What does it mean?"

"I don't know." He repeated the words slowly and without expression.

Eleanor sat up very straight.

"David, what does it mean? Is it meant for you?" She touched the initials with her finger and read them aloud: "'D. A. St. K. F.'—is that meant for you?"

"That's what I want to know." His hand dropped and she saw the hard set of his mouth. "That's just what I want to know."

"But—you're not married!"

"I was."

The words seemed to break something. It was like the breaking of a silence; but they had not been silent. Only for both of them something broke.

Eleanor did not speak. She looked at the slip of paper in her hand, and when she had read the words again she leaned back out of the circle of light, waiting.

"That's what I wanted to tell you about," said David.

"Yes."

"I've never told anyone about it."

She looked up then, distressed. What was coming? What had he done? The light showed her his face with the frown gone from it and only a sadness left. He half smiled at her, and the smile brought a mist to her eyes.

"It's all right—it's not anything that I mind telling you," he said simply. "It's only—when you've never spoken about a thing it's hard to begin."

Eleanor nodded.

After a moment he went on speaking, looking sometimes at her, but more often past her into the shadows.

"You remember I went to America? I suppose we both felt pretty badly just then. I wouldn't have gone if they hadn't packed you off to India. But I couldn't very well follow you—I hadn't a bean except what my father gave me—and I rather jumped at the idea of putting in a year in the States. I'd visions of making a fortune and coming after you—you know the sort of thing: *'Penniless Architect Wins Million Dollar Competition for New City Hall.'*" He laughed and shifted the papers on his table. "Well, it was nix on that; but I put in a pretty useful year in old O'Gorman's office. And then, when I was getting ready to come home, my father sent me some money and told me to come round by New Zealand and go and see old Bobby St. Kern and his family. Well, that was all right; they were no end good to me, and I stayed there six weeks. And as I'd just enough money to spare, I got a tramp passage to Sydney. I thought I might just as well see as much as I could whilst I was about it."

He paused, as if for a word; but the pause lengthened and deepened until it seemed a hard thing to break.

Eleanor broke it.

"Did you meet her in Sydney?"

"No." Another pause. Then quickly: "She was on board. You mustn't think there was anything then. There wasn't—I was thinking about you."

"Who was she?"

There was gratitude in David's eyes.

"She was only a kid—I never thought of her as anything else. Awfully shy and frightened, and no wonder. She'd been living alone with her father in a God-forsaken spot where they never saw anyone. He emigrated and buried himself there when her mother died three or four years before. And then he died, and there was just enough money to take Erica to Sydney, where there was a widowed aunt."

"Yes," said Eleanor, "I see."

"No you don't. There wasn't anything then; I was just sorry for her like anyone would be. And when we got to Sydney and the aunt didn't come on board to meet her, of course I said I'd get her ashore and all that. I thought it was odd the aunt not turning up; but of course our dates were a bit uncertain. Well, anyhow, when we got to the address, we found that the aunt had died suddenly a week before."

"Oh!" said Eleanor with just a little breath of protest. The story was bringing the boy of six years ago very vividly before her; as David spoke, voice, manner, and expression seemed to grow younger, more impulsive. It was easy to follow the steps by which he had walked, or blundered, into the trap which circumstance had laid for him.

David made an abrupt movement.

"Beastly—wasn't it, that poor kid with no money and not a soul in the world to care what happened to her except me?"

"Weren't there any other relations?"

"An aunt somewhere in England—her mother's sister. Erica wasn't even sure of her address. She thought she lived in London."

"What happened? What did you do?"

"There was a woman who said she'd been a friend of the aunt's. She took Erica in, and I went off to see my agents." He paused, turned to the table, and began to straighten some of the papers that lay there. After a moment he said: "There were letters for me, a whole bunch— I'd just missed a mail when I came away, and the St. Kerns had sent it on." He gave a short, half-angry laugh. "Most of the Family had written to tell me you were married."

Eleanor cried out. She had had her part, then in making the trap. That hurt very much.

David glanced at her in a detached sort of way.

"It was a knock," he said. "You won't think I've been holding it up against you—I don't want you to think that. But I want you to understand that it hit me. I was pretty well knocked out of time, and when I came round I was a bit off my balance. I really do want you to understand. You see, it was partly everyone writing like that. Grandmamma's effort was perfectly damnable. All the rest were quite well meaning, but they got me on the raw. You know the sort of thing the Aunts write, and Milly. I felt like knocking their heads together and going off the deep end. My father wrote me a very decent letter, though it made me angry at the time. He sent me some more money and told me not to hurry home if I didn't feel like it. It's a funny thing, you know, Eleanor, the way that things turn out. My father'd have had a fit if he'd known that money was going to pay Erica's passage."

"Go on," said Eleanor.

David frowned.

"I didn't plan anything—things just happened. Erica tried to get work, but people said she wasn't strong enough. I went to see her every day. She was a plucky kid, and she didn't tell me the woman was being a beast to her, until one day I came in and heard her slanging the poor little thing. She was a foul-tongued brute, and if she'd been a man, I'd have knocked her down. Erica caught hold of me like a scared child and cried. And the woman said, if I meant fair by her, why didn't I marry her? and I said, 'I'm going to.'"

There was a silence. After a while David went on.

"We were married. I took passages on the *Bomongo*. I didn't write to my father or anyone. I was awfully glad afterwards that I hadn't.

The reason I didn't write wasn't anything to be proud of. I wanted to put it across the Family—to arrive and spring Erica on them. Well, it never came off, as you know. The *Bomongo* went to bits in a gale ten days out from Melbourne. They got off a boat with the women, and it was never heard of. Erica was in it. I was in the last boat, and we were picked up next day. You know all that part. I stayed in Cape Town till there wasn't any chance of the other boat having survived. When everyone had given it up, I came home. As you know, I only just saw my father. I think I'd have told him if there had been time; but there wasn't. And when he was gone there didn't seem to be any reason for telling anyone else."

"You didn't tell anyone?"

"No—why should I?"

"Not Betty?"

"Betty was taken up with her own affairs. Francis was in the limelight at the moment—he'd just been making England a bit too hot to hold him, and I'd all that on my hands as well as settling my father's affairs." He hesitated, and then added: "I don't know if you can understand, but it got to feel exactly like a dream—as if it hadn't really happened, you know."

"Yes, I can understand that." Eleanor's voice was soft. "David—I do understand—all of it. But not this." She touched the newspaper cutting. "What does this mean?"

"That's what I don't know."

"David, if she were alive, you'd have heard long ago."

"That's what I've said to myself."

"She'd have written to you. David, she *must* have written to you. You—you hadn't quarrelled?"

"No, no."

"It must be a coincidence."

"That's what I said the first time."

Eleanor exclaimed sharply. She repeated his words:

"The *first* time!"

"Yes." He leaned over and took up the cutting. "This is the third, Eleanor."

She sat up straight, looking at him.

"David—when?"

"The first was three years ago. Look here, Eleanor, I'm telling you the whole thing. The Family had begun to think it was time I got married. Grandmamma gave the matter her personal attention. Betty was roped in and proceeded to ask a series of young things to stay. One of them came pretty often. She was a jolly little thing, and we got on awfully well in spite of Grandmamma. As a matter of fact she used to chaff me about it. Well, right in the thick of it all, this advertisement came out for the first time. I tried to find out where it had come from, but of course there was nothing doing. I wrote to the steamship company and to the solicitor I'd been to in Cape Town to ask whether they'd ever heard anything; and they said they hadn't. I couldn't think of anything else to do, and after a bit I put the matter out of my mind."

"It must have been a coincidence."

David looked away from her.

"The second one came out after your husband died."

Eleanor did not speak.

"I tried again to find out. I wrote to Cape Town again, and to the agents at Melbourne and Sydney. They said the same as before—they'd heard nothing." He paused for a moment and got up. "The third advertisement came out yesterday. Coincidence, Eleanor?"

"David, what do you really think?"

"I don't know what to think. If I'd ordinary initials—no one can pretend that there's likely to be another D. A. St. K. F. with a missing wife. If it's a practical joke, it's cruel and damned pointless. And if Erica's alive, why doesn't she write and say so?"

"How old was she?" said Eleanor irrelevantly.

"Sixteen—I told you she was only a child."

"You didn't tell me her other name."

"Moore—Erica Moore."

"Did you ever try and find the aunt you spoke of?"

David threw out his hand.

"I hadn't an idea how to set about it. She was Aunt Nellie, and her surname was Smith, I shouldn't wonder if there were thousands of Nellie Smiths."

"I should advertise," said Eleanor quickly.

"For Nellie Smith?"

"No—for Erica. I should put her name first—Erica Moore, and then say that anyone giving news of her would be rewarded,"

David walked across the room and back.

"Yes," he said, "yes. It couldn't do any harm."

He sat down at the table, wrote for a moment and laid the sheet of paper on Eleanor's knee. She read:

"ERICA MOORE.—Anyone giving information with regard to Erica Moore will be rewarded."

A fidgeting, hesitating hand fumbled at the door. Betty came halfway across the threshold and spoke querulously:

"I didn't think you could possibly know the time. The dressing-bell went ages ago."

Chapter Thirteen

DINNER WAS RATHER a silent meal. Betty alone upheld the conversation. She had had a letter by the evening post from Dick. She read it aloud, and then, taking it as a text, discoursed upon it.

David, who had heard it all before, produced no remarks. Eleanor, with a slight air of being somewhere else, said "Yes," and "Did he?" and "How nice, Betty!" Folly, who felt no interest at all in Dicky Lester, watched Betty between her lashes and decided shrewdly that it was not only Dicky's letter that had brought the colour to Betty's cheeks and the edge to her voice. "Jealous cat!" she said to herself.

After dinner David, with the air of a man who has had as much Dicky as he can swallow, introduced a new topic:

"By the way, I quite forgot to say Tommy Wingate's home. I ran into him last night. I've asked him to come down."

Eleanor looked up smiling, and Betty said "Oh?" in a half-offended tone. "You might have told me at once. Is he coming?"

"Yes—to-morrow. He's eating nuts with an aged uncle to-night, or I'd have brought him with me."

Folly, on her stool before the fire, looked from Eleanor to David.

"Who is he? Is he nice? Is he young? May I play with him?"

"Ask Eleanor," said David. "He's her property."

"Ooh! How exciting! Eleanor, may I flirt with him a little bit, just to keep my hand in?"

Eleanor laughed.

"Tommy will be delighted. He flirts nearly as well as you do."

"Ooh!" said Folly. She looked out of the corners of her eyes at Betty, and then whisked round and tugged at David's sleeve.

"David, you're not to read the paper. You're to listen and give expert advice. Which of my frocks shall I wear to-morrow so as to strike Eleanor's Tommy all of a heap?"

David laughed in spite of himself.

"It's no good—he's irrevocably Eleanor's."

Folly caught David's hand and pinched it vigorously.

"I don't want him for keeps. You haven't been listening. Eleanor's lent him to me to flirt with. Haven't you, Mrs. Grundy, darling?" She made an impudent face at Eleanor over her shoulder, then pinched David again, softly this time. "There! I've got Mrs. Grundy's leave! Even Betty can't say anything after that. Shall I wear this frock? Or does it make me look too good? I always think blue gives one a sort of maiden's prayer look. I've got a red frock you haven't seen—but perhaps that would shock him. George said it wasn't respectable."

David had a quick vision of a little scarlet Folly with green eyes full of laughing, beckoning mischief. He pulled his hand away from the fingers that had begun to stroke the place they had pinched, and said roughly:

"Tommy won't notice what you wear."

"You seem to have a great many clothes," said Betty in her most disagreeable voice.

"'M—I have. I like having lots; then I can wear the wicked ones when I feel good, and the little mild angel frocks when I'm going to run amuck." She blew an impudent kiss at David. "That's the way I keep the balance true."

"And who pays for the frocks?" said Betty.

Folly gazed at her artlessly.

"Oh, I can always find a man to do that," she said.

"Folly! How *could* you?" said Eleanor when they had gone upstairs.

"How could I what?"

Eleanor took her firmly by the arm.

"Come into my room. You're a little wretch, and I'm going to scold you."

Folly skipped on to the bed and sat there with one leg tucked up under her. With the heel of the other she drummed against the brass of the bedstead.

"Folly, you shouldn't—you shouldn't really! I hated to hear you say it."

Folly drummed.

"Say what? What *did* I say?"

"You said you could always get a man to pay for your clothes."

"So I can."

"Folly!"

Folly made large round eyes.

"I'm the cat with the eyes like mill-wheels, and Betty's the witch, and we're all in a fairy story—but I'm not quite sure who's the prince," she announced.

"Folly, you shouldn't have said it."

"Why not, if it was true?"

"It wasn't—it isn't."

Folly blew her a kiss.

"It is—it's perfectly true—I do get a man to pay for my clothes. I get George. And doesn't he grumble?"

She jumped down laughing and flung her arms round Eleanor's neck.

"I took you in! I shocked you! Oh, Mrs. Grundy, what a score! I'm games and games and games up on you!"

Eleanor shook her.

"Folly, it isn't a game. People have beastly minds—they believe that sort of thing quite easily. Betty believed it. You saw how she changed the subject. I only hope—"

"What?" said Folly. Her arms dropped. She looked at Eleanor defiantly. "Well, what do you hope?"

"I hope David didn't believe you."

Folly stamped her foot; her green eyes blazed out of a very white face. She said:

"I don't care a damn what David thinks!"

With the last word she had the door open and was gone. Her own door slammed and the key turned sharply.

It was a long time before Eleanor got to sleep. She woke with a start. Something had waked her, and for a moment she did not know what it was. Then the little click of the downstairs window came to her mind. That was what had waked her.

She listened intently, and heard the window close; her own window, wide open above it, carried the sound. She ran to it and leaned out. It was much later than it had been the other night, and it was cloudy, with a low mist everywhere. She looked, and could see nothing; and she listened, and could hear nothing at all.

She drew in shivering, more from strain than cold, for the night was soft. As she drew away from the window, she heard something, a faint sound which came from beyond her closed door. She opened it and stood there in the dark.

The passage ran from her door past the head of the stairs to the wing where Betty and David slept. The old schoolroom was there, and a spare bedroom. Folly's room faced the stairs. And it was on the stairs that something was moving.

With a quickness born partly of fear and partly of a sudden sharp anger, Eleanor put her hand on the switch outside her door and jerked it down. The light at the stair-head came on. The passage shone bright and empty.

Eleanor ran forward noiselessly. Halfway up the stair, with a black cloak thrown round her, stood Folly March, the fingers of her left hand resting on the balustrade, her eyes wide open and blank with fright. She looked up, saw Eleanor, and came up the remaining stairs with a rush.

"Ooh! You nearly killed me! Put the light out—put it out quick!"

She pushed open her own bedroom door, dragged Eleanor in, and turned out the passage light from the switch just outside. Then she shut the door and put on the light in the ceiling.

"Did you want to kill me? You nearly did."

"Folly, where have you been?"

Folly pulled off her cloak, rolled it into a ball, and flung it across the room.

"'M—" she said. "That's the question!"

She was in her nightgown, a flimsy transparent affair, white, with pink flowers on it. Her little feet were as bare and pink as a baby's.

Eleanor looked at the hem of the flimsy nightgown. It had been drizzling with rain all the afternoon; the mist was breast-high outside; park, and grass, and stone-paved walk must all be dripping wet. The little flowered night-gown was dry and crisp. The little pink feet were dry.

Folly stood looking at her toes. She shot an innocent glance at Eleanor's puzzled face, then she twiddled the toes.

"They're quite dry," she said with modest pride.

"Folly, where have you been?"

"On a broomstick over the moon."

"Folly, darling!"

"Didn't you know I was a witch? You can keep beautifully dry on a broomstick. Go to bed, darling. You can. It's quite safe—I never go for more than one broomstick ride at a time. And I really like moonlight best—it's more amusing."

She put her arm round Eleanor, hugged her, pushed her out of the door, and locked it in her very face.

Eleanor heard a smothered laugh:

"Good-night, Mrs. Grundy."

The light in Folly's room went out with a click.

Chapter Fourteen

NEXT DAY being Saturday, Tommy Wingate came down for the week-end. Miss Folly March seemed to approve of him; she certainly flirted with him to an extent that made Betty look down her nose, and provided a good deal of entertainment for the domestic staff. Tommy played golf with her, sang with her, and danced with her. But Folly

was shrewdly aware of the fact that Eleanor had only to beckon him
with a glance.

When she did, Tommy's gratitude was patent. He did not flirt with
Eleanor; he merely adored. He had never hidden, or desired to hide,
his devotion.

On Sunday evening he came down early, and found Eleanor early
too. She was standing by the fire, dropping fir-cones on to it and
watching them blaze. She wore a white embroidered shawl of China
crêpe over her black velvet dress; the long white fringes fell almost to
her feet. She turned to him, half laughing, as he came in.

"Don't they smell good? I love the fat green ones. Oh, Tommy!
Isn't it good to be home again?"

"It's good to be anywhere that you are," said Tommy, looking at
her through his absurd shining eyeglass. He thought her the most
beautiful woman in the world, and the most gracious.

"Thank you, Tommy. It's been ever so nice to see you."

Tommy leaned against the mantelpiece, one hand on the
marble edge.

"You'll see lots of me. Are you going to be in town?"

"For a bit."

"I can get up for week-ends. You'll let me come and see you?" His
jolly eyes were suddenly wistful like the eyes of a dog who begs for
what he knows he must not have.

Eleanor looked back at him sweetly and kindly.

"I shall love it," she said. Then she put her hand on his for a
moment. "Nice Tommy! But, Tommy, dear, don't be *too* nice to me."

"Why not?" said Tommy stoutly.

She just shook her head without speaking.

"I know it's no good now," he said without looking at her. "But
some day—"

Eleanor looked down into the fire. There were tears in her eyes.

"Oh, Tommy, that's all over."

Tommy squared his shoulders.

"That," he said, "is nonsense! You're twenty-five aren't you?
There's a frightful lot of time ahead of one at twenty-five."

"Yes," said Eleanor.

She stooped over the fire and pushed down a log with her hand. Tommy screwed his eyeglass firmly into his eye.

"When you're twenty-five there's no end of time to be happy in. That's what you want to get into your head. The other's all rot. You're meant to be happy, and I want to see you happy. Of course, I'd like it to be me; but if it isn't me, I'd like it to be some good chap who'll make you a thundering good husband."

"Tommy, dear, *don't!*"

"All right, I won't. You know I'm—well, I'm always there, and I always shall be there. You can bank on that."

It was at this moment that they both became aware of Folly with her hand on the half-open door. For once in her life she seemed to be a little taken aback. She looked over her shoulder, saw Betty behind her, and ran forward.

She had put on the scarlet frock. It suited the quiet Sunday evening about as well as scarlet paint would suit St. Paul's Cathedral. George March had been justified in his protest. The scarlet tulle left Folly's slim white back bare to the waist and stopped short a good two inches above the knee; there were no sleeves; there was very little bodice. There was, in fact, so little of it at all that if it had not been of a surprisingly vivid colour, it might have been mistaken for an under-garment.

Folly wore *the* curls on a silver ribbon. She also wore a dead white complexion and scarlet lips. Tommy looked at her with interest. Later on, after dinner, she took him away to the far end of the room, seated herself on the arm of a stiff, old-fashioned sofa, and said:

"Tommy, are we friends?"

Tommy didn't sit; he stood beside her with his back to the group by the fire.

"Rather!" he said.

"Are we old friends? You know, the sort that can talk home truths to each other?"

Tommy twinkled at her.

"Do you want me to talk home truths to you? Where shall I begin?"

"Stupid!" said Folly, swinging her feet.

She looked over Tommy's shoulder and was delighted to observe that Betty was watching them.

"Who are you calling stupid? I'm the brains of the Army."

"Then it's got very stupid brains. I'm going to it tell the home truths to you—that is, if we're really friends and you won't go through the roof. Well—shall I?"

"Are you going to tell me I've got a smut on my nose?"

"As if I should bother! It's your nose—you can have as many smuts on it as you like. No—I'm serious! 'M—I *can* be serious, Tommy, so you needn't look at me like that."

"All right, fire away!"

"Perhaps you'll be angry. All right, here goes. *Don't be a mug.*"

"What d'you mean?"

"I mean, don't be a mug. You are, you know. I came in and heard you."

"What did you hear?"

"I heard you being a mug. You were telling Eleanor that, whatever happened, you'd always be there, nice and handy for her to trample on when she wanted to."

Tommy stiffened a little.

Folly kicked her heels and made a face at him.

"There you go! I knew you would. Mind you, I don't suppose you've got a chance anyhow. If she marries anyone, she'll probably marry David. But if you have got the least scrap of a chance, you're simply chucking it away when you talk like that. Who's going to bother about a man who's always there? Go to the pictures and see some nice films about sheikhs—that's what you want. If Eleanor didn't think you were going to be lying about waiting to be picked up for the next hundred years or so, she might—"

Tommy shook his head.

"You don't understand. And look here, I think we'd better go back to the others."

"Mug!" said Folly, jumping off the sofa.

She went to the piano and played old-fashioned out-of-date song-tunes, all very sentimental and sugary. As she played, she watched the others. Betty and Eleanor on the sofa to the left of the fire; and

Tommy with his back to her leaning forward in his chair and talking cheerfully and discursively to Eleanor. Betty had a book. Sometimes she read it; sometimes she listened to Tommy. Every now and then they all laughed.

David sat on the other side of the fire. He was reading. His eyes never left his book, but he did not very often turn a page. Folly looked at him, and looked away. Eleanor's shawl had fallen from her shoulders; it lay on the sofa between her and Betty. Tommy was playing with the fringe, plaiting and unplaiting it.

Folly struck a loud banging chord, jumped up, and ran across to Eleanor. She held her elbows and shivered ostentatiously.

"Eleanor, may I have your shawl?"

"You certainly want it," said Betty pointedly.

Eleanor smiled and nodded.

Folly caught it up by a handful of fringe, shook it out, and made a little sheeted ghost of herself. Then she trailed across the hearth, picked up her stool, and carried it round to the corner between David and the wall. Here she sat herself down chin in hand and kept silence for a long ten minutes. Then David heard a dejected voice at his elbow:

"David!"

"What is it?"

"Are you angry with me too?"

David looked round. There was something forlorn about this little white ghost with all its flaunting scarlet hidden away. He had never looked at Folly quite as he looked at her now.

"Silly little thing! Who's angry with you?"

"Betty is—and Tommy is. Are you?"

"No."

"But you didn't like my dress—did you?"

"No, I didn't. Why on earth did you get it?"

A flicker of impudence came and went.

"I got it in Paris, partly because George said I wasn't to, and partly because I thought it was like my name."

David's eyes laughed.

"Are you as scarlet a folly as all that?"

"'M—sometimes. But I didn't mean that. My name's not really English folly, but French *follet*, and I got it from an old French gentleman, Monsieur Renault, who came and stayed with us when I was five. He heard them call me Flora, and he said it was a name much too serious. Ooh! I can hear him saying it now—'*beaucoup trop sérieux.*' He said I was *Feu-follet*—Will-o'-the-Wisp. And after that everyone called me Folly. Sometimes I hate him, because I think I might have been ever so good if they'd gone on calling me Flora."

Her face came just a little way above the arm of David's chair; it was tilted up to him. David looked down at sad green eyes, a white face, and a painted scarlet mouth. Suddenly, vividly, he remembered that he had kissed Folly, and that Folly had kissed him. He pushed his chair back a foot and picked up his book. In another moment he would have kissed her again under Betty's very eyes.

He held the book between them and looked hard at it. *Feu-follet*—Will-o'-the-Wisp—Fire-folly—Wildfire. The words slipped through his mind, each name a little dancing tongue of flame floating over dangerous places—dark, dangerous places where a man might drown.

After a moment Folly moved too. She turned slowly round upon her stool and sat quite still, with one hand propping her cheek, and mournful eyes that looked into the flames—and looked long. The white China shawl fell round her to the ground. It was the colour of ivory, and the raised flowers and birds and butterflies embroidered on it looked as if they were carved in ivory. Folly herself was so still and so white that she too might have been a little ivory figure with the firelight playing on it.

David never looked at her once.

Tommy went off next morning after an early breakfast. David drove him to the station, and came back to find Betty and Eleanor at the toast and marmalade stage, with Folly on the fender-stool alternately eating an orange and reading extracts from the Births, Marriages, and Deaths. She kissed her hand to David as he came in.

"We're all weeping for our Tommy. I'm trying to cheer the others on their way. 'M—Mrs. Mulberry Beam has a son—only she doesn't put it like that. It's, 'Mrs. Mulberry Beam—Genevra Jones—a son,

Theophil Mortimer Delange.' Ooh! What a name! I must have some orange after that!"

"You're simply plastering *The Times* with juice," said David. "Suppose you hand it over." Folly dropped her orange and clutched the paper. "I haven't nearly finished. Betty, give him some tea to keep him quiet. 'M—Brown has a boy, and Smith has a girl, and the Robinsons have got twins."

"Don't you ever read anything except the Births, Marriages, and Deaths?" said David, between amusement and impatience.

"'M—I read the Agony Column. I'm just getting to it: 'Constantia B—Return the books, and all will be forgiven.' I expect that's thieves really—and this one too: 'If Ernest has any doubts, J. S. M. will set them at rest.'"

"Come on, give me the paper, Folly!"

"I've *nearly* finished. Betty's poured you out a nice cup of tea. Go and drink it. Here's another: 'Erica Moore.—Anyone giving information with regard to—'" She stopped and looked across the top of the paper with a puzzled frown. "Erica Moore—Erica *Moore*—I know that name—I've seen it somewhere. Ooh! It says, 'will be rewarded!' Now if I could only remember about it, I might get a simply enormous reward!"

David had walked to the window. Eleanor looked at him helplessly. She ought to be able to stop Folly; but she couldn't. And then quite suddenly Betty, who was filling the teapot, caught her sleeve in the kettle and pulled it over with a crash. *The Times* was forgotten. Betty, very white, twisted her handkerchief about her wrist and left the room.

Folly came up to the table and touched the kettle with a wary finger.

"It's not very hot," she said. "It couldn't possibly have burnt her." She looked mischievously at Eleanor.

"It startled her. Betty's rather easily startled."

"'M—*she is*," said Folly with her hand on the kettle.

Chapter Fifteen

JUST A LITTLE LATER, when Folly was throwing out crumbs to the birds, Eleanor put a hand on her shoulder.

"Folly, will you come to the study for a moment? David wants to ask you something."

In the study David was standing at the window with his back to the room. He did not turn round when they came in. Eleanor shut the door. Then she put her arm round Folly and said:

"David wants to know if you can help him. It's that thing you read at breakfast—the advertisement about Erica Moore. You said you'd heard the name before. Can you remember where you heard it?"

Folly shot one glance at Eleanor and then looked down.

"I've heard it," she said. "Yes, I have."

"Where have you heard it?"

"'M—I don't know."

Eleanor looked anxiously at David; but David did not move.

"Folly—it's rather serious. Do try and remember."

Folly flashed her another look, suspicious, defiant, and a little frightened.

"I can't—I don't know where I heard it. Why do you want to know?"

"Are you sure you know the name?"

"Yes, I was—when I read it, I was sure. It came, and it went"—she flicked her fingers in the air—"just like that. I read: 'Erica Moore,' and I had a little lightning picture of knowing something about her; and then it was gone. Eleanor—what's the matter? Who is she? Why do you want me to remember? Who is Erica Moore?"

"My wife," said David. He did not turn round, and his voice was hard and forced.

Folly gave a little gasp. It was so faint a sound that it did not reach David. For a moment all her weight came on Eleanor's arm.

Eleanor did not look at her. She waited till Folly said in a small choked whisper:

"David hasn't got a wife. Why did he say that?"

A feeling of acute distress swept over Eleanor. She was between David and Folly. If she had been alone with either of them, she could have found something to say. She felt Folly pinching her arm with hard, shaking fingers, and she heard Folly's voice say again very urgently:

"Why does he say it?"

It was David who answered. He gave an odd laugh and said:

"Because it's true."

Folly let go of Eleanor and went back a step or two until she caught the edge of the writing-table and leaned against it.

"How is it true?" she said, staring at David's back.

Eleanor looked from one to the other. Then she spoke quickly:

"It is true, Folly. They were married in Australia; and on the way home the ship was wrecked, and David thought his wife was drowned. He had every reason to think so. And then the other day there was an advertisement in the Agony Column; it had David's initials, and it said, 'Your wife is alive.'"

Folly threw up her head.

"There might be millions of people whose initials were D. F. Why should it be David?"

"It wasn't just D. F.; it was all his initials—D. A. St. K. F.—David Alderey St. Kern Fordyce."

Folly's hands came together and clung. She didn't speak.

Eleanor said: "The advertisement you read was David's. We thought—"

She stopped with a bewildered feeling that she did not really know what they had thought or expected. Not this queer tangled thread which led to Folly—no, not that at any rate. She went on speaking because when the silence fell it fell so heavily:

"You see, if you know anything—if you can remember anything, it might be a great help."

"I can't remember—it's gone."

"Did you think you'd known her, or that you'd heard the name somewhere?"

"I didn't know her. It was just the name. I think I saw it—I think I saw it written—I think—"

Her voice stopped. She looked past Eleanor at David, who had not moved. After a long dragging minute she went to him and touched his arm. When he turned, she was there, close to him. She said:

"I can't remember. I'll try."

She was very white.

"Don't try too hard. It's more likely to come back if you don't."

"I did try—nothing came."

"Stop trying, and it will probably come of itself."

She nodded. Then, without another word, she turned and ran out of the room.

Eleanor, standing where Folly had left her waited to see whether David would speak. She felt a bewildered constraint. When David and Folly spoke to one another, it was as if they were speaking in a language which she did not know—so few words—such simple words; but they left her with the feeling that she had been listening to something which was not meant for her. There was a sense of strain, a sense of fear, as if the meaning which eluded her held something which would be terrifying if she could grasp it.

David was looking again into the dull grey mist which lay beyond the window at which he stood. It thickened continually, coming up like smoke between the trees; one moment they appeared as half-smudged impressions, and the next were blotted out of sight.

Eleanor became aware that she had nothing to say to David if David had nothing to say to her. She went softly out of the room and shut the door.

Chapter Sixteen

DAVID WAS LUNCHING at the other side of the county with a prospective client. Later in the day he telephoned to Ford to say that as the fog was getting worse every minute he would stay the night and go on up to town next morning.

Eleanor went back to London by an afternoon train, taking Folly with her. They did not speak of David or of his affairs. Folly, who had been gay and impudent at lunch, had a long silent fit, and hardly spoke at all. After dinner she stopped playing with Timmy, sat back on her heels, and said:

"I suppose David wrote and told you at once when he married that Erica person?"

Timmy, who had been left on his back, made an agile recovery, darted under a chair, and crouched for a spring.

Eleanor was vexed to find herself blushing.

"No—he didn't tell anyone."

"I suppose he told his father," said Folly in an accusing voice.

"No, he didn't."

"Why didn't he?"

"It all happened so quickly. She was left stranded in Sydney."

Folly gave a little laugh. Her small figure, in its straight, black frock, was stiff and upright. Timmy watched her with orange eyes; the tip of his tail twitched.

"I expect she took good care to be stranded where there was a man to pay the bills."

"Folly! Don't! She's dead."

"Is she? I thought she was alive. You can't have it both ways. If she's drowned, I'll say 'Poor Erica!' in a proper funeral voice; but if she isn't drowned, then she's a horrid, designing cat who's just been waiting to *pounce* on David."

At the word, uttered with great energy, Timmy pounced; a swift, furry rush carried him right up on to Folly's shoulder, where he was caught, slapped, and kissed.

Folly got off her heels and made a lap for him.

"Little serpent cat!" she said. "Eleanor, will you lend him to me to come out with me on my broomstick? He'd love it. You're a witch-kitten, aren't you, Timkins?—a bad, worst, wicked, furry-purry witchling?"

She cuddled him as she spoke, and he slipped purring into the sudden sleep of kittens, his head thrown back and a tip of pink tongue peeping out between white milk-teeth.

"Well?" said Folly. "Go on telling me about the Erica person. She married David, and she wouldn't let him tell anyone."

"Folly, she was only sixteen and quite alone."

Something looked out of Folly's eyes.

"When I was sixteen I knew a lot," she said.

Eleanor did not doubt her. She went on hastily:

"David married her, and a few days afterwards they sailed on a ship that went down. David put Erica into the second boat, and it was never heard of again. He got away in the last one, and they were picked up next day. The second boat was never heard of at all."

"Why didn't he tell anyone?"

"He didn't want to. And when he got home his father was dying."

"He told Betty," said Folly.

"No—he never told anyone till he told me the other day."

Folly nodded.

"Betty knows—he must have told her."

"He didn't."

"Well, she knows. She jumped like anything when I read that out about Erica Moore—she jumped so that she upset the kettle, and she pretended she'd burnt her hand."

"I don't see how she could know. David said she didn't. You know David and I were both frightfully taken aback when you suddenly said 'Erica Moore'; and I expect Betty saw that there was something wrong. She's a nervous sort of creature."

"She's a vinegar cat," said Folly. "I hate vinegar cats. Timmy, my angel, if you grow up into a vinegar cat I shall drown you. I *will*. I shall take you broomstick-riding and drop you into a bottomless lake, and you'll be a good riddance of bad rubbish."

She tickled Timmy under his chin and he made a little growling sound in his sleep. Folly darted a look at Eleanor and resumed:

"Why did David have to marry the Erica person? Hadn't she got any relations? Who'd she been living with?"

"Her father in New Zealand. He died. She went to Sydney on the same boat as David—she was going to stay with an aunt. When she got there the aunt was dead."

"And you believe all that?"

"It's what David told me."

"Of course David believes it. She vamped him."

"Folly, I really don't think—"

"Pouf! Of course she did! She vamped him, and she married him when he was all alone with no one to protect him; and then she pretended to be drowned. And now she's getting ready to pounce. Why should she go and advertise now? Tell me that."

"I don't know," said Eleanor disingenuously; but she blushed again.

"I do. I know quite well. She thought David was thinking about getting married, so she got ready to pounce."

"Folly, wait a minute. It wasn't the first advertisement. There'd been one three years ago, and another last autumn year."

Folly stared at her.

"It's mean," she said. "It's like a snake. Why doesn't she write to David or come and see him?"

"Folly, I don't believe it's Erica—I can't. She was so young, and David was so good to her—and they hadn't quarrelled. Why should she do anything like that?

"Why should anyone?"

"I don't know. That's just it—I don't know. It's like being in a fog."

"'M—" said Folly. "Didn't she have any relations that weren't dead? They might know something."

"There was an aunt in England—her mother's sister. Erica didn't seem to know the address."

Folly made a face.

"Can't David find her? What was her name? Who was she?"

"I think she let lodgings," said Eleanor. "I think her name was Nellie Smith."

"Ooh!" said Folly. She scrambled to her feet, upsetting the slumbering Timmy. "Ooh!" she said, and pressed a hand to each of her flushed cheeks. They burned like fire and her eyes sparkled. "I saw it! Ooh! I saw it quite clearly."

"What, Folly? What?"

"Erica Moore—the name, you know. I've remembered! It came just like that—blip! And I saw it—her name all funny and neat on the next date to mine in Miss Smith's birthday book."

"Oh," said Eleanor. "Folly, are you sure?"

"Of course I'm sure—I'm always sure about things. It was Miss Smith, where George and I were in rooms just before I went out to India nearly three years ago. And she brought in her birthday book and said would I write my name in it? She was that sort, you know—birthday books, and woolly mats, and awful enlarged photographs of all her relations. And she said would I write my name, and then she would always pray for me on my birthday? She was a nice old thing really, so I wrote it on the twenty-fifth of June. And Erica Moore was on the twenty-sixth just under mine. And I said, 'Who's that?' And she said, 'It's my niece, my poor sister Chrissie's daughter.' And she told me a most awful long story about her poor sister Chrissie; but she didn't tell me a single word about Erica."

Eleanor had turned quite pale. The fog was lifting; but what was behind it? She tried to speak steadily.

"Folly—have you got the address? Can you remember it?"

"Martagon Road—no, Martagon Crescent. It runs out of Martagon Road, and it's *much* more select. 16, Martagon Crescent, Bayswater."

Chapter Seventeen

DAVID REACHED HIS OFFICE at half-past ten next day. His secretary, Miss Barker, came in with his letters—a very efficient lady with sandy hair done in a bun and features which even David's Aunts considered respectable.

"Good-morning, Miss Barker."

"Morning, Mr. Fordyce. A Mr. Wilde rang up yesterday—introduced by Mrs. Homer Halliday. He wants to build a house as a wedding present for a nephew—about three thousand. I made an appointment for three o'clock this afternoon. And a Miss Down rang up and said she wanted to see you personally, so I gave her ten forty-five. Oh, and Mrs. Rayne rang up a quarter of an hour ago. She said she'd ring you up later."

David was opening his letters.

"Then Miss Down will be here directly. Did she say what she wanted?"

"No, she didn't say."

Miss Down was shown in a few minutes later. David had an impression of an over-dressed person in crude, bright colours which did not match. She shook hands with a hard, nervous grasp, sat down with her back to the light, and broke into voluble speech:

"I hope you don't mind my coming in like this and taking up your time. Time's money—isn't it? I'm in business myself, so I know all about that. And I don't want to take up your time on false pretences, either, because 'honesty is the best policy'—isn't it? And I can't be sure that I'm going to build a house, because there is such a thing as not being one's own master, and circumstances alter cases—don't they? But I thought I might as well call on you and find out what a small house would cost if I was in a position to have one built—and I don't say whether I am or whether I'm not." She paused, possibly for breath.

David thought her an odd person. Looking at her with courteous attention, his first impression resolved itself into details. Miss Down wore a hat of brilliant magenta-pink felt and a scarf of bright cerise; her mulberry-coloured coat showed glimpses of a salmon-pink jumper; she had on loose Russian boots to the knee and red kid gloves stitched with white. He judged her to be three or four and twenty years of age. Her features and complexion, rather thrown into the background by so much bright colour, were of a nondescript character, but quite passable.

"Well," he said pleasantly, "what can I do for you, Miss Down?"

"I don't know—I just thought I'd call. But you'll quite understand that I don't want to rush into things. 'Least said, soonest mended,' you know."

She drew off her right-hand glove as she spoke, disclosing a very pretty hand with exquisitely tended nails. David noticed with a little surprise how white and soft it was.

"Of course you wouldn't be committing yourself in any way. I expect you want to know what different types of houses cost? Is that it?"

"Well, it might be."

"Would you like to see some sketches? Perhaps you could give me an idea of the type of house that interests you and what you were thinking of spending?"

Miss Down dropped her glove and bent over to pick it up.

"Oh, I couldn't go as far as that. It's best to be quite fair and aboveboard—isn't it?"

"Yes, of course."

There was a pause.

"What does a bungalow cost?" said Miss Down.

"Well, it would depend on the size, for one thing. If you could give me an idea of what you're prepared to spend, I could show you plans and sketches."

"Well," said Miss Down, "I don't know. The fact is, I don't quite know how I'm placed, and it would all depend."

She exhibited a trace of confusion and looked down at her gloved left hand. The third finger, tightly encased in crimson kid, undoubtedly wore a ring—not a wedding ring, because there was a very distinct bulge in one place.

David concluded that Miss Down was engaged and wished him to be aware of the fact. He said "I see," and smiled again.

"I wish *I* did," said Miss Down with a jerk. "I wish *I* did. But I can't say I do. Gentlemen are things you can't depend on, and that's a fact—though I suppose you won't agree with me."

There is a certain awkwardness about discussing with a strange damsel the probabilities of the gentleman upon whom she has set, if not her affections at least her expectations, coming up to the scratch.

"Gentlemen do let you down so," said the lady. "Now *don't* they? Look at the papers—full of it! Married ones too, and old enough to know better!"

David wondered whether she had called upon him to discuss the prevalence of divorce.

"About your bungalow—" he began; but Miss Down broke in:

"What d'you think of a gentleman that marries a girl and leaves her without a bean? Here to-day and gone to-morrow, and the poor girl left to grin on the wrong side of her face. Wouldn't you call it a cruel shame?"

Miss Down had no particular accent, but when she said "shame" she made a little more of it than most people do; her voice was not exactly common, but it had an edge. Her colour had risen, and she stared at David.

"Yes, I should. It sounds a low-down trick."

"A gentleman that'd do that would deserve pretty well anything that he got, wouldn't you say?"

"I suppose so. About this bungalow, Miss Down—perhaps you'd like to think it over and let me know when your plans are more settled?"

Miss Down got up.

"Yes, I'll think it over. It's always better to think things over—isn't it? Pity more people don't do it, especially about marrying—isn't it? 'Marry in haste and repent at leisure.' We used to play proverbs when I was a child, and it's wonderful what a lot of good advice you can get from them. Well, I'll think things over and let you know. I thought I'd like to call and see you before I decided about anything."

The telephone bell rang at David's elbow. He put the receiver to his ear and heard Eleanor's voice say "Hullo!"

He said: "Hullo, Eleanor!"

"David, is that you?"

"Yes. What is it? Nothing the matter?"

"No. David, Folly has remembered."

"*What!*"

"Yes—last night. The name was in a birthday book."

"A birthday book! Whose birthday book?"

"Miss Smith's—Miss Nellie Smith's. She *did* let lodgings, and George March stayed there with Folly just before he went out three years ago. Miss Smith asked Folly to write her name in her birthday book. And she says Erica's name was under hers, in the next space. She seems quite sure about it."

There was a pause. David's hand tightened on the telephone.

"Does she know the address?"

"Yes. Will you take it down? 16, Martagon Crescent, Martagon Road, Bayswater."

He wrote the address down and repeated it aloud.

"Is that right?"

"Yes, quite right."

There was another pause. Into the middle of it came the sound of the closing door.

David said, "Thank you, Eleanor," and rang off.

Miss Down was gone.

Chapter Eighteen

Eleanor was having tea by herself that afternoon, when David was announced. He came in, looked round quickly, and said:

"Where's Folly?"

"She's out. Did you want her?"

"Yes, I did. I'm on my way to see Miss Smith. Thanks awfully for ringing me up—and I wanted to see Folly first to find out a little more."

"I'm so sorry. Sit down and have some tea. It's quite fresh. Honestly, David, I don't think she could have told you very much. I asked her a good many questions."

David sat down.

"When was Folly there? Three years ago?"

"Not quite three years ago. George came home after the divorce, you know. He was at home a year, and then he went out again and took Folly with him, though she wasn't quite seventeen. And just before they sailed they were in Miss Smith's rooms for a week or two."

"I see. She's sure about having seen Erica's name?"

"Yes—quite sure. She asked about her, and Miss Smith just said she was a niece. She told her a lot about Erica's mother; but she didn't tell her anything at all about Erica—Folly said so particularly."

David drank his tea at a gulp and set down the cup.

"I wanted to see her. Where's she gone?"

Eleanor looked worried.

"She's gone to see her mother."

"Her mother!"

"Yes. She's in town, worse luck, and likely to stay. I'm most frightfully bothered about the whole thing. Floss is a most odious woman, and Folly has a sort of obstinate loyalty to her."

"Oh, well," said David impatiently. Then: "She married the chap she went off with, didn't she?"

"Yes. Leonard Miller. I thought she was out in Australia with him, but she isn't. He's there; and she's here, with a most awful crowd of people round her—that dreadful St. Inigo man for one. And I can't keep Folly away—I've no authority."

"Where's George March?"

Eleanor laughed.

"George is dangling on the edge of matrimony. I expect to hear of the engagement any day."

"What!"

"Yes—really."

"Who is she?"

"A Mrs. Hadding—large, cheerful, managing, and very well off. She was on board with us. She'll do splendidly for George, but Folly won't stay in the same house with her for five minutes. That's what worries me so."

David got up.

"I shouldn't worry. It's no use." He laughed a little. "Don't play at being Grandmamma. You're not really a hundred."

"Folly makes me feel five hundred," said Eleanor. She laughed too, but a little ruefully.

"*Don't*. What's the good? You can't run other people's shows. If they can't run 'em themselves, they're bound to smash up. Well, I'm off."

"You'll let me know, David?"

"Yes, of course. But I don't expect anything. I don't see—no, she can't know anything. But I'll let you know."

Martagon Crescent consisted of thirty narrow houses tucked away behind a row of gloomy shrubs and a tall iron railing. David rang the bell of No. 16, and almost immediately the door opened upon a dark passage very feebly lighted by a single jet of gas.

"Miss Smith?" said David.

It was a little girl who had opened the door. She said "I'll tell her," and ran away into the dark.

In a minute she came back again.

"She says, is it about the rooms?"

"No," said David, "I want to see Miss Smith."

"Then will you come in?" said the girl.

She took David past the first door and showed him into a back room. There was a small fire on the hearth, and the gas-bracket was lighted. The girl shut the door and went away, leaving David with a queer feeling that he had been expected.

He stood in the middle of the room and looked about him. There was a horsehair sofa with a round bolster and a red woollen antimacassar. The carpet was drab, and the wall-paper had turned mustard colour with age, but the bright pink curtains were quite new. A rosewood table in the corner held a case of stuffed birds, a large Bible, and two photograph albums. Each of these objects had its own wool mat crocheted in pink and green loops. Over the mantelpiece was an illuminated text. It proclaimed, "Vanity of vanities; all is vanity," and its faded colours made a very fitting commentary on the text. Prussian blue, crimson lake, bice green, and gold leaf were all gone away to the same dreary dun. On the left-hand wall hung a verse from Timothy—"Flee youthful lusts"—and over the door by which David had entered was the reminder that "Wine is a mocker."

Pope's couplet about the people who

"Compound for sins they are inclined to,
By damning those they have no mind to,"

jigged into David's mind. He wondered what Miss Nellie Smith was like.

And then the door opened and Erica's aunt came in. She was a very little, blanched person, and she looked frightened. It was the look of fright that stirred David's memories of Erica, and not any real likeness.

Miss Smith wore a grey stuff dress with an old-fashioned collar which came high up round her throat, where it was fastened by a mournful and majestic cameo brooch which displayed a lady weeping on a tomb. The brooch was so large that you saw it before you saw Miss Smith, who was not large at all. She had grey hair, which she wore in a fringe very tightly controlled by a hair-net; her features were small and neat. She was much older than David had expected.

She did not offer to shake hands, but stood just inside the door. Something very insistent said to David: "She knows who you are."

He came forward.

"Miss Smith," he said, "my name's Fordyce—David Fordyce." And again something said: "She knows."

"Yes," said Miss Smith timidly. "You wanted to see me? Was it about the rooms? Won't you sit down?"

She sat down herself on the shiny black chair that matched the horsehair sofa. David sat down too. Miss Smith folded her hands in her lap. He saw that the left hand, which lay beneath the other, was shaking very much. It shook, and it picked at a fold of the grey stuff dress.

"Miss Smith," said David, "I've come to ask if you can tell me anything about your niece, Erica Moore."

Miss Smith swallowed nervously. She said, "My niece, Erica Moore?" in a fluttering voice.

"Yes," said David. "I knew her. I would be very glad if you would tell me anything you know."

"I—don't—know—"

"I told you my name was Fordyce. Had you by any chance heard my name before?"

He looked hard at her, and she winced. Her right hand weighed suddenly on the one beneath it.

"It's a Scotch name, isn't it?"

"Yes," said David dryly, "it's a Scotch name."

If he pushed her to it, she would lie; and for the life of him he couldn't do it. Instead, he said quickly:

"Miss Smith, please don't be frightened. I don't want to hurt anyone; I only want to know whether you can tell me anything about Erica that I don't know already. You see, Erica was my wife."

She said "Oh!" but without conviction. If she was trying to express surprise, she did it very badly.

"She knows; but how does she know?" The thought came and went. The conviction that had been growing in him brought confusion in its train. How could she possibly know? Erica had told him that she didn't know her aunt's address; she had not written to tell anyone of their marriage. His mind went to their fellow-passengers. To them she was Mrs. Fordyce, not Erica Moore. Still, it was just possible.

"When did you last hear from Erica?" he said.

Miss Smith brightened a little.

"From New Zealand, Mr. Fordyce, just after her father died. She said she was going to Sydney to her father's sister. It was her mother who was my sister, you know—much younger than me, as you can guess. She didn't make a happy marriage, Mr. Fordyce. And she was so pretty. She was only my half-sister, but I brought her up; and then after she married I hardly ever saw her again." She spoke in a quick undertone as if words were a relief.

"And that was the last you heard from her?" said David.

Miss Smith was silent. Then she caught her breath and said:

"That's the last letter I had from her."

"The last letter. Did you hear in any other way? Did you know that Erica was married? Did you hear that she was drowned in the *Bomongo*?"

"I didn't hear she was drowned."

"But you heard something. Miss Smith, won't you tell me what it was?" He leaned towards her. "You see, I must know. I met Erica when she was all alone; and when she got to Sydney and found her aunt was dead, we got married. And we sailed in the *Bomongo*. She went down. Erica was in a boat that was never heard of. I made every inquiry. There never was any question of survivors from that boat. That's five years ago. Three times in the five years there's been an advertisement in *The Times* under my initials saying that my wife was alive. I'm trying to get to the bottom of it. I think you know something. Won't you help me by telling me just what you know?"

Miss Smith looked at him with a sort of terrified surprise.

"I don't know anything about any advertisement," she said. "I don't indeed. No, Mr. Fordyce, I don't."

Here was obvious relief at being asked something which she could truthfully deny. David was very considerably taken aback. She knew something. But if she didn't know about the advertisement, what did she know? Was it possible that she didn't know anything at all? He decided that it was not possible. But he had no reason for so deciding.

He was aware that something was being withheld; he could only guess at what that something might be.

"Did you not see *my* advertisement, then?" he asked. "It was in Monday's *Times*. I asked for information about Erica."

"We take the *Mirror*," said Miss Smith. "I don't know anything at all about any advertisement."

"I hoped so much that you would be able to help me. I don't want to bother you; but if you do know anything, don't you think that I ought to know it too?"

Miss Smith didn't speak. She looked down at her hands.

"Miss Smith—won't you help me?"

She made no answer.

David's temper caught.

"I want a straight answer to a straight question. Have you had any news of Erica since the *Bomongo* went down?"

Miss Smith went on looking at her hands.

"I think I've a right to ask that question. I think I have a right to insist on your answering it."

Miss Smith looked up. She was trembling, but a curious frightened dignity showed in face and voice.

"It's five years since the *Bomongo* went down," she said.

"What do you mean by that?"

"It's five years ago, Mr. Fordyce. Why did you wait five years? Why didn't you come to me before?"

"I didn't know where to find you."

Miss Smith looked down at her hands; they had stopped shaking. She did not exactly sniff, but the tip of her nose moved. David realized that he was being given the lie.

"You don't believe me? Well, I can't make you; I can only tell you the facts. Erica told me she had an aunt in England, and that her name was Nellie Smith. She said she had forgotten her address."

Miss Smith's nose twitched again.

"She wrote to me after her father died," she said.

"She told me she had forgotten your address. I can only tell you what she told me. How many hundreds of Nellie Smiths do you suppose there are in England? I've only found you now by accident."

"Yes, Mr. Fordyce. May I ask you how you did find me?"

"I have cousins of the name of March. Perhaps you'll remember that Mr. George March and his daughter stayed in your rooms about three years ago."

"Yes, Mr. Fordyce. But that's three years ago."

"I told you I advertised for news of Erica. Miss March saw the advertisement, and she remembered the name—Erica Moore. She says she wrote her name in your birthday-book when she was here, and that Erica's name was on the same page."

"Yes, that's right," said Miss Smith. She looked uncertainly at David. "I'm sorry I doubted you, but five years is a long time for a gentleman to wait before he so much as troubles himself to ask whether his wife is alive or not."

The resentment in her voice fairly took him aback.

"Miss Smith, what do you mean? I made every inquiry that I could possibly think of. I stayed in Cape Town till I was called home to my father who was dying. I employed a solicitor, and I have written to him from time to time. Will you tell me what more you think I could have done?"

She made no answer. Whilst David waited, she looked up at him in a flurried way, and then down again.

"Miss Smith, will you answer the question that I asked you? Have you heard anything about Erica, or haven't you?"

Miss Smith got up. She could not turn any paler, but the lines about her mouth deepened. David had been wrong. She would not lie, however hard she was pressed. She stood under her illuminated texts, and she looked, not at David, but at the big Bible with the frill of pink and green wool standing up all round it in loops.

"I can't answer your question, Mr. Fordyce," she said. "I'm not at liberty to answer it."

David got up too. He felt as if he had been struck very hard and unexpectedly.

"Miss Smith—what do you mean?"

"I can't tell you. You must go away. I can't tell you anything."

She shook and tottered. David caught her arm and put her back into her chair.

"Is Erica *alive*?"

She leaned back and closed her eyes.

"Miss Smith, for God's sake!"

"I can't." She said it in a thread of a voice.

After a minute she opened her eyes and looked at him imploringly.

"I mustn't. Will you go?"

"How can I go?"

The tears came into her eyes.

"I—can't—tell—you. I'm—not at liberty. If you'll go away, I'll write to you. I'll ask."

David bent over her and took one of her hands. He was shocked to feel how cold it was.

"You'll ask leave to tell me. Is that what you mean?"

"Yes," said Miss Smith.

She groped for a handkerchief and began to cry.

Chapter Nineteen

DAVID WAS DINING that evening with Mrs. Homer-Halliday, the lady who had insisted upon four bathrooms being introduced into the small Tudor house which she had bought as a week-end cottage. She was one of those charming middle-aged American women who possess perfect taste and the means of expressing it. David had had an introduction to her when he first went to the States, and added gratitude for much kindness to a sincere admiration of her many charming qualities.

They dined at The Luxe and were to go on to a private dance given by the Lane-Willetts. David walked to The Luxe and was glad of the cold, stinging air. He had come away from Martagon Crescent feeling very much as if an earthquake had shaken the whole fabric of his life to its foundations. Erica's aunt, with her honesty, her trembling dignity, and her terrified reticence, had made a far more profound impression upon him than the three advertisements which he had tried to dismiss as either malicious or irrelevant. He was in no mood for his engagement; and yet there was relief in the necessity for keeping it.

It was a pleasant party of eight. Mrs. Homer-Halliday had David on her left and talked to him a good deal. They were halfway through dinner, when he looked across the room and saw Folly March at a table with three other people. Two of them were men of a sufficiently raffish type, one bald and flushed, the other a pale, unwholesome youth with red hair. Facing Folly across the table was a large fair woman with sleepy eyes and an applied complexion. She wore a great many rather unconvincing pearls and conveyed so unmistakably the impression of the woman who has dropped into the half-world that David received a violent shock. What was Folly doing in a public place with a woman of this kind? Then, with a still greater hock, it came to him that Folly was with her mother—that this was Mrs. Miller.

He looked away quickly, but in spite of himself his eyes went back to Folly. He had a profile view of her. She wore the little white dress with the frills. The broken coral necklace had been replaced by a string of equally infantile blue beads—not the big ones of the passing fashion, but the little oblong sky-blue beads which children used to thread for their dolls in the seventies and eighties. There was a silver ribbon in her hair; the little dark curls just hid her ears.

"What a perfectly sweet little girl!" said Mrs. Homer-Halliday. "I'm sure you know her—or is it only that you'd like to know her?"

David found her smiling archly at him.

"I beg your pardon?"

"*Now*, Mr. Fordyce, don't you pretend you weren't looking at the little girl with the blue beads!"

"She's a cousin of mine," said David.

"Well, I've lost my heart to her. I'd love to have you bring her to see me one day. Do you know the people she's with?" Her tone changed ever so little.

"No," said David, keeping to the letter of the truth. He felt no desire to explain Mrs. Miller.

Mrs. Homer-Halliday changed the subject.

Some time later David was waiting for the rest of his party in the lounge, when he saw Folly again. She was with the red-haired youth who had been her partner at dinner, and she wore a sparking mutinous air that made her very much the Will-o'-the-Wisp.

David felt a strong desire to kick the red-haired young man very hard. The feeling surprised him a little. Under the frowning intensity of his gaze Folly looked across a crowd of people and saw him. At once her face changed. Without nod or greeting she slipped through the intervening groups and came to him.

"David! Did you see her?" The thrill of excitement in her voice struck an answering thrill from David. He nodded. "Eleanor told me you were going to see her. *Do* tell me."

Neither of them had mentioned Miss Smith's name. They were suddenly on a note of such intimacy that everything was taken for granted. David dropped his voice:

"I saw her. She wouldn't tell me anything."

"Does she know anything to tell?"

"Yes, I think she does. She said she wasn't at liberty to tell me anything."

"What did she mean?"

Folly's eyes were bright and blank.

"She was going to ask—there was someone she was going to ask whether she might tell me."

"What is there to tell?" said Folly.

"I don't know. She seemed to know about me—to be expecting me."

"How could she?"

Mrs. Miller bore down upon them, and in a moment Folly was changed; the eager note dropped from her voice.

"Who's your friend?" said Mrs. Miller. She put her hand on Folly's shoulder, a large white hand gemmed to the knuckles.

"It's David Fordyce. How much of a cousin are you, David?"

"Fifth cousin six times removed, or something like that."

"Oh, the Fordyces are too much for me. I don't pretend to keep up with them," said Floss Miller. She shrugged the shoulders she was so proud of, laughed, and looked sideways at David out of those sleepy eyes.

Considering that the Fordyce family had dropped her, David thought this remark showed some assurance. He disliked Mrs. Miller more than he had ever disliked a woman at first sight. She wore a plain and well cut black gown with an air which made it seem flaunting. She had certainly had too many cocktails. The hand on Folly's shoulder filled him with a sick disgust.

"Well, so long—must be going," she said. She looked back over her shoulder as she drew Folly away. "Come and see me—27, Maudsley Mansions." Her eyelids narrowed and she smiled. Just for a moment her resemblance to the Mona Lisa was startling.

Folly went a yard or two with her mother and then ran back.

"That's Floss," she said defiantly.

"So I guessed."

"Why did you look at her like that?"

"Folly, how did I look?"

Folly laughed angrily.

Like all of you do—like all you Fordyces do; as if you were too good to live; as if you couldn't bear to see her."

David was really shocked.

"Folly! I can't think why you should say such a thing."

"It's true—you're all like that. And I came back just to tell you—" She choked and stopped.

"Folly—*please* don't!"

She looked at him with a wide, strange look. Then it changed; resentment came up like a flame.

"I don't care for any of you. Floss's friends are good enough for me—they don't pretend anyway. I'm going with her now—we're going to dance. You're much too good to come, I suppose."

"I'm afraid I've got another engagement. My party's waiting for me now."

"So is mine." She dropped her voice to a furious whisper. "It's like the sheep and the goats—isn't it? I shall probably meet Stingo and make it up with him. Run along to your sheep, or they'll begin to bleat." She slipped into a laugh, gay and impudent. Her eyes mocked him; the tip of a scarlet tongue just showed. And then she was gone.

Chapter Twenty

DAVID HAD HARDLY GOT to office next morning, when Eleanor rang him up.

"David, did you know Francis Lester was in town?"

"Good Lord! No! There must be some mistake.

"There isn't. Folly met him last night. It appears he's a friend of her mother's."

"There must be some mistake. Is Folly there?"

"I'll call her."

He heard her voice raised; it came faintly as she moved away from the telephone: "Folly! Folly! David wants—" The rest was lost.

A moment later, Folly, gay and impudent:

"Hullo, Mr. Grundy! Temper better this morning?"

"I was going to ask about yours," said David dryly.

"'M—mine's feeling better, thank you. Did you ring up on purpose to ask about it?"

"No—Eleanor rang me up. Folly, is it true that you met Francis Lester last night?"

"'M—I danced with him. He dances divinely."

"It can't be the man I mean."

"'M—it is. He asked after you, and after Betty, quite *nicely*. He explained about being a cousin right away at the start. Is that all? Because I'm really having my bath, and Eleanor's old lady will make Eleanor buy her a new dining-room carpet if I go on dripping on to it much longer. I've only got a towel on. Good-bye, Mr. Grundy *dear*."

She rang off.

David bent his mind to drainage.

A quarter of an hour later the telephone bell rang again. He picked up the receiver, and a woman's voice said: "I want to speak to Mr. Fordyce."

"Speaking," said David. He did not recognize the voice. It had that metallic quality which makes some voices so unpleasant on the telephone.

"You are David Fordyce?" said the voice.

"Yes."

"You advertised for news of Erica Moore?"

David's hand closed hard on the receiver.

"Yes."

"May I ask why you described her as Erica Moore and not as Erica Fordyce? She *was* Erica Fordyce, wasn't she?"

"Yes. Who am I speaking to?"

"To someone who knows that Erica Moore was Erica Fordyce. You haven't said why you advertised for Erica Moore."

"I should think that would be obvious. Anyone who had any information would know that she had been Erica Moore. I naturally had no wish to make my private affairs public property."

"Meaning you didn't wish your family to know of your marriage?"

"You can put it that way if you like. May I ask who you are?"

"You can ask," said the voice.

David made a strong effort to keep down his temper.

"I suppose you didn't ring me up just to say that sort of thing. It's rather waste of time really. Don't you think so? The point is, have you any information to give me?"

"Quite a lot," said the voice.

"Then if you have, don't you think it would be better to let me meet you? I don't consider this telephone conversation at all satisfactory. If you'll forgive me for saying so, I shall want to be convinced of the authenticity of any information about my wife."

A hard, unmirthful laugh came to him along the wire:

"I'm afraid you'll have to talk to me this way or not at all. Now listen, David Fordyce. You met Erica Moore on your voyage to Sydney five years ago. The boat was called the *Susan Peterson*; the master's name was Quaid. You landed at Sydney on the first of February. Erica stumbled going down the gangway, and you saved her from a nasty fall. You drove with her to 120, Langdale Street, where her aunt, Mrs. Foss, had been living. When you got there, you found she had died a week before. Erica was taken in by a Mrs. O'Leary who lived at 125 in the same street. She was a widow with one son called Robert. He had red hair and freckles like his mother." The voice paused, and then went on again: "Well, how does my information strike you? Is it accurate?"

David was dumbfounded; the mass of small details, the hard antagonism with which they were presented, fairly staggered him.

The voice went on:

"As you don't say anything, I take it that silence gives consent. On February 10, 1922, you married Erica at a registry office in a street with a church at one end of it. Erica didn't know the name of the street. You were married at half-past eleven in the morning. There was a thunderstorm going on, and you sheltered in the office until it was over."

"Who are you?" said David. "For God's sake stop all this! If you've anything to tell me, don't beat about the bush."

"You asked for proof that I knew what I was talking about. Are you satisfied? Or shall I tell you what Mrs. O'Leary said when you had such a row with her the day you made up your mind to marry Erica? She said, 'If you mean fair by her, why don't you marry her?' Didn't she?"

David pulled himself together.

"You are telling me things that I know. Have you got anything to tell me that I don't know?"

"Monday comes before Saturday," said the voice. "Do you remember buying Erica a ring with turquoises? Would you know it again if you saw it? It had three forget-me-not flowers set side by side. She liked bright colours, and she fancied it; and you bought it for her the day after you were married. You got the wedding ring at the same shop—the name was Andrews. And Erica wanted her initials put inside her wedding ring, and the date. So you'd know the ring again, even if you didn't know Erica."

"Who—are—you?" said David. His lips were dry.

There was no answer; the line had gone dead. When he got the exchange, it was to be told that the other party had rung off. Further questions, and, perhaps, an urgent note in his voice, produced the information that the call had come from a public office.

David sat long and stared at the wall in front of him. Behind all this closely detailed information there was some motive which he could not divine. There was something vaguely horrible, as if Erica were being called up for a malignant purpose. The voice was dreadfully hostile. There was something that shocked those faint boyish memories of his.

As he sat there, he realized how faint they were, how little he had known of the timid child he had married, and of that little how dim a memory survived. He tried to call up Erica's face, but it would not come. A little shrinking figure in black—he could see that; but the small immature features eluded him. She was pale; her eyes were neither blue nor grey, and her hair neither light nor dark. She was in black for her father.

Suddenly he remembered her saying that she hated black. He could see the gesture with which she picked up a fold of her skirt and said: "I hate it! I love bright, bright colours. How soon do you think I can wear colours again?" He saw and heard her quite plainly; and he heard himself asking her what colour she liked best, and her eager answer: "I like pink best of all—bright pink, like roses."

Looking back, he felt the old pity stir. She had been so starved of all the colour and gaiety of youth. He guessed at a stern, unhappy home—no companions, no toys, no amusements. A solitary visit to Aunt Nellie had been remembered and treasured. "I went with the Sunday-school for a treat all the way to Epping Forest;" and, "When I stayed with Aunt Nellie, we used to play games every evening." David had laughed and asked what games—cards?—to be met with a shocked, "Oh no! Cards are wicked. Aunt Nellie wouldn't have them in the house."

"What games then?"

"Oh, parlour games. Lovely! Backgammon—and Scripture characters—and spillikins—and proverbs. I liked proverbs best of all."

It stirred his pity now as it had stirred it then. How could this little pitiful creature be a threat, and what link was there between her and that hostile voice?

He went over in his own mind the fortnight between the marriage and the shipwreck. In Sydney, Erica had known no one to whom she could have confided all these details. If Mrs. O'Leary had known some of them, there were others that she could not know—the little blue ring; the initials inside the wedding ring; the hour and place of the marriage. He had taken Erica away from the woman's house four days before, and they had not met again. There remained the second landlady and the other passengers on the boat. It was possible that Erica had told one of them all these details, and that they had been remembered for five years. It was possible; but it was supremely unlikely. Erica was timid and reserved to the last degree, and on the *Bomongo* she had hardly spoken to any of the other passengers. She had not spoken much, even to him.

But over and above everything else, there was the absence of motive. Why, after five years, should all these trivialities be focussed into an unexplained and implacable resentment?

He could find no answer to the question.

Chapter Twenty-One

THE AFTERNOON POST brought David a letter from Miss Nellie Smith. She wrote:

"DEAR SIR,

"I am sorry I cannot give you any information, as I am not at liberty to do so. My niece will communicate with you. It is no use asking me anything.

"Yours truly,

"E. SMITH."

David read the letter three times. From its cold formality the two words "my niece" struck him. Her niece. What niece? Erica had told him that her mother had no relations except Aunt Nellie. Yet Aunt Nellie had a niece; and the niece would communicate with him. Someone had communicated with him already.

After a long time he took up his pen and wrote:

"DEAR MISS SMITH,

"I should be very grateful if you would give me your niece's name and address. I did not know that you had any niece but Erica. I want to assure you that I have not, and never have had, any other motive than a desire to find out all that can possibly be found out with regard to Erica, and then to do whatever is right and just. I can do nothing whilst I am kept in the dark. Will you tell your niece this and ask her to treat me with confidence? I can assure you that she will not regret doing so.

"Yours sincerely,

"DAVID FORDYCE."

He dined that evening with Eleanor. She greeted him with "Oh, David, Betty's been here! And I hope I didn't do wrong."

"What did you do?"

"Well, I told her Folly had seen Francis Lester."

David whistled.

"Well, it was really very difficult not to—she brought the conversation round so. David, don't be angry, but I believe she knew."

"Knew! Knew what?"

"Knew that Francis was in town—knew that he'd met Folly last night."

"What makes you think so?"

She lifted her clear, candid eyes.

"It's so hard to explain how one gets an impression. I can't explain. I think she'd been seeing him—I think she had come up to town to see him."

"That's a bit far-fetched."

"Perhaps it is. You're not vexed, David?"

"No—she'd have to know. It's rotten his turning up like this. I can't think what she ever saw in the fellow; but she was awfully fond of him."

The door opened and Folly danced into the room. She made David a bob curtsy and twirled in front of Eleanor in a short, gold frock that glittered under the lights.

"Things being proper and improper are so funny! This morning, when I had a huge bath-towel on, it would have been frightfully improper for me to see David, though I was all covered up from my chin to my toes; and to-night, when I'm not covered up at all, anyone can see me and I'm perfectly proper."

"Are you?" said David dryly.

"Honi soit qui mal y pense," said Miss Folly March in a tone of conscious modesty.

Folly, it appeared, was going out after dinner. She was meeting Floss, and they were going somewhere to dance; hence the new gold frock. When dinner was over Folly would not wait for coffee.

"I'll have coffee with Floss. I'm to pick her up at her flat. I'd have dined there, only I wanted to see if Mr. Grundy would pass my frock."

She danced up to Eleanor and kissed her on the cheek.

"Bye-bye. David's going to take me down and catch me a taxi."

"Am I?" said David.

"'M—you are. If you were really nice you'd come along and dance with me. But the *very* least you can do is to get me a taxi."

Out on the landing she slipped her hand into his arm.

"Let's walk down. I hate lifts—they're like a Channel crossing stood on end."

The flat was on the second floor. Just round the turn of the stone stair Folly stood still.

"I told you I should probably make it up with Stingo."

"Did you?" His tone was indifferent.

"Yes, I did. I danced with him. He dances divinely."

David said nothing. Perhaps his face spoke for him. Folly, standing one step above him, tapped with a little gold shoe.

"Why shouldn't I make it up with Stingo if I like?"

"Oh, certainly—if you *like.*" His voice was coldly contemptuous.

"I told you I'd probably make it up with him—and I did. Why shouldn't I? You look down your nose at him and *snoop*; but he isn't any worse than anyone else."

"If you don't know a rotter when you see one—"

Folly jerked a round white shoulder. Her anger slipped from her.

"What's the good of talking like that? You're all the same, really. Any man'll go just as far as you'll let him." Her tone was bleakly matter-of-fact. "Floss told me that when I was fifteen. She said any man would get you into a mess if you gave him a chance."

David felt something; he did not know what. He said, "You're talking nonsense," and turned to go on down the stair.

Folly jumped two steps and caught him up.

"I always do talk nonsense—don't I? David, don't *run*." She hung on his arm and pulled him round to face her. "I've got something to show you."

"What is it?"

"Something frightfully exciting. Prepare to be *thrilled*." She caught his hand. "David, my hair's growing ever so fast. I shan't want my little bought curls any more. I've promised them to Timmy. He does *love* to bite them, and he shall have them all for his very own. My hair's simply racing."

She was tugging at his hand and pinching it all the time.

"Feel!" she said, and dragged his hand against her cheek.

The dark colour rushed into David's face. He stepped back.

"Are you trying to see how far I'll go?"

The violence of his own anger surprised him.

Folly looked up at him with green mischief between her lashes.

"Perhaps I am."

"Thank you," said David. "I'm not taking any. You can play those tricks on St. Inigo."

Folly sighed.

"What a nasty temper you've got, David Fordyce!"

He made no answer.

When he had got her a taxi he went back to Eleanor. He had Miss Smith's letter in his pocket. It had been in his mind to show it to Eleanor and to tell her about his strange telephone call; but the letter remained unshown and the confidence un-given.

Eleanor had just poured out the coffee when the click of a latch-key made them both look round. A moment later the door opened and Folly stood on the threshold. She had shed her coat in the hall. A blue gauze shawl was wrapped about her; the gold of her dress came sparkling through it. She was brightly flushed.

"Folly I!" said Eleanor.

David said nothing.

Folly came in and shut the door behind her. She flicked a corner of her shawl at David.

"This is really a white sheet, and I'm a good, humble penitent on my way to the shrine of Grundy."

"Folly, what *do* you mean? Why have you come back?"

"David said he'd rather I didn't go," said Folly meekly.

David lifted his eyes and looked at her. The look informed Miss Folly March with a good deal of plainness that she was a little liar.

Miss March acknowledged the compliment by dropping her lashes so that they rested becomingly on modestly blushing cheeks.

"He said he didn't think Stingo was a nice companion for me, so I came back."

Eleanor poured her out some coffee. The situation was a little beyond her, and the air too electric for her taste. She began to talk to David about Betty.

Folly went to the piano and played hymn tunes.

Chapter Twenty-Two

DAVID HAD ARRANGED to sleep in town all that week. He made an early start on Thursday morning and drove down into Berkshire with Mr. Wilde to see the site which he had bought for his nephew's house. He got back in the early afternoon.

"Mrs. Lester called," said Miss Barker. "She said she'd look in again after lunch."

Betty came in half an hour later.

"I wanted to see you," she said in a more than usually plaintive voice.

David recollected Francis and his affairs with a prick of the conscience. Betty would be likely to want to see him. He said, "What's the matter?" and wished the interview well over. On every previous occasion when they had discussed Francis, Betty had wept and taken dire offence. It is not easy to combine the offices of trustee and younger brother.

Betty sat down in a chair by the window.

"Francis is back," she said.

"Yes," said David, "I heard yesterday. I hope—" He did not say what he hoped, but he looked affectionately at Betty.

"Why shouldn't he come back?" she said in an accusing voice; a hard, unbecoming flush mounted to her cheeks.

David was silent. There really were a good many reasons why Francis Lester should stay away. To have been expelled from his club for card-sharping does not assure a man a welcome.

"Why shouldn't he come back?" The flush rose higher. "You never liked him. If there'd been anyone to help him five years ago, he need never have gone—but there wasn't."

"Betty, what's the sense of raking things up?"

Betty opened her bag and took out a handkerchief. With a premonitory sniff she said:

"I'm sure I don't want to rake things up. I only want you to be kind to poor Francis."

David had no fancy for the rôle.

"Look here, Betty—"

Betty applied the handkerchief to her eyes.

"I do think you might try and understand. No one knows how hard it's been for me all these years."

"My dear girl, I've been awfully sorry."

"What's the good of being sorry? I want you to be kind to Francis."

"But hang it all—"

"You won't—I know you won't." She choked on a sob.

"Betty, what on earth do you want me to do?"

"I want you to be kind."

David lost his temper.

"Good Lord, my dear girl, the man's not a puppy-dog! I can't pat him on the head."

Betty buried her face in her handkerchief.

"You're frightfully unkind!" She stopped to sniff and blow her nose. "I knew you would be—I knew it wasn't any use asking you."

"You haven't asked me anything yet."

"Because I knew it wouldn't be any use." She sniffed loudly and dabbed her eyes.

"Betty, what do you want me to do?"

She dropped her handkerchief into her lap and sat up straight.

"I want you to let me have some of my capital."

"For Francis? Certainly not!"

"David—if you'd only listen! A few thousands would pay his debts, and we could start fresh. Oh you don't know what it would mean to me!" She leant forward, flushed and tremulous.

David felt very sorry for her. He stopped being angry.

"My dear girl, I can't possibly let you part with any of your capital. I'm responsible for it. As a matter of fact, I haven't even got the *legal* right to let you play ducks and drakes with it."

She locked her hands together.

"I knew it was no good. You don't care—Francis might starve, and you wouldn't care. If you cared at all, I'd ask you to lend me the money. But it wouldn't be any good." She paused, and then added, breathlessly and quickly: "Would it?"

"No," said David, "it wouldn't. Betty, for the Lord's sake, don't begin to cry again! Miss Barker's in the next room and she'll think I'm murdering you. Now look here, it's no use my beating about the bush. Francis behaved very badly five years ago. I don't know where he's been or what he's been doing since then. If he's pulled up and means to go straight, I don't want to stand in his way. I'd help him to a moderate extent if it was a question of his making a start somewhere abroad. Quite frankly, England's not possible. I'd help him to start abroad if there was anything to show that he really meant to pull up. But I can't touch your capital; and I'm not going to break into my own."

Betty stopped crying. She pressed her lips tightly together and looked bitterly offended.

"Thank you very much for your *kind* offer," she said in withering tones. "I suppose you expect me to be *grateful*!" She walked to the door and opened it, sniffing. "I suppose you expect me to say *thank you*!"

David shrugged his shoulders. He had a certain unwilling sympathy for Betty's husband. Behind him the door banged.

Ten minutes later the telephone bell rang.

David said: "Hullo!"

The voice that answered him was the voice that had given him all those details about himself and Erica yesterday. It said:

"Hullo! You *are* David Fordyce, aren't you, and not a clerk?"

"Yes, I'm David Fordyce."

"I thought so. Well, I just rang up to ask whether you've been thinking over my credentials?"

"You haven't given me any credentials. I'm very glad you've rung up, because I want to ask you some questions. I had a letter yesterday from Miss Smith—Miss Nellie Smith, Erica's aunt. It you will hold on for a moment, I will read you what she says." He took the letter from his pocket-book, unfolded it, and read it aloud. "You see, Miss Smith says, 'My niece will communicate with you.' Am I to understand that you are Miss Smith's niece?"

There was no answer, but the line was still active. David repeated his question.

"Silence doesn't always give consent," said the voice.

"Are you Miss Smith's niece?"

"Has Miss Smith got a niece?" replied the voice.

"That was what I was going to ask you," said David. "I do not understand Miss Smith's reference to her niece, because Erica distinctly told me she was an only child, and that her mother had no relations except Miss Smith."

"That does make it difficult," said the voice. "Of course, some people would say, if a person only had one niece and then wrote a letter and said their niece would communicate with you, that they might mean the only niece they'd got. Some people might take it that way, you know."

"I put Erica into the *Bomongo's* second boat myself," said David steadily. "Neither the boat nor anyone in her was ever heard of again."

There was no answer. After a moment the voice said:

"How certain you are about things! Now that's settled, perhaps you'd like me to go on where I left off yesterday? I've got a lot more interesting things to tell you."

"I should like to hear anything you can tell me. But before you begin, I'd like to say that up to the present you've told me nothing that

Erica might not have repeated to someone in Sydney, or to someone on the *Bomongo* who survived."

"Very well—hearing's believing—I'll go on. Erica was in a cabin with three other women on the *Bomongo*. Perhaps she told one of them the things I'm telling you. She was the sort of girl who'd rush and confide in the first stranger she came across—wasn't she?"

"No, she wasn't," said David.

"Perhaps she told Mrs. Manners. She was one of the people in the cabin—a big, domineering woman with a fretful invalid daughter. Then there was a Miss Baker, a girl of Erica's age, who was so sea-sick that she never left her berth. Perhaps she told her."

David was silent. Erica had been terrified of Mrs. Manners; she had disliked Miss Manners and the Baker girl. It was in the highest degree improbable that she had ever told them anything about herself.

"Well, I'll go on," said the voice. "On the ninth day out a bad storm got up. On the tenth night the passengers in the *Bomongo* were ordered into the boats. You went along to Erica's cabin about ten o'clock, and you stayed there because the women were all so frightened. Some time later there was a crash and the boat heeled over. A man ran along the passage shouting for everyone to come on deck. You got Erica and the Baker girl up the companion and out on to the deck; and there Eva Baker got separated from you. One of the officers told you to put Erica into the second boat. She cried and clung to you, and didn't want to go; the noise was frightful; she was beside herself with terror. One of the other passengers helped you to get her into the boat. Shall I tell you the last thing she said to you? When I've told you, you can think it over. It was just before you put her into the boat. And everyone in the boat was drowned; so you can think out which of those drowned people could have told me what Erica said to you. She said, '*Oh, David, don't, don't make me go! Oh, David, I'm so frightened! David, let me stay with you! I'd rather be drowned with you than go in that dreadful boat!*'" The voice stopped speaking; there was a little click at the further end of the line, and then silence.

David put his head in his hands. The voice had softened on the piteous words until it might have been Erica herself, saying them again in hurried, shaken tones. The memory of her terror swept over him. Five years ago—the wind; the driving rain; the darkness; the slippery slanting deck; Erica clinging to him; horror of darkness; horror of shipwreck—and a girl's frightened cry—words sobbed out and heard only because the trembling lips were so near. He had had to use force to unclasp the desperate clinging hands. It had been a very bitter thought to him that if he had let her stay, she would have been safe. *"David, let me stay with you! I'd rather be drowned—"* But she had been drowned because he had not let her stay.

Chapter Twenty-Three

WHEN AT LAST David lifted his head, it came to him with a shock that he was not alone. There was someone sitting in the chair which Betty had drawn forward—a little silent figure sitting motionless with folded hands. There was a moment of grey uncertainty; and then he saw that it was Folly March who sat there—not Erica come back from the depths of that angry sea.

He sat up, stiff in every limb. He had a dazed feeling of having been somewhere out of time and space, somewhere between past and present—torn. The darkness, the storm, receded; Erica's voice died away from his straining sense. But for a moment or two the familiar objects around him were thin and insubstantial, like things seen in a dream. Folly might have been some little wandering wraith of herself. She sat mournfully still and mournfully silent, her dark fur coat open over a darker dress, her face very pale and smudged beneath the eyes with a black shadow that looked like a bruise.

He made a great effort and said: "What is it?"

Folly did not speak. She gave a little sigh with a catch in it.

The sound of his own voice steadied David. The past was the past again. The things about him became more solid. He repeated his question:

"What is it? Is anything the matter?"

She shook her head.

"Did you want to see me?"

She spoke then in a ghost of a little husky voice.

"I wanted to see someone."

She seemed so quenched that he turned from his own affairs.

"Where's Eleanor?"

"Grandmamma sent for her."

"What for?"

"A pie-jaw, I expect." There was a momentary green flicker in the mournful eyes. "It's generally a pie-jaw when Grandmamma sends for anyone, isn't it? I expect it's about me."

"What's the matter, Folly?"

Folly shivered as if she were cold.

"Feeling lost dog," she said. "I do sometimes. It's perfectly beastly." She paused, looked down at her folded hands, and said in a stiff little voice: "George is married."

"George!"

"'M—George. She's a Mrs. Hadding. I knew he'd do it the minute he got away from me. They got married yesterday. I got his letter just after Eleanor went to be pie-jawed. That's why I had to come here."

"I say, I'm awfully sorry."

"I expect it's quite a good thing really. She's all right. I couldn't live with her—that's all. That's why I'm feeling lost dog."

"Perhaps you'll feel different about it after a bit. It was bound to knock you over at first."

She shook her head.

"No—I shouldn't ever feel any different. There are people you can live with, and people you *can't* live with. She's one of the can't's. I shall probably go and live with Floss"—David suppressed an exclamation—"but of course, I don't know that she wants me. Floss is only fond of me in patches, you know—when there isn't a man. And George isn't fond of me at all."

"Folly! Don't!"

It was the dispassionate tone in which she said these things that made them rather dreadful.

"George told me once that he didn't believe I was really his daughter," she said in the same matter-of-fact voice, only on the last word it suddenly failed and she sat dumb.

David looked away. There was something incredibly painful in the conviction with which she spoke.

He said: "Eleanor—" and stuck. And then:

"Eleanor likes having you."

"Eleanor will get married," said Folly. "And if I tried to live with Aunt Milly, I should blow right up."

"She's an awfully good sort."

"'M—she is. But she'd make me carry parcels and go to mothers' meetings, and I should blow right up. I've never seen Aunt Milly with less than *five* parcels; and they have things like red flannel and mustard plasters in them. I should blow up."

Under the stimulus of conversation Folly was reviving a little. There was a certain zest in her voice, and a faint gleam in her eye. "Of course it's a pity I can't come and live with you. Grandmamma and the Aunts always say that what I want is a chaperon; I think you'd make such an awfully good one. *Strict! Ooh!*" said Folly. An authentic imp looked out of her eyes for an instant.

It is to be doubted whether any man is really pleased at being told that he would make a good chaperon. David was not pleased; also he was far from certain of his ability to sustain the part.

"Well, Eleanor isn't married yet."

Folly looked at him sideways. Then her lashes dropped.

"Don't let's talk about me. Let's talk about you." She leaned forward and asked eagerly: "Have you heard from Miss Smith?"

"Yes, I heard yesterday."

"What did she say?"

The letter was lying on the table in front of him. He took it up and gave it to Folly, and heard her draw a very quick breath.

"What does she mean?"

David found her looking at him in a surprise that was tinged with fear.

"I don't know, Folly. That's just it—I don't know."

"David, what does she *mean*? She didn't have another niece; she only had Erica. She told me so her very own self. She told me Erica was the only relation she'd got left in the world—she told me so."

Folly's voice sounded rather frightened; she held the arms of her chair very tightly.

David looked straight in front of him and said, "I don't know;" and there was a strained, unquiet silence.

Folly broke it.

"She says—someone will write. She says—her niece will write. Has—anyone written?"

David made an abrupt movement.

"Someone's been telephoning to me."

"Oh!" said Folly on a little gasping breath; and then: "Who?"

"I don't know. I don't know the voice. I don't know anything." He flung round and faced her. "It's a woman who rings me up—from a public call office. She has a beastly voice—hard, mocking; and she seems to know everything that I said or did when I was with Erica. It's damnable."

A look of terror swept over Folly's face. It was like a quick cloud passing. She said in a whisper:

"Who is she?"

David lifted his hand and let it fall in a gesture of helpless negation.

"Is it—Erica?"

The whisper was hardly sound at all; but it reached David and shocked him to his feet. He got up with a jerk. That hard, mocking voice—and Erica, whose piteous wail still beat against his ears: "David, don't make me—don't make me go!" Yet it was that hard voice which had called up the piteous one and, repeating the piteous words, had softened and become piteous too. He felt a horror that he had never felt before. If this was Erica, if it was Erica's voice that had mocked him, what had the years made of her; what searing, hardening change had passed upon the child that he remembered?

Folly got up slowly and came slowly a step nearer to him. Then she stopped, her eyes wide and full of fear. She looked, not at David, but at the space between them; and she looked at the empty space as if some bodily presence filled it.

She said "Erica!" in a faint gasp; and then: "David—was it Erica?"

David felt cold. The room was cold, as if a cold wind were blowing through it. He turned away from Folly's eyes. Neither of them spoke.

After a moment Folly began to move towards the door. She walked very slowly and stiffly, and it took her a long time to turn the handle, and a long time to close the door between her and David.

Chapter Twenty-Four

ELEANOR MEANWHILE had gone to have tea with Grandmamma and the Aunts, arriving, as bidden by Aunt Editha, not later than half-past three—"as Grandmamma is anxious to have a little talk with you, dear girl, and she does not care about talking much immediately after a meal."

Eleanor was met in the hall of Mrs. Fordyce's house by Aunt Editha, who embraced her warmly.

"My dear girl! So nice to see you! We haven't had a real talk yet. But, of course, you must go to Grandmamma now—she's expecting you and—yes, my dear girl, we must have our little talk; only just now Grandmamma will have heard the bell ring, and she mustn't be kept waiting."

At the top of the stairs, Aunt Mary:

"Eleanor, you're a little late. And—oh, my dear, flowers again!"

Eleanor laughed.

"Did they take you in, Aunt Mary? I didn't forget. And my violets aren't real this time."

"Grandmamma doesn't care about artificial flowers," said Miss Mary in a fluttered, disapproving sort of way. "I think—I really do think it would be better if you were to take them off. Grandmamma feels so strongly about things like sham jewellery, and imitation lace, and—and artificial flowers."

Eleanor removed the violets, and was ushered into the drawing-room. Now that the room was no longer filled by a crowd of people, Aunt Editha's birthday chintzes had a most startling effect; they certainly made everything else look very shabby. And yet Eleanor felt how much she would have preferred the unrelieved shabbiness.

Grandmamma sat in her usual chair by the fire. She wore a black cashmere dress with *lisse* frilling round the neck, and over the dress a grey golf jacket of a rather superannuated appearance. Her collar was fastened by a brooch containing the intertwined and plaited hair of her parents and nine brothers and sisters; the shades ranging from the flaxen of John, deceased as an infant, through Roger, sandy; Alexander, undeniably red; Editha, auburn; and Frederick, dark brown, to Papa and Mamma, one iron and the other silver grey.

Eleanor received the kiss of disfavour. Grandmamma's eyes dwelt so bleakly on her grey coat and skirt that she was glad she had left the violets outside.

In a minute or two the full tide of august displeasure was sweeping over her. Folly had hit the mark when she announced that Eleanor was to be scolded on her account. It appeared that someone had told James Alderey, whose wife had told Milly March, who had told Aunt Editha, who, of course, had at once informed Grandmamma, that Folly had been seen dining in public with that abandoned creature, Florence.

"I allude, Eleanor, to poor George's former wife. And I have sent for you to ask how you can reconcile it with your conscience to allow Flora—who is, I understand, in your charge—to associate with such a person."

Eleanor bowed before the storm, only to find that meekness had a most disastrous effect upon Grandmamma. After ten minutes or so Mrs. Fordyce was enjoying herself, and was addressing Eleanor very much as she might have addressed the erring and impenitent Floss herself. By the time she had said all that she had to say on (*a*) the prevalence of immorality; (*b*) the proper treatment of social offenders; (*c*) the lightmindedness and total lack of respect for morality displayed by young persons in general, and Flora in particular; and (*d*) the awful responsibilities attaching to the charge of a young girl, Eleanor was rather battered. There were side excursions into the divorce laws, modern education, etc.

When the peroration had been reached, Grandmamma pushed back her wig, which had been resting on her left eyebrow, took a fresh breath, and began on second marriages, with a very long digression into marriages between cousins, together with a few poignant expressions of opinion on the immorality of the proposal to remove the word "obey" from the marriage service. In common with all other masterful ladies who have ruled their own husbands with a rod of iron, Grandmamma held extremely strong views on this subject. She imparted them to Eleanor with fluency and vigour until the tea was brought in.

Having talked herself out for the time being, she relaxed a little, and Eleanor was allowed to converse with the Aunts. She found them all agog over Milly's hints that George was contemplating matrimony.

"I do hope a wise choice, dear girl," said Aunt Editha.

Eleanor, aware of the catechism that would follow, refrained from saying that she knew Mrs. Hadding. She merely said she hoped so too.

"A strong hand is what Flora needs," said Mrs. Fordyce, speaking with so much energy that she spilt her tea. "If George can induce the right person to take charge of his far worse than motherless daughter, it will be well. Firmness and wise counsel are what Flora needs, and what you, my dear Eleanor, are yourself far too young and inexperienced to supply."

The tea-party proceeded upon this note of majestic gossip. Awful warnings were recalled from the family annals and from elsewhere; homilies founded upon these sad cases flowed as freely as did the tea. Aunt Editha said "Quite true," and "Yes, *indeed*" at intervals. And everyone except Eleanor felt sorry when she rose to go.

On the way downstairs Eleanor retrieved her violets. Out of the presence, she was reviving rapidly, and by the time she had pinned on her flowers in the hall, she was sufficiently herself to say:

"Grandmamma seemed quite pleased about George marrying again."

"Oh, dear girl, but *George* is a man!" said the scandalized Aunt Editha.

Eleanor laughed and kissed her warmly.

"That does make a difference—doesn't it? But, darling, prepare for a shock—*Mrs. Hadding is a widow.*"

She ran down the steps without waiting to see how Aunt Editha bore the shock.

Chapter Twenty-Five

DAVID WENT ROUND to Martagon Crescent that evening. No. 16 showed no lights. He rang and knocked for a quarter of an hour and heard no answering sound. He came away to wait for tomorrow with an increasing sense of strain. Yet to-morrow brought no relief. The telephone bell rang often enough, but the voice that had repeated Erica's last words to him was silent.

Friday and Saturday passed. He went again to Martagon Crescent, only to come away, as before, from a dumb, unanswering house.

On Saturday Tommy Wingate came up to town for the week-end. Milly March, rushing into Eleanor's flat at three o'clock in the afternoon full of her brother George's marriage, found him there before her and "*actually* holding Eleanor's silks for her to wind."

Milly, as usual, was encumbered by innumerable parcels. She had left the ham, the Stilton cheese, and three pounds of apples in the hall, but several minor brown-paper packages reposed in her lap and littered the carpet around her chair. She remained until half-past six, hoping against hope that Tommy would go, and then came away only because she had promised to look in on Grandmamma.

She fluttered the Aunts a good deal by her description of Tommy and her suspicions that Eleanor was dining with him. "She *said* she was going out to dinner, and they were talking about plays."

The Aunts took it by turns to stay with Grandmamma on Sunday morning. It was Miss Mary's turn for church next day. Neither she nor Aunt Editha commented on the fact that she was starting an hour earlier than usual; but she arrived at Chieveley Street in very good time to ask "dear Eleanor" whether she would care to accompany her to church.

"Dear Eleanor" was not alone. At barely a quarter past ten Captain Wingate was seated at her piano picking out tunes with one finger. Eleanor had the grace to blush.

It ended in Tommy accompanying both ladies to church, after which he and Eleanor walked Aunt Mary to Grandmamma's door, and then went off together.

It was after receiving Miss Mary's report that Miss Editha St. Kern decided that she could not let the afternoon pass without going round to Chieveley Street. "The dear girl may be feeling quite embarrassed. Young men are sometimes quite impervious to hints. I shall go round, and I shall take dear Eleanor the book I promised to lend her as soon as I got it back from Bertha. Bertha enjoyed it greatly."

With the book neatly done up in brown paper, Miss Editha rang Eleanor's bell. The rather stern parlourmaid who presently told her that Mrs. Rayne had gone out for the afternoon could not possibly be suspected of prevarication.

"Gone out?" said Miss Editha.

"For the afternoon," said the parlourmaid.

"Is Miss March at home?"

The parlourmaid hesitated, and Miss Editha walked into the hall.

"Ah, I see she is. Then you needn't announce me—I'll just go in." And in she went, to find Folly curled up in a big chair with a book. Timmy lay asleep on her knee in an abandoned attitude, all stretched out and furry.

"Don't get up," said Aunt Editha brightly. "I wouldn't disturb that darling pet of a kitten for worlds. I'll just take this chair beside you, and we can be quite cosy. Well, Flora, my dear, this is very nice. It was such a disappointment to find that dear Eleanor was out; but the next best thing to finding her is to find you, my dear. Dear Eleanor has gone out with Captain Wingate, I suppose?"

"'M—" said Folly. "Look at Timothy, Aunt Editha! Isn't he funny? He always yawns when I tickle his chin."

"I was just thinking how nice it would be to have a cosy little chat with you, Flora dear." Aunt Editha stroked Timmy absent-mindedly with one finger. "About your father's marriage, you know. Now tell me, was it a great surprise to you?"

"Oh no."

"That is well. I *am* so glad of that. And now, dear child, tell me—have you met this lady?"

Folly nodded.

"How delightful—how very delightful! Dear child, you will be such a happy family. I feel sure of it. So sensible of your dear father to choose a contemporary of his own—so *very* sensible. I hear from Aunt Milly that he has made a most judicious choice, and that you will now have that kind, wise guidance which you must so often have felt the need of."

Folly was stroking the pads of Timmy's paws; the little transparent claws came curving out of their velvet sheaths and then sank back again. She fixed a mournful gaze on Miss Editha's face.

"I shall probably go and live with Floss," she said.

"With—Floss? You mean—Oh, my dear child!"

"'M—" said Folly. "I expect I shall."

Aunt Editha patted her hand. She was terribly shocked, but never too much shocked to be kind.

"Dear child, pray don't talk like that. I know how terribly hard it has been for you. But, believe me, brighter days will dawn—they will, indeed. I feel sure that your dear father has made a very wise and happy choice, and that you will come to rejoice in his happiness like a good, unselfish child. And now we won't talk about it *any* more. When did you say dear Eleanor would be back?"

"I don't know."

"Is she out to tea?"

"I expect so."

"My dear—well, perhaps you would both come round and have supper with us this evening?" This was a really brilliant inspiration, and quite impromptu.

"Thanks awfully, Aunt Editha, but we're engaged."

"Are you going to Aunt Milly? She didn't mention it."

"Oh no," said Folly. She pulled Timmy's whiskers, and was bitten for her pains.

Aunt Editha smiled her kind, bright smile.

"Now, don't tell me. You must really let me guess. Is it Frank and Julie?"

Folly shook her head.

"Dear Uncle St. Clair then? No? The William Fordyces? My dear child, where can you *possibly* be going?" Aunt Editha was flushed, and her voice trembled a little.

All at once Folly's mood changed. Aunt Edith was kind. She did try to find things out, but she was *kind*; and she was really, really fond of Eleanor. She was even fond of the wicked little Will-o'-the-Wisp who had been teasing her. She put both hands on Aunt Editha's arm and squeezed it.

"We aren't really going out at all; Tommy and David are coming here. So you couldn't guess—could you?"

"Tommy?" said Aunt Editha, pleasantly fluttered. "Is that Captain Wingate? And do you call him Tommy, dear child?"

"'M—" said Folly. She stopped squeezing the arm and patted it instead. "Everyone calls him Tommy—he's that sort. But I thought you knew him. David and Eleanor seem to have known him for ages and ages and ages."

"Wingate?" said Miss Editha. "Wingate—Wingate? David had a schoolfellow of that name, older than himself, I think. Yes—yes! And his parents used to live in the same neighbourhood as dear Eleanor's parents. That would be it! Of course, such an old friend, it makes all the difference. Dear Eleanor would naturally enjoy meeting him again— to be sure—very pleasant for them both. Dear child, you've quite set my mind at rest. And now I must be getting back to Grandmamma."

Folly let her out. On the threshold Miss Editha turned and hugged her.

"Such a nice talk, dear child! So cosy!"

She forgot to leave the book that Bertha had enjoyed so much.

Chapter Twenty-Six

DAVID FOUND a faint relief from strain in Tommy Wingate's cheerful company. At supper Tommy was full of talk. The solemn parlourmaid had gone out, and they waited on themselves.

After supper they sat round the fire and talked about the times when Tommy was Wingate major and a most tremendous swell, and David was his fag. Eleanor, it appeared, was then chiefly remarkable for the length of her pigtail and the way in which it was apt to betray her by catching in trees and bushes when she was in headlong flight from the boys. They went on remembering very happily, and Folly, curled up on the floor at Eleanor's feet with her head against Eleanor's knee, forgot all about George and Floss and being lost dog.

When Tommy said good-bye, he said: "May I come next week, Eleanor?"

Eleanor first met his eyes frankly and answered with an "Oh yes—do," and then quite suddenly blushed and dropped her lashes.

David went away feeling more rested than he had done all the week. That schoolboy past had been a very pleasant place to wander in.

At midday on Monday he was rung up again.

"Well, David Fordyce?" said the voice.

David made his own voice as coolly indifferent as he could:

"Who is speaking?"

There was a laugh.

"That won't go down, you know."

"Don't you think it's time you told me your name?" said David.

"I'm going to. As a matter of fact my card is probably somewhere on your table at this moment. I left it there when I came to see you."

David fumbled amongst his papers and picked out a card. It was of the size used for men's visiting cards, and written across it in pencil with printed letters were the words *"Miss Heather Down."* There was no address.

Miss Down—the girl in the bright pink hat who had talked so oddly. He asked quickly:

"Are you Miss Down? I have her card."

"Miss Heather Down. Well, David Fordyce, you've had the week-end to think things over, and I should like to know what conclusion you've come to?"

"I haven't come to any conclusion at all. I should like to meet you and talk things over."

"All in good time."

David struck the table with his hand.

"Miss Down, what's the good of all this? If you wished to rouse my interest, you've roused it. I can't believe that you want to torture me."

The voice said: "Can't you?"

"No, I can't. Will you tell me plainly whether you believe Erica to be alive?"

There was a long pause. Then the voice said:

"What do you think, David Fordyce?"

"I don't know what to think. I have believed her dead."

"Since when?"

"Since the wreck of the *Bomongo*."

In a sort of hesitating way the voice said: "Erica survived that wreck." Then with vehemence: "You know very well she did, David Fordyce."

"I do *not*."

"You say that?"

"Of course I say it."

"Then you've got a nerve. Do you think I know so much, and don't know that Erica wrote to you?"

"Erica wrote to me?"

"You know she did."

"Miss Down, that's a most extraordinary assertion. If I had received a letter from Erica, how could I possibly have believed that she was dead?"

"I never thought that you believed it. It suited you to pretend you believed it—that's all."

"I never received any letter from Erica—I can swear it."

"You swore to love and cherish her. Pie-crust promises—weren't they? What's the good of your trying to bluff me? I can tell you what was in the letters."

David exclaimed sharply.

"I know too much, you see. Do you still think you're talking to a stranger, David Fordyce?"

A feeling of the most sickening dread touched David.

"Tell me who you are, then."

"Can't you answer the question yourself? If you can't, take a dictionary and look up my name. That may help you."

"What do you mean?"

"Look in the dictionary. And then if you want to see me, you can come round to Martagon Crescent. I shall be there at nine o'clock." She rang off.

David sat looking at her card. Miss Down—Miss Heather Down. The feeling of sickening dread touched him again. It was as if he were in the dark, in a place unknown, and there, upon the darkness, could see a formless image drawing together, taking on form and outline.

He got up, went to the bookcase, and took down "The Oxford Dictionary." The leaves turned under his fixed gaze. He was scarcely aware that it was his own hand that turned them. Halfway down a right hand page he saw the word Heather, and read on: "A species of *Erica*." He shut the book and put it back on the book-shelf. The image had taken shape; and with all his heart and mind he rejected it.

He went back to his table and sat down. The horrible moment had passed; he felt clear and cool to coldness. Heather Down—Erica Moore. The name was merely a punning translation. He rejected the name and its implications. He rejected the whole attempt to convince him that Erica lived. Then, as he sat there, things began to come back to him—little odd things. Miss Down in her bright pink scarf. Erica's voice saying: "How long must I wear black? I do love bright colours. I like pink best of all." Miss Down sitting in that chair over there and using odd old-fashioned proverbs to point her nervous jerky speech. Erica saying to him: "We played parlour games—backgammon and spillikins and proverbs."

Like the tiny waves that wash against the foot of a cliff and undermine it, these thoughts came lapping against the set determination with which he rejected Heather Down's preposterous claim. If it were a claim, why had it not been made before? The thing that she had said came sharply into his mind. She said that Erica had written. Impossible! If she had written, why had he not received her letter? She had not written. She had not survived the wreck of the *Bomongo*. The whole thing was some barefaced attempt to impose upon his credulity.

At this point the little lapping waves began again. Whoever Heather Down might be, or whoever she might claim to be, she had, or fancied she had, some grudge against him. The resentment in her voice sounded real enough. He began to go over his interview with Miss Smith.

The little waves went on lapping.

Chapter Twenty-Seven

AT THE CORNER of Martagon Crescent, David looked at his watch. It was nine o'clock. He walked slowly to the door of No. 16 and rang the bell. The same little girl whom he had seen before let him in. David supposed her to be some sort of maid-of-all-work—a small peaked creature who looked ten, but who was probably fifteen.

He followed her into Miss Smith's parlour. The single gas jet burned noisily and filled the room with its stale fumes; a small, weak fire dwindled on the hearth. The room was cold as well as stuffy. Beneath the predominating smell of gas other odours lurked—the fustiness of a very old carpet, faint traces of furniture polish, and the peculiar smell of linoleum.

The door opened and Miss Down came in. She wore the same pink hat in which she had visited the office, a salmon-coloured jumper, and a bright cerise golf-jacket. Her manner was nervous, and her colour very high. She made no attempt to shake hands, but crossed between David and the fire and remained standing near the rose-wood table with its pink and green woolly mats and its family Bible.

David turned so as to face her. His first feeling was one of extreme relief. She was at least two inches taller than Erica; and he judged her to be three or four years older.

He said: "Good-evening, Miss Down."

She made no reply to the greeting, and before the nervous intensity of her look David felt a faint return of his old horrified dread.

After waiting to see if she would speak, he said:

"Miss Down, you have made a most extraordinary assertion. You say that my wife survived the wreck of the *Bomongo*. You *do* say that?"

"Of course I do. The proof of the pudding's in the eating, isn't it?"

"What do you mean by that?"

"Are you going to pretend that you don't know what I mean?"

"There's no pretence about it."

"There are none so blind as those who won't see." Her manner was at the same time nervous and self-assertive; she was obviously in a state of great excitement.

David said coolly: "Am I to understand that you claim to be Erica?"

Her bright flush deepened.

"And if I said 'Yes' to that, David Fordyce?"

David's eyebrows lifted.

"I really shouldn't advise you to make that claim." Tone and manner were as quiet as could be, but Miss Down started as if he had struck her.

"And why? You'll have to tell me that, you know. You've got a grown woman to deal with now, not a poor little frightened child like you had five years ago.

"That," said David, "is one of my points Erica would not have been twenty-two until next June. You don't seriously ask me to believe that you are only twenty-one?"

Miss Down tossed her head.

"There are things that make you old before your time. It doesn't keep a girl young to be married and deserted before she's seventeen."

David looked her straight in the face.

"You're a couple of inches taller than Erica was."

Miss Down pounced on the last word.

"Was," she repeated." You've said it—haven't you? Are you going to say that a girl of sixteen can't grow a couple of inches, especially after a long illness? Are you going to say that?"

"No, I'm not. But I'm going to say something else. You're not Erica, Miss Down, and you can't make me believe that you are."

As he spoke, David believed his own words—believed them utterly. But in the next instant he was shaken. The girl standing opposite to him looked down quickly at her left hand. It was the look, the turn of the head, which he had seen in Julie on the day of Grandmamma's birthday party. Julie had looked down sideways at her new wedding ring, and the look had brought Erica to him—Erica looking down, Erica looking sideways at the ring which he had given her. Heather Down had looked sideways just like that.

David's eyes went to her left hand and saw a narrow gold circle about the third finger.

The impression passed; but it had shaken him. He went on speaking:

"I think you must realize that you can't just make assertions like that and expect to be believed. Have you any proof of what you say? Have you any evidence at all to show that Erica survived the wreck?" David looked hard at her as he spoke.

The light of the gas jet showed ends of dark brown hair under the bright hat. He thought that Erica's hair was a little lighter. Miss Down would certainly say that the hair of a girl of sixteen usually does darken, especially when it is kept short. Erica's eyes were between blue and grey; and so were Miss Down's. The brows had the same arch, and the features in both cases were of that rather nondescript and indeterminate kind which do not leave any very definite impress.

When David tried to call up a picture of Erica, his most vivid recollection was of her small shrinking form, her black dress, her pallor, and her shyness. Heather Down was certainly not pale. But there again she would say, no doubt, that a girl who has just lost her father and been thrown on the world at sixteen may very well be pale.

She might have read his thoughts, for she threw up her head and said defiantly:

"I've more colour than I used to have."

"You are not Erica," said David. But his voice lacked the conviction with which he had spoken before.

"I'm Heather Down."

David shrugged his shoulders.

"You might as well call yourself Erica Moore and have done with it. Why don't you? Is it because you're afraid to take a name which you know you've no right to?"

The girl dropped her voice to a lower note:

"If you're so sure that I'm not Erica, why do you trouble yourself about me? You can snap your fingers and go away like you did *before*. You can marry again. There's nothing to stop you, is there as long as you're sure that Erica's dead?"

"I want to ask you two questions," said David. "There have been three advertisements in the last three years, giving my initials and saying: 'Your wife is alive.' Did you put them in?"

"No, I didn't," said Miss Down, with what was obviously a stare of astonishment.

"But you saw my advertisement—the one in which I asked for information about Erica."

Miss Down smiled scornfully.

"Yes, I saw that. I thought you'd waited a good long time before you put it in."

"And why did you wait five years before you came forward with this claim of yours?"

"Tell me what I've claimed!" Her voice had real passion in it. "You married a poor friendless girl, and you deserted her. She wrote to you, and you never answered her letters. How can a girl who is ill and friendless, and who hasn't got a penny in the world, come across the sea to make a claim on the man who's deserted her? I had to work and save money before I could come over. And you say, why did I wait five years? I didn't wait. There were two letters; and you never answered them."

"I never had them."

Heather Down dived into the pocket of her golf jacket and drew out a yellowish printed slip.

"When there was no answer to the first letter, I registered the second. Here's the receipt. Do you still say you didn't get that letter?"

David took the slip and looked at it. It was dated December 7, 1922, and the address was to David Fordyce, Esq., Ford, Fordwick, Surrey. He stared at it until the letters ran together and his own name was a formless blur. He looked up at Heather Down with eyes that saw her differently. He did not feel sure about anything any more. He said, simply and gravely:

"I never had the letter—I didn't indeed. If it ever arrived, there'll be some record of it at the Fordwick office. I—Miss Down, do you really mean that Erica wrote?"

She nodded, watching him.

"You can keep the paper if you like."

"I must make inquiries. I must go down to Ford."

His manner was altered, shaken. He looked at her suddenly with a desperate appeal.

"Who are you?"

"Miss Smith's niece," said Heather Down.

She leant over the rose-wood table and opened the big Bible; the leaves fluttered under her fingers until she found what she was looking for—the space between the Old Testament and the New.

David looked at the page with its heading of Births, Marriages, and Deaths. The page was almost full. At the bottom he read, "Christina married William Moore;" and then Erica's name and the date of her birth. His eye travelled up the page. Above Christina was Ellen—that would be Aunt Nellie, twenty years older than the little after-thought sister; and above Ellen the names of the parents, William John Smith and Ellen Riley, and the date of their marriage, a year before the birth of Ellen.

David looked from the page to Heather Down.

"Your name's not here."

She shut the Bible with a nervous jerk.

"Did you think it would be there?" she said.

Chapter Twenty-Eight

DAVID LEFT MARTAGON CRESCENT with his mind set wholly upon the letter. He must go down to Fordwick and see if it had ever been received there. He kept his thoughts to this point with a most determined effort. If he relaxed, he found that he was remembering Heather Down's quick sideways glance at her ring, or the way in which her voice had softened when she repeated Erica's piteous cry to him on the *Bomongo*, the cry which only he and Erica had heard. He would not let his thoughts relax or take in more than the road to Fordwick, which he would travel as soon as it was light next morning, and the questions which he would ask of Mrs. Perrott, who had kept the post office there for five-and-twenty years. All through the watches of the night he travelled that road and asked those questions. A cold, grey dawn brought the relief of action.

It was only half-past nine o'clock when he walked into the post office and rapped upon the counter. The post office was also a general shop. There were tins of biscuits and tins of cocoa; garden seeds and garden twine; tin-tacks; bacon; tea; potatoes; acid drops, and peppermint bulls-eyes.

The door behind the counter creaked and Mrs. Perrott emerged, stout, comfortable, motherly, with a take-your-time-and-let-me-take-mine sort of air. She beamed on David, to whom she had sold peppermints and acid drops in infancy.

"Well, Mr. David—I *never*!"

"Good-morning, Mrs. Perrott," said David.

"Nasty damp morning again, I'm sure—and so it was yesterday. But they say rain's needed."

Mrs. Perrott reached the counter and leaned upon it.

And what can I do for you this nasty morning, sir? Are you just off to town?"

"Just *down* from town." David leaned on the counter too. "I've come down on purpose to ask you something, Mrs. Perrott."

"Me, Mr. David! Well, I'm sure anything I can do for any of the family, and for you in special sir—"

"It's about a registered letter," said David quickly.

"Well now!"

"It's a very important letter, and it was registered. I don't know how long you keep the records of that sort of thing; but it's some time ago, I'm afraid."

"How long ago would it be, sir?"

"More than four years."

Mrs. Perrott shook her head slowly.

"We don't keep nothing more than two years. Didn't you get the letter, sir?"

"No, I didn't. I've only just heard that it was sent."

"Well, I'm sure! And it was important?"

He nodded.

"Isn't that too bad, now!" said Mrs. Perrott. "Where would it have been from, sir?"

"South Africa—Cape Town. I've got the receipt."

He laid it down on the counter, and she took it in her hand, turning it this way and that as if the faded yellowish slip were a puzzle that might give up its secret if it were looked at long enough.

"Well, well, it's too bad," said Mrs. Perrott.

She watched David go out of the shop and start up his car. Then she went back to the room behind the shop, where her niece Etta, who did a little dressmaking, sat sewing at the bright blue stuff which Gladys Brown had just brought her in to make up.

Etta looked up as she came in, her pretty, pert face all screwed together.

"Gladys is going to look a fair show in this blue," she said discontentedly. "Funny how a girl with a bad complexion never knows it. A fair show she'll look. And if she thinks dressing bright is going to make Charlie look at her, well, she's made a bit of a mistake."

Mrs. Perrott looked indulgently at the blue stuff.

"Well, I liked a bit of bright colour myself when I was a girl—and Gladys has got a good heart if she hasn't got a good skin."

She took up her duster and began to dust the room slowly and methodically. It was a small room with a window looking out on a garden which was so full of cabbages that it was astonishing to think that Etta and Mrs. Perrott could ever exhaust the supply. Pressed closely against the glass were three fine geranium plants in pots, and on the mantelpiece, on either side of an old-fashioned wooden clock, there were hyacinths just coming into flower—a red hyacinth in a tall purple glass full of water, and a very bright pink hyacinth in a dark blue glass; their long stringy white roots showed through the coloured glass like seaweed moving in deep water.

Mrs. Perrott dusted the clock very carefully. It had belonged to her great-great-grandmother, Beulah Long, and she "thought a sight of it." She didn't hold with people who got rid of the things that come down to them and let them go to auction. She polished the face of the clock whilst she told Etta how Mr. David had come in about a registered letter that had never reached him:

"Four years ago and more. And, of course, I had to tell him we didn't keep nothing more than two years."

"Was there money in it?" said Etta, staring.

"He didn't say—but he did seem put out."

Etta was sewing with quick, jerky stitches.

"It's just like that old machine to go wrong when I've got all this work in! There's a wonderful bargain in *The Lady*—here, where's it got to? Listen to this: '*Banjulele, quite new. Would take sewing machine in exchange.*'"

Mrs. Perrott swung round, duster in hand.

"No, you don't, Etta, my girl!"

"But—Aunt—"

"There's no buts about it. The machine was your blessed Aunt Emma's, and if ever there's an angel in heaven it's her, though I'm her own sister that says it. And I wonder at you, Etta—yes, I do—to sit there and say to my face that you'd do an irreligious thing like selling your Aunt Emma's machine to a stranger for a horrid Christy-minstrel banjo that's only fit for a black-faced nigger singing vulgar songs on Margate sands!" Mrs. Perrott was quite red in the face as she finished.

Etta gave a pettish jerk of her shoulder and said: "Oh, well—"

Mrs. Perrott went on dusting in an offended silence. It was about five minutes later that she suddenly exclaimed.

"What's the matter?" asked Etta rather sulkily.

Mrs. Perrott sat down in the nearest chair.

"Well, I never! But I suppose it couldn't have been that one."

"What *are* you talking about?"

"Well, to be sure—but I don't suppose it could have been."

"Gracious, Aunt! Have you gone dotty?"

Mrs. Perrott looked at her reprovingly.

"There's no one in the family on either side, nor as far back as I know, that hadn't all the use of their intellects the same as the Lord meant 'em to have, right up to their last dying day. Very good strong mem'ries they all of 'em had, especially my great-uncle, Ebenezer William, that could always remember as he heard the bells rung in this very church for the battle of Waterloo. I don't say I'm quick nor full of book-learning, and I don't know that I hold with all this book-learning that goes on nowadays. There's good books and there's bad books, and I'm no scholar, nor ever was. I mayn't be quick, but I'm sure. And it's come back to me that there was a letter like Mr. David was asking for."

Etta stared and said "Gracious!" again.

"It's come back to me," said Mrs. Perrott.

"But, Aunt, there's hundreds of letters for Mr. David in four months, let alone four years."

"There's not so many registered letters. And I tell you how I remember about this one—if it was the one that Mr. David's asking about. I'll tell you how I remember it. It come the last week of September, and blazing hot weather. And old Masterson that gave up being postman at Christmas that year—let me see, it was 1922—September 1922 it was, and a very sudden heat—and Masterson comes in and he says, 'Well, missus, I'm in hopes as you haven't no letters by afternoon post anyways.' And he gives me the bag. And there was two or three bills, and I said, 'They'll wait nicely, and no one the wiser nor the worser off.' And then there was the foreign letter for Mr. David, and I said, 'This'll have to go whether or no.' And poor Masterson he leans on the counter and mops his face, and he says, 'Missus, I'm done.' I can tell you he frightened me a bit. But I got him to a chair, and I made him sit quiet, and I fetched him a drink." Mrs. Perrott stopped speaking. Her duster lay on her lap; she began to pleat it into neat straight folds.

"Well? What happened?" said Etta curiously.

"Happened?" said Mrs. Perrott. "Nothing happened. I left Masterson to keep the shop, and I took the letter up myself. And that's how I come to remember about it."

"Then Mr. David got it?"

"I suppose he did," said Mrs. Perrott, getting out of her chair.

She went on dusting until everything in the room was spotless. Then she went through into the shop, and with infinite care and pains, she wrote a letter.

Chapter Twenty-Nine

DAVID REACHED HIS OFFICE at about eleven. There was a formidable amount of work waiting to be tackled; but the first thing that he did was to write a letter. He took pen and paper, dated the sheet, and wrote:

"DEAR MISS DOWN—"

There he stopped, and for a moment rested his head upon his hand. Miss Down—Erica—was he writing to Erica? He said, "No," and had the feeling that he was pushing against a cold conviction that gathered weight as he withstood it. He straightened up and went on with the letter:

"I have just returned from Fordwick. I am unable to trace any registered letter posted over four years ago, as they do not keep the records for more than two years. I wish very much to see you again. I am sending this letter by District Messenger. I shall be in office till six. If I do not hear to the contrary, I will come to Martagon Crescent at nine o'clock.

"Yours sincerely,

"DAVID FORDYCE."

When he had sent the letter off he addressed himself to his arrears of work.

It was about three o'clock in the afternoon when Miss Barker opened the door and said:

"Miss March would like to see you, Mr. Fordyce."

Folly had hardly waited to be announced. She scandalized Miss Barker a good deal by passing her in the doorway instead of waiting in the outer office to be told that Mr. Fordyce would see her. Miss Barker had, fortunately, closed the door before Folly perched herself on the corner of the table with her feet dangling.

David looked up with a very decided frown and saw her in her red hat and dress looking impishly at him.

"I say, look out! There are papers all over the place."

"I don't mind them," said Folly. "I like kicking my heels. I haven't got the red ones on to-day. You were quite right about my being followed in them; and I didn't want anyone to follow me here."

"You've no business to come here," said David.

"Why on *earth* not? An office is a frightfully proper place, and that girl out there is the real chaperony sort—I should think even the Aunts didn't mind your having her."

"Did you come here to talk about Miss Barker?" said David gloomily.

"No-o—not specially. Are you busy?"

"I was." David's frown had become ferocious.

Folly opened her green eyes very wide.

"What an awful temper you have got, David! Doesn't it hurt when you frown like that? I should think it would sprain your eyebrows. It would be horrid for you if you had to have them in splints. I do wish you'd be careful."

"Folly, I really am busy. Why did you come?"

"Because I really, truly had to see you."

"Why?"

She crossed one knee over the other.

"I thought of something. I've been thinking of it a lot, and I thought I ought to tell you about it."

"What is it?"

Her voice arrested his attention; there was a little stammer of hesitation in it.

"David—that advertisement."

"Which one?"

"Not yours; the one with the initials and 'Your wife is alive.'"

"Yes?"

"Do you know who put it in?"

"I thought, of course, that it was Miss Smith or—her niece. But they didn't seem to know anything about it; they seemed surprised—really surprised."

"'M—I expect they were. Would you like to know who put it in?"

David stared at her. She had clasped her hands about her knee and was leaning a little towards him.

"What do you know about it?"

"I know who put it in."

"How can you possibly know?"

"I do. I can tell you who put it in—and it wasn't Miss Smith or her niece."

"Who was it?"

"Betty," said Folly in an odd, wavering tone.

She jumped down from the table as she said the name, and stood a yard from David watching his face. A dark anger passed across it.

"What on earth do you mean?"

Folly stood her ground.

"I mean what I said—Betty put it in."

"Is this a joke? Do you think this is a subject to joke about?"

"I'm not joking. I came to tell you something because I thought you ought to know. But if you're going to look at me like that and go through the roof like a bomb—well, you can just find out for yourself; I won't tell you anything more!" She stamped an angry foot, and on the last word her breath caught in something uncommonly like a sob.

The anger went out of David's face.

"Folly—are you *serious*?"

He saw the glint of tears.

"I'm never serious—am I? No one ever takes me seriously."

David got up and stood between her and the door.

"Look here, you've gone too far. You can't say things like that about Betty unless you're prepared to substantiate them."

The tears were gone. This time it was a different kind of glint that he saw.

"Ooh! You do use long words! What does sub-what's-his-name mean? It sounds horrible!"

"Prove," said David impatiently. "You've said a thing about Betty, and I can't let it pass. You've got to prove it."

Folly went back to the table and leaned against it. With a little cool nod she said:

"All right. I came here to tell you, so I will. It's not because of your saying 'must,' you know."

"Well?"

"Betty did put it in—at least I think she did. And I came to tell you because I thought you ought to know. I didn't tell anyone else—I didn't tell Eleanor. But I thought you ought to know."

"Go on," said David.

"That advertisement came out on Thursday—the day I went up to town and Stingo was a beast. I looked in the paper afterwards and I saw it—after Eleanor told me, you know. I went through the old papers and looked till I found it."

"Yes, it was Thursday."

Folly nodded.

"On Friday night, after we came back to Ford, Eleanor took me into her room and scolded me—after we went up to bed, you know. And I lost my temper—I do lose it sometimes, but not nearly so often as you do—and I damned out of the room. And I went away into my own room, and hours afterwards I thought I'd go along and see if Eleanor was awake, because a dreadfully good feeling came over me and I didn't feel as if I could bear her to go on being dreadfully angry with me all night and perhaps have a dream about being angry with me—because I do truly love Eleanor, and when I truly love someone I can't, can't bear them to be angry with me."

As she said this Folly's hands came together and pressed one another and her eyes were full of light; her face was very pale. The light in her eyes hurt David with a sudden piercing pain. He looked away, and then looked back again.

"Go on," he said.

"I opened my door," said Folly, "and I heard someone else opening their door, away on the left. So I looked; and it was Betty's door. The door was open when I looked, and there was a light in the room, so that I could see her come through the door. I did see her, David. But she didn't see me. I didn't want her to see me, so I shut the door all but a chink, and I heard her go past my door and down the stairs. I waited for her to put the light on, but she didn't; and when I looked out her door was shut, and all the passage was dark, and all the house downstairs was dark, and—and I didn't like it a bit—I *didn't*," said Folly. "You wouldn't have either. *Nobody* would."

"Well?"

"Ooh! It was horrid! I didn't feel as if I could shut my door, and I didn't feel as if I could open it. And I waited a most frightful long time, and Betty didn't come back, and I began to think about people disappearing in the middle of the night, and burglars, and all the creepy-crawly stories I'd ever heard. And I got so frightened I simply had to do something, so I opened my door, and I went on tiptoe to the top of the stairs, and I listened. And it was like vaults and caverns and dark places in the sort of dream where you can't see anything; and there wasn't a sound. I wanted to go back to my room most awfully, but I thought I'd go a little way down the stairs first and see if there was a light anywhere. I thought if Betty was in her sitting-room she'd have a light and I should see it under the door. I went halfway down, and I hung over, and I looked, and there wasn't any light, but I could hear Betty talking. I couldn't hear what she said, only just her voice going up and down. Then she stopped, and a man said something."

David exclaimed sharply:

"Folly! What are you saying?"

Folly screwed up her face.

"I nearly fell over the banisters. You needn't look so shocked—it was only Francis. But I didn't know that till afterwards."

David came over to her and caught her arm.

"Folly, what's all this nonsense? Francis Lester at Ford—in the middle of the night?"

Folly nodded lightly and impudently.

"'M—he was—talking to Betty—in a dark room. Wasn't it shocking? And when I didn't know it was Francis—Ooh! I really did very nearly fall crash over the banisters in a deadly swoon, I was so shocked. *Betty!*"

David dropped her arm.

"Go on," he said shortly.

"When I stopped nearly swooning I thought I'd better go away. I didn't think it was my business to chaperone Betty. It didn't seem much use either, so I began to go upstairs. I didn't go very fast, because I was feeling all tottery with the shock." Her eyes danced wickedly. "And I'd only gone a few steps, when I heard Betty give a sort of choky cry, and I had a most dreadful thought that it might be a burglar after all, and that he was *murdering* her. So I ran right down the stairs and up to the door, and I turned the handle frightfully gently and opened the least little chink—and the room was quite pitchy dark. And just as I opened the door, Betty sniffed, and I thought he couldn't be murdering her, because I don't believe that even Betty would sniff if she were being murdered. She does sniff a lot—doesn't she?"

David frowned impatiently.

"David! What a perfectly horrible face! All right, I *am* going on. I was just going to shut the door and go away when Betty said, 'David took *The Times* to town with him yesterday, so I didn't know for certain if it was in.' Then she said, 'Francis, I wish we hadn't. He looks awful.' And Francis said, 'Don't be a fool! Do you want him to get married?' And of course I felt much better as soon as I knew it was Francis, and not a burglar or a horrid scandal. And I shut the door, and I wouldn't have told anyone ever, only I thought you ought to know."

"Folly—is this true?"

"You've got a very unbelieving mind," said Folly. "I told you it was true before I began. But of course, at the time, I didn't know in the least bit what they were talking about. But when I read out your advertisement at breakfast—you know, the one wanting information about Erica Moore—Betty knew the name as soon as I read it, and she jumped like anything, and upset the kettle and pretended she had burnt her hand. She hadn't really burnt it, because the kettle was nearly cold. And when Eleanor told me about the other advertisement—the one that said your wife was alive—I thought and thought, and I began to feel certain that Betty was talking to Francis about it."

"Folly—you're not making this up?"

She gave a little resigned sigh.

"What a frightfully high opinion you've got of me! You'd better let me finish telling you what happened, and then I'll go away. I've got to where I shut the door, haven't I?"

"Yes, is there any more?"

"Lots," said Folly. "I nearly died of fright for one thing—but of course you wouldn't mind about that. Well, I started to go towards the stairs; but I hadn't gone halfway, when I heard the morning room window shut. And I felt my way back along the wall. I was only just past the door when it opened and Betty came out. She nearly touched me, and if she hadn't been crying, I expect she'd have known there was someone there. She went straight upstairs—I don't think it's the first time she's walked about the house in the dark like that. I waited till I heard her door shut, and then I went up too, and when I was nearly up—Ooh! I had such a fright! The light over my head went on like a flash of lightning, only it stayed there."

"Who turned it on? Betty?"

"No—Eleanor. She'd heard the window shut. Her room was just over the sitting-room, you know."

"Well?"

Folly sparkled.

"It was frightfully funny! She thought I'd been having an assignation out in a nice dank wood, and she looked at my toes and they were dry. And I told her I'd been broom-stick riding. I do love to make Eleanor's eyelashes curl! I got her so puzzled and shocked she didn't know where she was."

David took no notice of this.

"Folly—all that about Betty is true?"

The mischief sank deep into her eyes like a stone sinking in a pool; they looked mournfully at David.

"You don't ever believe me. You won't believe me if I say it's true."

"Yes, I will. You're sure it was Betty?"

She nodded.

"And sure of what she said?"

She nodded again.

He said, more to himself than to her:

"But why? Why on earth?"

"She doesn't want you to marry. That's what Francis said—he said, 'Don't be a fool! Do you want him to get married?'"

He looked at her in horror for a moment.

"Folly, I can't believe this. No, I don't mean that I don't believe what you say. But you only heard a few words. I think there must be some other explanation. You see, I simply can't believe a thing like that about Betty."

"I see," said Folly. "It's nice for Betty. It must be nice to have someone who—can't—believe—things against one." She went on looking David straight in the face, but the words came slower and slower and at the last were hardly audible.

There was a pause. Then she said:

"I thought you ought to know."

Before he knew what she was going to do, she had walked past him and opened the door. The sound of Miss Barker's typewriter came tapping through the silence.

Folly said, "I'm *frightfully* sorry I came," and shut the door.

Chapter Thirty

DAVID WENT BACK to his work. About an hour later he found that he had stopped working. Betty—all this business about Betty and Francis. He went over it slowly, carefully, and at the end could only fall back on his loyalty to Betty and Betty's loyalty to him. There must be an explanation.

All the time that he had been working, and all the time that he had been going over Folly's story, the thought of Folly herself had been pricking him. The sound of her voice coming slower and slower hurt and went on hurting. She had come to do him a service, and he had made her frightfully sorry that she had come. On a sudden impulse he rang up Chieveley Street. It was Folly herself who answered.

"David speaking. Folly, is that you?"

"Yes, it is. What do you want?"

"I want to thank you."

"I don't want to be thanked."

"I don't want you to be sorry you came," said David. "The more I think about it, the more I feel sure that there's some explanation of what you heard. But I think I ought to know what it is, and I think you were perfectly right to come and tell me. I'm most awfully grateful to you for trying to help me."

Silence.

"Folly!"

"'M—"

"Are you there?"

"Yes, I am."

"Folly, I hated your saying it must be nice to have someone who can't believe things against you. Do you think I'd believe things about you?"

"'M—you would—everyone would—j-just like lightning."

"Don't talk nonsense! You know I wouldn't believe anything."

A pause. Then:

"W-wouldn't you? Not if people stood in rows and said they'd seen me?"

"Of course I wouldn't."

"Not if Grandmamma, and the Aunts, and Betty, and everyone said it?"

"Not unless you said it yourself."

"Ooh!" said Folly with a little crow of triumph. "David, I l-love you!"

The words came with a rush and were followed by a silence which seemed to stretch between them unbroken and unbreakable. Through this silence there beat a heavy, inaudible pulse. David found his hand clenching on the receiver. He could not have spoken a word to save his life.

When the silence had lasted a very long time it was broken by a tiny click. Far away in Chieveley Street Folly had rung off.

David hung up the receiver and drew a long breath. Folly's little pleased laugh; her lightly, childishly spoken words; and then the silence which left behind it this dazed sense of something only just averted—

He went doggedly back to his work. At nine o'clock he was ringing the bell at No. 16, Martagon Crescent. Heather Down opened the door.

She said, "Come in," and he followed her into Miss Smith's parlour.

"Well?" said Miss Down with a trace of defiance in her voice.

"You got my letter?"

"Yes, I got it."

He had come determined to test everything that he could recall of feature, voice, and manner; but in the actual presence of Heather

Down his memory of Erica faded into something as dim as a just remembered dream. The bright colours which Miss Down affected were confusing to the eye; her features made but a slight impression. She wore to-day a jumper suit of the brightest shade of Reckitt's blue; an orange and brown scarf was knotted about her throat; her hair was entirely covered by the bright pink hat in which she had paid him her first visit.

"Well?" she said. "What about it?"

"I couldn't trace the registered letter," said David. "They don't keep the records. You say there were two letters. I've come here to-night to ask you to tell me what was in them."

She was leaning against the end of the horsehair sofa, her hands behind her. She gave him a quick, Searching look.

"Erica wrote the letters."

"Yes," said David. "Can you tell me what was in them?"

He thought she eyed him warily.

"You're asking me if I can tell you what was in the letters that Erica wrote to you. A girl doesn't show that sort of letter to anyone else."

"No—I suppose not. Can you tell me what was in the letters?"

He kept his eyes on her face. If she were Erica, she would know what was in the letters. If she were Erica telling the contents of those five-year-old letters, surely there would be something that would ring true enough to convince him. If she were not Erica, could she produce anything that would pass muster? What Erica might be to-day he did not know; but he thought he knew what kind of a letter the Erica of five years ago would have written. Also, supposing Heather Down was not Erica, she could not be absolutely sure that Erica's letters had not reached him; and in that case she would be afraid of making a slip. With a shock he realized that he was accepting the fact that Erica had survived the wreck. These thoughts did not so much pass through his mind as remain there; he did not at any time throughout the interview entirely lose sight of them. They were vividly present as Heather Down answered his question with another:

"You want to know whether I can tell you what was in the letters?"

"Yes."

"Do you mean word for word?" Her voice hesitated a little. "I couldn't say that I'd remember word for word anything I'd written five years ago."

Did the hesitation mean that she was hedging? He watched her as he said:

"No—I didn't mean that. Can you give me the gist of the letters?"

"Both of them?"

"Both of them."

"Well, I can do it. I suppose you think you're testing me. For all I know, you've got the letters in your pocket." She stood up with a nervous jerk. "All right—I can do it. Are you going to write down what I say?"

David had taken out a notebook and pencil.

"Yes, if you don't mind."

Heather Down laughed.

"Why should I mind?"

She pulled a chair up to the rose-wood table and sat down. Her right arm lay on the polished wood. She slid her fingers nervously to and fro along the dark markings. Her eyes followed the movement.

"I'm ready," said David.

He too had drawn a chair up to the table. The notebook lay open. He watched Heather Down and waited, pencil in hand, for her to begin.

"Dear David." She said the words in a sort of embarrassed whisper, then looked up jerkily. "It begins like that."

"The first letter?"

"Yes, the first letter. It begins, 'Dear David.'" He wrote the words painfully.

"Yes?"

"'I have been ill. I can't write much. I didn't know who I was till just now. They have been very kind. Please come quickly.

'ERICA.'"

David wrote the words as they were spoken. They fell slowly one by one, and he wrote them down. The unbearable conviction that they were Erica's words bore down upon him like some crushing weight. He wrote her name, and after a long minute he looked up.

"Is that all?"

"The first letter." Her voice was very low. Yes, that's all of it." After a pause she said: "There was a covering letter from the people she was with. I don't know what it said—I didn't read it."

"Their name?" The words came sharply.

"I won't tell you that just now. Do you want the second letter?" She had gone back to tracing the pattern on the table.

"Yes."

She began again:

"'DEAR DAVID,

"'Did you get my letter? I wrote three months ago to tell you I was alive. I thought perhaps you would think I had been drowned—a lot of people were. Will you write and tell me what to do? I am better, but I am not well yet. Will you write to me?
'ERICA.'"

"There's a postscript," said Miss Down without looking up. "It says: 'Will you tell Aunt Nellie that I wasn't drowned?'"

David wrote the words. The letters appalled him; they were just such letters as Erica, deserted, might have written.

"That's all," said Heather Down. "You never answered. You never came."

"I never got the letters. They never reached me."

Her voice went away to a sobbing whisper:

"That's what you say."

"It's true."

There was a very painful silence. David broke it with an effort.

"Will you swear to what's in those letters—that Erica wrote them?"

Miss Down pushed back her chair and jumped up.

"Oh yes, I'll swear to it—on the Bible if you like. I've nothing on my conscience that I can't swear to." She leaned over and rested her hand on the big Bible with its worn brown leather cover rubbed shabby at the edges. "I don't mind taking my Bible oath to the letters. Did you think I would? Did you think I made them up? I swear that

that's what Erica wrote—as near as anyone could remember after more than four years."

She took her hand away, and he saw that it was shaking.

"There! I've sworn to it!"

David got up with the notebook in his hand.

"Will you put your hand back on the Bible and swear that you're Erica?"

Miss Down flushed scarlet.

"No, I won't. If I'm Erica, I'm your wife. And if you don't know me and won't own to me, do you think that I'd make any claim on you? Do you think I've come to try and get money from you?"

She went back to the sofa and stood against it.

"Do you think I'd take a penny from you? Do you think I want a man that deserted me and doesn't even know me? Swear that I'm your wife? No, thank you, David Fordyce—not much I won't!"

The extraordinary, sudden passion in voice and look produced an effect of vehement sincerity. If she had sworn, David would have believed her less. He stood and looked at her with a sort of horror.

Heather Down threw out both bands.

"Go away! What are you stopping here for? I wish you'd never come! I wish I'd never seen you!"

As she threw out her hands, David saw again the palm of her left hand a glint of blue. What he had taken to be a wedding ring was a ring with blue stones in it, turned round so that only the plain gold band showed whilst the hand was closed or lying palm downwards. He stepped forward, caught her by the wrist, and put a shaking finger on the blue stones. They made three blue flowers—three forget-me-not flowers.

It was the ring he had given Erica.

Heather Down looked him straight in the face her eyes full of bright angry tears.

"You've forgotten the girl, but you remember the ring!" she cried.

As he met her look, unbelief came up in him like a flood. He dropped Heather Down's wrist and stood back from her. The unbelief began to ebb away. The instinct to get away before he was betrayed into some irrevocable word or act turned him to the door.

He went out of the room and out of the house.

Chapter Thirty-One

DAVID GOT Mrs. Perrott's letter next morning. She wrote:

"DEAR SIR,

"I have remembered something about a letter as may be the one you was asking for. Hoping this may be of service to you.

"Yours obediently,

"BEULAH PERROTT."

David took his car and went down to Fordwick. He was thankful for the need of action. To sit in office with a thousand conjectures coming, going, jostling, and contradicting one another, and making his attempt at work a farce, was an experience from which he was glad to escape.

If Mrs. Perrott was surprised to see him so soon, she did not show it. She gave him her usual greeting, remarked upon the weather, and inquired after his health. After these polite preliminaries she seated herself in a leisurely fashion and asked what she could do for him.

"I got your letter this morning," said David.

Mrs. Perrott nodded.

"I thought maybe you would."

"I've come down to have a talk with you about it."

"To be sure," said Mrs. Perrott comfortably. "And I'd ask you into the sitting-room, only Etta's got her sewing all over the place, and we can be private here. Post office business is post office business, and dressmaking is dressmaking, and I don't hold with mixing them, but if you come through this side of the counter, I can give you chair."

"I'd rather stand," said David. "I've been sitting in the car." He leaned on the counter. "You say you've remembered something about a letter."

"It come back to me after you'd gone, all of a sudden-like, when I was dusting. I'd me duster in me hand, and it come over me just like a flash."

"Will you tell me about it?" said David patiently.

Mrs. Perrott began to tell him:

"You remember Masterson, Mr. David, that was postman before Brooks, and gave up Christmas four years ago and went down Bournemouth way to a daughter that was married to a wheelwright?"

David said he remembered Masterson.

"Well," said Mrs. Perrott in her slow, even tones, "I was dusting me hyacinths, and I suppose it was they put me in mind of Masterson. His wife couldn't abide the smell of them, so he never raised any. But he always noticed mine, and when they come into bloom he used to go through into the sitting-room a-purpose to sniff at them. He used to say he liked a real good scent that you didn't have to guess at. So I suppose it was seeing the buds on my hyacinths made me think of him, and then it all come back."

"Yes?" said David in an encouraging voice. He had known Mrs. Perrott for twenty-five years, and he knew that when she started to tell a story she had to be let alone to tell it her own way.

"I was quite took aback," said Mrs. Perrott comfortably. She settled herself in her chair and crossed her arms. "It come over me as plain as plain. Masterson he come in with the afternoon post-bag, and he lumps it down on the counter, and he says to me, 'Missis,' he says, 'I hopes as you haven't no letters that's any way special this afternoon, because I'm fair done.' And sure enough he did look bad. Well, I opened the bag, and there were half a dozen things that were no matter if the people didn't get them for a month o' Sundays—and so I told him. And then, at the bottom of the bag, if there wasn't a letter for you, Mr. David! Well, I looked at it, and I saw that it was foreign— Cape Town was the postmark—same as you was asking about. Well, when I saw that, I said, 'This one'll have to go up to Ford, whether or no.' And poor old Masterson he catches hold of the counter and he says, 'Missis, I'm done!' It fair gave me a turn the way he said it."

"Well?" said David.

Mrs. Perrott heaved a large sigh.

"*Well* it was in the end, but it gave me a turn at the time. I got him into a chair and I give him a drink, and by-and-by he come round a bit. And then I began to think about the letter, and it come to me as I'd take it up to Ford myself and let Masterson mind the shop. Etta was away staying with her mother's sister that spoils her so."

"You took the letter yourself?"

David felt that unless he spoke quickly he would probably have to listen to the life-history of Etta's mother's sister.

Mrs. Perrott was recalled to her tale.

"I took it," she said. "I put on me hat and I went up across the fields, and, my goodness, wasn't it hot! I didn't wonder as Masterson—"

David interrupted her.

"Hot!" he exclaimed.

Mrs. Perrott nodded.

"The heat was that heavy I was pretty near melted. If I hadn't had my numbrella, I don't know what I *should* have done."

"Hot!" repeated David. "In December, Mrs. Perrott?"

"I didn't say nothing about December, Mr. David. It was September—the last week of September, and as hot as an oven on baking-day."

"September!"

"Last week of September."

David pulled out his pocket-book, extracted the receipt, and pushed it across to Mrs. Perrott. She picked it up and looked at it, a puzzled frown gathering on her large placid face. She read, "December the seventh," and repeated the words twice over. In the end she said firmly:

"September it was, and there's no getting from it."

"Then it wasn't this letter," said David.

"Seems as if it couldn't ha' been," Mrs. Perrott agreed.

David's thoughts were racing. He had not received any South African letter in the latter part of 1922; the last communication from the Cape Town solicitor had reached him in June. If Mrs. Perrott remembered a letter with the Cape Town postmark in September—in the last week in September—The words broke off in his mind. The thought broke off. Other words came—Erica's first letter; not the second one which she had registered, but that first one, posted in September.

Again the thought broke. Heather Down hadn't said when that first letter was posted; but if the second one was registered on December 7th after Erica had waited in vain for a reply, that would certainly put the first letter somewhere in September. How long would she wait before she wrote again? Two months certainly, perhaps three—probably somewhere between two and three months. September—yes, the first letter might have come to Fordwick post office on that hot day in the last week of September. Once again, and with the same sense of shock, it came to David that he was believing Heather Down—he was accepting her account of the letters as true.

All this passed very quickly whilst Mrs. Perrott was fingering the faded receipt. She looked up from it now and repeated slowly: "It seems as if it couldn't ha' been this one."

"Mrs. Perrott," said David earnestly, "go back to that hot day you were telling me about. Just put yourself right back there and go over what happened. You took the letter out of the bag, and you saw that it was addressed to me. Can you remember anything about the writing on the envelope?"

Mrs. Perrott shut her eyes.

"The bag was on the counter, just about here." She reached out a groping hand. "An' I put my hand in and felt around, and out come the letter. Yes, that was it—one of those longish envelopes like bills come in—white—yes, it were a white envelope. That's come back to me quite plain, that it were white."

"Was it registered?" The question came quick and low.

Mrs. Perrott opened her eyes in surprise.

"Why, if I hadn't clean forgotten that it was a registry letter you was asking about! Well, that settles it—don't it?"

"It wasn't registered?"

"Oh no," said Mrs. Perrott. She looked vexed. "To think of me being so stupid, now! I can't think what's come to me or what made me think it was, and I'm sure I'm sorry to have troubled you for nothing."

"Perhaps you haven't troubled me for nothing," said David. "Will you go on and tell me just what happened after you said you'd take the letter for Masterson?"

"There isn't anything more to tell," said Mrs. Perrott, in a flustered, disappointed manner. "I'm sure I'm that vexed at being so stupid—and however I done it I can't think." She pushed the receipt across the counter. "Here's your paper, sir, and I'm sure I'm very sorry."

David took up the receipt and put it away in his pocket-book.

"Don't you bother about that, Mrs. Perrott. You took the letter for Masterson and you went up to Ford with it. And when you got to the house, I hope they gave you a cup of tea after your walk. Did they? And can you remember who you gave the letter to?"

Mrs. Perrott blinked at him.

"Well, to be sure, if that isn't kind! And I'm sure Mrs. Williams and me is always the best of friends, and many's the cup of tea I've had with her, and she with me."

"Did you give the letter to Mrs. Williams?"

"'Twould ha' been to Williams I'd ha' given it if I'd ha' got to the house, because, seeing I'd come up with a letter, I should ha' gone to the front door with it."

"Well, didn't you?"

"I should ha' done if I'd got so far as the house. But being such a hot afternoon, I was glad enough to be saved the quarter of a mile."

"You didn't go up to the house?"

"Not when there wasn't no need to, though any other time I'd ha' been pleased enough to see Mrs. Williams."

David very nearly banged on the counter.

"Mrs. Perrott, for the Lord's sake, what did you do with that letter?"

Mrs. Perrott stared at him in rebuke. She didn't hold with young gentlemen losing their tempers. She said, in a dignified, offended tone:

"Some might say that I done wrong; but my own feeling was as how I ought to get back to poor old Masterson just as quick as ever I could, and I took Miss Betty for a godsend, and no mistake."

"Miss Betty!"

"Mrs. Lester, I *should* say." Mrs. Perrott was still on her dignity.

"Did you give the letter to my sister?"

"I give it to Mrs. Lester," said Mrs. Perrott, relaxing a little. "And I'm sure I took her for a godsend, as I said. I was that hot with hurrying, and when I see Miss Betty coming down the drive and out of the gate, I just took and give her the letter and got home again as quick as I could."

There was a pause. Then David said:

"You're quite sure you gave the letter to Mrs. Lester?"

"I'm certain sure—Gospel certain sure, Mr. David."

David straightened himself up very slowly.

"Thank you, Mrs. Perrott," he said in rather an odd voice. "I'm sorry if I was impatient just now, but the letter was such a very important one. Of course"—he half turned to go, and spoke without looking at her—"of course the letter you gave Mrs. Lester wasn't the one I was inquiring about."

"Seems it couldn't ha' been," said Mrs. Perrott in her easy voice.

Chapter Thirty-Two

DAVID DROVE SLOWLY up to Ford. Twice in as many days someone had dipped into the tangle of his affairs, pulled out a thread, and laid it in his hand. Folly's thread and Mrs. Perrott's thread both led to Betty. That the two threads were entirely disconnected made the coincidence just a trifle startling.

David was not in a position to disregard anything that might either substantiate or discredit the statements made to him by Heather Down. Heather Down said that there had been two letters, of which the second was posted in Cape Town on December 7th, 1922; and she supported this statement with the documentary evidence of a post office receipt. Mrs. Perrott declared positively that a South African letter with the Cape Town postmark had arrived at Fordwick post office during the last week of September, '22, and that this letter had been delivered to Betty.

David left his car at the front door and went into the house in a puzzled, troubled mood. He found Betty at the writing-table in her sitting-room. There was a paper before her with rows of figures on it.

This much David saw, and then she pushed a sheet of blotting-paper over it and swung round in her chair with a startled exclamation:

"David! I hadn't an idea you were coming down!"

"Nor had I," said David.

He was wondering if those long columns of figures had anything to do with Francis Lester's affairs. If they represented his debts, there seemed to be plenty of them. He frowned, and noted that Betty was flushed and undeniably cross.

"I do wish you'd let me know when you're coming! Your room's not ready or anything. Of course men never think of such a thing—but in this weather mattresses require to be *aired*."

"Who do you suppose airs the mattress I sleep on in town? Anyhow, I'm not staying—I've far too much on hand."

"You're always away now," said Betty fretfully. "I'm sure I wish I could afford to be away as much as you are. One might as well be buried alive as be down here by oneself in the winter. And really, David, I think you might let me know when you're coming. I don't suppose there's anything for lunch, and it puts the servants out so."

"I shan't be here for lunch." David's tone was dry. It was occurring to him that, after all, he was the master of the house, and not a rather tiresome guest, as anyone might have supposed from Betty's tone.

"What on earth have you come down for?" said Betty. "You haven't—there's nothing wrong, is there? Not—not Francis?"

"Good Lord, no!" What on earth should be wrong with the fellow? What an ass Betty was about him!

"It's so startling your turning up like this. I do think you might let me know!"

"I've come down on business. I want to know if you can help me about it."

It was extraordinarily difficult to begin, extraordinarily difficult to put the matter in a way which would not give Betty cause for offence—it was so easy to offend Betty, and so hard to placate her. David made an effort and plunged:

"I've just been told of two very important letters which never reached me."

Betty flushed.

"I'm sure I always send on everything as soon as it comes. I'm most particular about it. You'd better go and talk to Mrs. Perrott. She's a lazy, careless old thing, and no more fit to run a post office—"

"The letters I mean ought to have reached me more than four years ago."

Betty jerked back her chair and got up.

"Good gracious! What old history! I shouldn't have thought any letter was worth worrying about after four years."

She went over to the sofa that stood in the window and began to shake up the cushions with her back to David.

Suddenly and irrelevantly he remembered that it was the click of this window which Folly had heard when she stood barefoot in the dark hall with the house asleep behind her; and, in this room without a light, whispering about him and his affairs, Betty—Betty and Francis Lester.

He was silent for long enough to make Betty turn and look at him. Her odd, uneasy expression made him say quickly:

"The letters were so important that I'm bound to try and trace them. I've come down to-day because Mrs. Perrott wrote and said she remembered something about one of them. She says she remembers a letter with the Cape Town postmark coming for me one day in the last week of September, '22."

Betty laughed scornfully.

"My dear David, how on earth could she possibly remember one letter out of hundreds—and all those years ago? It's perfectly ridiculous!"

"There weren't hundreds of letters from South Africa. And she remembers this one because old Masterson was taken ill after he brought her the post-bag, and she started to take the letter up to the house herself."

"And dropped it in a ditch on the way, I suppose!" said Betty with another laugh.

She had half turned back towards the window, and stood against the end of the settee idly turning and poking one of the fat pink cushions. The room was all rather too pink for David's taste—too garlanded, too floral. The bright rose-colour was very unbecoming to Betty's sandy hair and Betty's lines.

"I suppose she dropped the letter. One doesn't like to say so."

Betty's repetition of the phrase roused David to speech. He said slowly and heavily:

"Mrs. Perrott says she gave the letter to you."

"To me!" said Betty. Her voice rose sharply. "My dear David!"

"She says she met you just inside the gates and gave you the letter."

Betty picked up the pink cushion and dropped it again.

"And do you mean to say you believe a word of all that rubbish? As if anyone could remember *one* letter nearly five years afterwards! The whole thing's too ridiculous for words! What do you think I did with it if she gave it to me?"

"I don't know. You might have put it down somewhere and forgotten it. You might—half a dozen things might have happened. Betty—the letter was so important that I'm bound to ask you if you can't remember something about it."

Betty's manner changed. Without looking at him, she asked:

"Who was it from?"

David hesitated, then plunged again.

"It was from my wife."

"Oh!" said Betty with a sort of gasp. "Your—David! What do you mean?"

"I didn't tell anyone because I thought she was dead—I thought she was drowned. Now I am told she is alive. I am told she wrote me those two letters in the autumn of '22. I never got either of them."

He looked at Betty as he spoke. He could see only the back of her neck and part of an averted cheek. Both neck and cheek were crimson.

"Who—told—you?"

"Told me what?"

"Who told you she was alive?"

"There was an advertisement."

"Who told you about the letters? There wasn't anything about them—"

"In the advertisement? No, there wasn't, was there? Look here, Betty, what do you know about all this? What do you know about the advertisement?"

"I—I read it."

She had turned round now and was staring at David.

David came towards her with a look on his face which she had never seen there before.

"Tell me what you know about it. Tell me at once. Do you hear? *Tell me!*"

He had her by the shoulders. The heavy grip, the look on his face, made a stranger of him. She flinched and burst out crying.

"Don't look at me like that! You're hurting me—oh, you're hurting me!"

"I'll kill you if you don't tell me," said David in a low, steady voice.

"I will—I will. David, let go! Oh, you're hurting me!"

He let go and stood back as she dropped into the corner of the sofa sobbing. He was full of the shuddering rage of a man betrayed on his own hearth. He stood back from Betty because he could not trust his hands. He was in horror of himself and of her. Betty and Francis plotting against him in this damned pink room! There was a frieze of roses with the heavy heads of bloom dropping down the white paper; there were wreaths of pink and crimson roses on the Aubusson carpet; roses crawled on the chintz of every chair, and the fat pink cushions bulged on top of them. Francis and Betty had stood here whispering in the dark!

Chapter Thirty-Three

THE SILENCE LASTED so long that Betty stopped crying. Her sense of injury and self-pity passed into cold, constraining fear. David hadn't moved at all; he stood with his hands clenched looking past her. It was David, whom she had never been afraid of in her life; and she was so much afraid that she could not speak. The ticking of the old gilt clock on the mantelpiece seemed to grow louder and louder.

Betty sat huddled up in the sofa corner just as she had fallen when David thrust her away. The pink cushion that should have been behind her shoulders had slipped sideways and was crunched up under her right elbow. She wanted to move it to shift her position, but the cold fear held her motionless.

The clock went on ticking.

David spoke at last. He spoke, but he didn't move.

"Tell me what you did with that letter."

Betty was able to move again. When David spoke, she stopped being so much afraid of him. She began to grope for her pocket-handkerchief.

"I—I didn't—"

"Tell me what you know about the letter. You had better not tell me any lies."

"Oh!" said Betty. "How can you!"

"Go on—tell me what you know. You'd better. You'd better tell me the truth."

Betty sniffed into her pocket-handkerchief.

"How can I tell you anything when you speak to me like that? I'm sure it was an accident that might—that might have happened to anyone."

He turned a cold, dark look upon her.

"You're not making yourself very clear. What was an accident?"

"The—the letter was. It might have happened to anyone." She sniffed again and with more heart.

"You had an accident with the letter. Is that what you're asking me to believe?"

She had a momentary spasm of fear at his tone.

"I—I—really, David, I don't see why you should blame me. It was Mrs. Perrott's fault for giving it to me."

"*Will* you tell me what happened? You admit that Mrs. Perrott gave you the letter."

"She ought to have taken it up to the house," said Betty. "She'd no business to give it to me like that."

"What did you do with it?" said David.

Betty put the pink cushion behind her shoulders.

"I slipped it into the pocket of my jumper, and when I got back to the house I should have given it to you, only the telephone bell rang, and—and it was Francis."

"He wasn't in England."

An odd look crossed Betty's face.

"He was often over here when nobody knew. He used to let me know, so that I could meet him somewhere. He—he didn't use his own name of course. I'm sure the way he was *persecuted* was shameful— everyone turning against him except me. If you'd stood up for him, things might have been very different."

"We won't discuss Francis. You're to tell me about the letter."

"I am telling you—and then you'll see how unjust you've been. Francis wanted me to come to him at once. He was quite stranded—ill and without money to pay for anything. I can't bear to think about it—he had a most dreadful time."

"You went to him?"

"Of course I did. I had to tell you something, so I told you old Nurse was ill and I was going to look after her. And I forgot all about your wretched letter—anyone hearing suddenly that their husband was ill would have forgotten a thing like that."

David drew a long breath. He had himself under control again. He said sharply:

"You forgot about the letter. When did you remember it?"

"Not till I got back again—not—oh, not for a month at least. And I don't suppose I should have remembered it then, only I was putting away my summer things and I felt something crackle when I was folding up the jumper I had on that day, and I put my hand in the pocket, and there was the miserable letter."

"Yes," said David. "And why didn't you give it to me then?"

Betty sat up straight.

"*Really*, David, anyone would think I was a *thief*!" She gave a little angry laugh. "Perhaps when you've got your temper back you'll see that I did what I thought was the *kindest* thing to *you*."

David's eyes narrowed.

"You haven't told me what you did. I don't think I'll start thanking you till I know."

Betty took an aggrieved tone.

"I did what I thought was the *best* thing to do. I was naturally *very* much upset when I found the letter, and I thought I'd better just look at it and see if it was important."

"You mean you read it."

"I thought I ought to look at it. And I got a most *dreadful* shock when I found it was from someone we'd never heard of, who said she was your wife."

David clenched his hands again. He could not trust himself to speak. *It was true.* Erica had survived—Erica had written. It was true.

Every trace of colour left his face; his lips were stiff as he said:

"You kept the letter back."

Betty sniffed loudly.

"It was the most dreadful shock I've ever had, except—things about Francis. I was most *terribly* upset."

"You kept the letter back."

"David, you're most unreasonable. You don't seem to think what a shock it was to find you'd been secretly married for goodness knows how long. I was so upset I didn't know what to do."

"You kept the letter back." His voice was quite low and expressionless.

"It was out of kindness to you," said Betty, "and you ought to be grateful to me instead of looking like that. At first I was too upset to think. And then I read the letters again, and I realized that you'd been thinking this girl was dead. And the letter from the people she was with said how ill she was, and I thought it would be dreadful for you to hear she was alive and then perhaps find out that she'd died after the letter was sent off."

Everything Heather Down had said was true. There had been a letter from Erica, and a covering letter from the people she was with, just as Heather Down had said.

"What did you do with the letter?"

"I put it away," said Betty. "I—I asked Francis what I had better do, and he said I was quite right not to raise your hopes. He said he'd got a friend in Cape Town and he'd write and ask him to find out how things were before we told you anything. It was all for your own good and to save you anxiety. But, as Francis said, if she'd been alive and getting better, there'd have been more letters—and there hadn't been. So he said not to do anything until he heard from his friend."

"There was another letter," said David.

"It came at Christmas." Betty's tone was quite eager. "Francis said his friend must be away, because we hadn't heard from him. And then, just after Christmas, there was a registered letter for you from Cape Town."

"Go on," said David.

"You were away for a couple of days. I couldn't send it on to you without explaining about the first one. You *can* see that, I suppose?"

She flushed at the contempt in his voice as he said:

"It was awkward—yes."

"David, I think you're most unreasonable. You don't try to understand my position."

"I wasn't thinking about your position. What did you do with the second letter?"

"Francis said we'd waited so long that it was no good being in a hurry. He said he'd send a cable to the address she wrote from, asking for news. He said—"

David's mind was wholly fixed upon the letters.

"What did you do with the letter—with both the letters?"

"I'm telling you what I did."

"Did you destroy them?"

"No, of course I didn't."

"You've got them still?"

"Yes, of course I have."

"Give them to me."

"But—"

"I don't want anything but the letters. Give them to me at once!"

Betty got up. She said something under her breath and went across to the writing-table.

"Are they there?" He spoke roughly.

"*Really*, David!"

"Are the letters there?" His voice took a tone that frightened her again.

Her hand shook, and the bunch of keys she was holding jingled. With a little clatter she unlocked one of the small drawers of the bureau and pulled it out. It was a small deep drawer full of letters tied up in packets. She began to take the packets out. At the bottom of the drawer there were two letters in long-shaped envelopes. Betty took them up and turned with them in her hand. She began to speak, to say something. But David did not hear what she said. He took the letters from her hand and went out of the room, shutting the door behind him.

Chapter Thirty-Four

DAVID WENT INTO HIS STUDY with the letters. He sat down in his writing-chair and laid the envelopes side by side on the table before him. Both the letters were addressed in the same clear commercial hand. He remembered Erica's childish scrawl and frowned.

After a moment he took up the first letter. Betty had not torn the envelope; she had steamed open the flap. The little bitter thought went through his mind that if it had suited Francis Lester, the flap would have been stuck down again, and he, David, would never have known that the letter had been read.

He took the two enclosures out of the envelope, and was stabbed at once with a painful sense of pity. This was Erica's own hand, weaker and more childish than he remembered it. She had written in pencil, and the marking was faint—so faint as to be almost illegible. He read slowly and with difficulty the words which he had slowly written to Heather Down's dictation:

"DEAR DAVID,

"I have been very ill. I can't write much. I didn't know who I was till just now. They have been very kind. Please come quickly if you can.

"ERICA."

When he had read her name he took up the enclosure, written in ink in the same hand that had addressed the envelope. He read:

"DEAR SIR,

"Your wife has been ill in my house for some months. She has only recently been able to tell us who she is and to give us your address. Without wishing to alarm you, I should say it would be as well if you could come to her without delay.

"Yours faithfully,

"L. BAKER."

The letter was dated September 4th, 1922, from an address in Cape Town.

David took up the second letter. It had been registered, and the postmark bore the date of December 7th. The flap of the envelope was open, but not torn. This letter too had been read.

This time there was no enclosure, only the same weak pencil scrawl under the heading "Tuesday."

"DEAR DAVID,

"Did you get my letter? I wrote three months ago to tell you I was alive. I thought perhaps you would think I had been drowned—a lot of people were. Will you write and tell me what to do? I am a little better, but not very much. Will you write to me?

"ERICA.

Under the name a postscript very badly written:

"Please tell Aunt Nellie that I'm not drowned."

When a little time had passed, David took out his notebook and read the letters as Heather Down had given them to him. They were almost word for word what Erica had written. The most important difference was in the second letter. Erica had said, "I am a little better, but not very much." In Heather Down's version this had become: "I am better, but I am not well yet." It was just such a difference as would be natural enough if Erica, recovered, were remembering what she had written in the dispirited mood of illness.

David put the letters away in his pocket. There were things that he must ask Betty; but he had to master himself before he could meet her. He had trusted her utterly, and she had done this horrible thing to him. That she or anyone else should have read these simple, piteous appeals unmoved was unbelievable. Yet it had happened. Betty, reading them, had not been moved at all; she had thought of herself, of what Francis would say. It was quite unbelievable; but it had happened.

Time went by. Instead of decreasing, David's sense of shock and bitterness increased. It seemed impossible that he should meet Betty. And whilst this sense of impossibility was at its height the door opened and Betty came in.

She held the door in her hand and said fretfully:

"David, *are* you staying to lunch? I must tell the servants something."

"Come in and shut the door," said David. "I want to speak to you."

She did come in then, and stood by the big armchair. Her manner was one of offence.

"I want to speak to you about those letters. You'd better sit down."

She jerked an angry shoulder, but did as she was told.

"You didn't seem to want to hear what I had to say just now."

"I wanted to read the letters first. You can go on now. Why didn't you give me that second letter?"

"I told you," said Betty in her most annoyed voice. "Francis said it was no good to raise your hopes, and he'd send a cable to find out what had happened."

"Yes?"

A little of the assurance went out of Betty's manner.

"It was all for your own good. I'm sure I went through a dreadful time."

"What was the answer to the cable?"

"I didn't hear anything for ten days. Francis was abroad again. I kept writing to him. At last I said I should give you the letters, and he wired 'Don't.' And then he wrote and said Erica was dead."

David repeated the last word.

"Yes"—she spoke quickly and nervously—"the cable said so, and what was the good of my giving you the letters after that? It would only have raked things up and upset you."

David set his face like a flint; his voice rang harshly:

"The cable said that Erica was dead?"

"Yes."

"And in the following October you and Francis put an advertisement in *The Times* under my initials to say that my wife was alive."

Betty began to sniff.

"You were flirting with Angela Carr. Francis said you'd marry her. David—don't look at me like that! You don't give me time to explain. Francis said he'd made more inquiries, and that there was a mistake about the cable. He said Erica was alive, and—and—I suppose you think I ought to have let you commit bigamy."

An awful patience descended upon David. To Betty, right and wrong simply meant things convenient or inconvenient to Francis— what Francis approved was right; what Francis disliked was wrong; what Francis asserted was fact. On this basis the whole unbelievable affair was simple enough. He looked calmly at Betty's flushed, angry face. His calmness stung her more than his anger had done.

"It's all very well for you, but it was most unfair of Father to leave you Ford and cut me off with a wretched six hundred a year. If I'd had to live on it, we should simply have starved—and, as Francis said, once you got married, you wouldn't want me here, and you wouldn't go on paying Dicky's school bills either."

It was like being in a dream—the familiar room, and Betty saying this sort of thing to him. He seemed to have got past any feeling about it. There was just that strange patience which endured through some horrible dream. He put his head in his hands and stared at the ink-marks on his blotting-pad.

It was clear now where most of Betty's six hundred a year had gone. He had sometimes wondered how she managed to be so hard up and to produce a succession of unpaid bills for him to settle. She lived at Ford without contributing a penny to the expenses; Dick's school bills came to David as a matter of course. He answered Betty's complaint on that score first:

"Why do you say things like that? You don't really believe them. I told you I would pay Dick's bills."

"You wouldn't have gone on if you had married," said Betty fretfully. "Francis said—"

David traced an ink-stain with his finger.

"I'd rather you didn't quote Francis. If I said I'd do a thing, I should do it." He looked up at her. "Let's get back to the advertisement. It said Erica was alive. *Is she alive?*"

Betty hesitated, sniffed, dabbed her nose.

"Francis said—"

In a perfectly expressionless voice David cursed Francis.

Tears of anger sprang into Betty's horrified eyes.

"David! How dare you!"

"*Is Erica alive?*" said David.

Betty sniffed again.

"I—I don't know."

David went on looking at her.

"You kept back the letter because she was dead; and you put in the advertisement because she was alive. You can't have it both ways."

"Francis said she was dead; and then he said it was a mistake."

"Why did he think it was a mistake?"

"He didn't say."

"And you didn't ask him?"

A pause.

"Did you ask him?"

"Yes, of course I did."

"What did he say?"

"He said to the best of his belief she was alive."

"And you left it at that?"

Betty sniffed.

"Did you believe what Francis said? Did you think Erica was alive?"

"I didn't *know*. *I* suppose you think I ought to have let you commit bigamy. You don't seem to realize that it was all for your own good. And, as Francis said, it was better to be on the safe side, because it would have been most frightfully awkward if you'd married again and she'd turned up afterwards."

David looked down at his blotting-paper. Erica's letter had lain there—the little weak scrawl in which she had asked him to come to her. His calm broke suddenly.

"Can't you realize what you've done? She must have thought I'd deserted her. If she's alive, that's what she thinks now. If she isn't alive, she died thinking it. Betty, what have I done to you that you should do this horrible thing to me?"

"I did it for the best," said Betty in a fluttered voice. "You don't understand—you don't think how difficult it was for me. You don't— What was the use?"

It was like trying to talk to a person who is hopelessly deaf; she didn't hear him. He spoke without looking at her:

"You'd better go."

Betty got as far as the door.

"Francis always said what an awful temper you had. I think you ought to beg my pardon."

David lifted his head.

He said: "Do you want me to kill you? I shall if you don't go."

Chapter Thirty-Five

DAVID WENT BACK to town without breaking bread in his own house. He drove between wet hedges under a wet sky. There was rain on the wind-screen and rain on the long shining road that took the grey reflection of the sky. He felt as if his mind was full of a grey mist in which thoughts moved dimly and were lost. His ceaseless effort was to clear the mist away so that he might think. Little by little the formless thoughts began to take form and to become apparent.

The letters—it all came back to the letters. Everything that Heather Down said about the letters was true. She said that Erica had survived the wreck. That was true. She said that Erica had written. She gave, almost word for word, the contents of Erica's letters. If these things were true, they were so many reasons for believing what she said about other things. He owed her amends for disbelief. If she were Erica, how much more did he owe her? An appalling weight of obligation rested upon him. If she were Erica, deserted, penniless, ill, what could he do to wipe out these memories and fulfil the trust he had undertaken?

When he reached London he wrote to Heather Down:

"I must see you at once. I will come in an hour unless you ring me up."

He signed his name and sent the letter, as before, by District Messenger.

When he had had some food, he walked to Martagon Crescent. He did not know what he was going to say to Heather Down, but he thought that he would know when he saw her.

It was Miss Smith who opened the door to him. She did not open it very wide, and she stood there in the entrance looking fixedly at him with a strange, frightened look.

"You're to come in," she said, but she did not stand aside. She leaned against the door and went on looking at him. "She's in there." She looked back across her shoulder. "You're to go in."

David moved to pass her. He had to touch her arm, and he felt it tremble. He said quickly under his breath, "Miss Smith," and at once she shut the door with a slam.

"It slipped—it slipped out of my hand. She's waiting. You're to go in."

As she spoke, she went down the passage in front of David and pushed open the sitting-room door. He went in, and heard the door jerk to behind him.

Heather Down was sitting by the rose-wood table. Or was it Heather Down? David stood still with every pulse drumming. She was bare-headed, and she was dressed in black. She looked slighter, she looked younger. She sat in a drooping attitude with her head bent; her hands were in her lap. The ring with the three blue flowers spanned the third finger of the hand that lay uppermost, and below it was the plain gold of a wedding ring that had not been there before. The half-averted face was pale, the lashes wet; her brown uncovered hair lay smoothly about the brow and down-bent head. Figure, attitude, dress, all recalled Erica only too vividly. Where before he had looked at Heather Down and searched for a hint of Erica, he now looked at this drooping black-robed girl and, thinking first of Erica, scanned the pale features for something to remind him of Heather Down.

He stood there struggling for composure, and all the time she neither spoke nor made any sign. In the end David found voice. He said:

"I have traced the letters."

As he said it, the bright, sudden colour in her face made her Heather Down again.

"The letters?" she said.

"I have traced them."

She looked up at him, and the resentment in her eyes struck him like a blow.

"You had them all the time."

He shook his head.

"You had them. Letters don't go astray and then turn up again like that. Do you think I'm a born fool?"

"I don't know what you are. If I knew—" He broke off. "If you are Erica—"

"If I'm Erica," said Heather Down. "Well, what then?"

David came a step nearer.

"Are you Erica?"

She looked down at the ring on her finger, the quick sidelong look which had brought Erica back to him before. This time she touched the ring, slipped it slowly from her finger, and laid it on the table between them.

"That's the ring you bought me, isn't it? You recognize it, don't you?" She touched the other ring, the wedding ring, sliding it up to the joint and back again. "One wedding ring looks like another—doesn't it? Shall I take this one off and let you look at it? You had initials put inside the ring you gave your wife. You've forgotten such a lot that I shouldn't wonder if you've forgotten that. Have you?"

"No, I haven't," said David.

She pulled the ring off with a jerk and threw it down beside the other.

"Look at it then! Look at it and see whether it's your ring or not."

David picked it up and turned it to the light. It was the first time there had been daylight in the shabby room. The bright pink curtains were draw back; the gloomy dirty sky looked through a dirty window-pane. The corners of the room faded into dusk; the texts were illegible. What visibility there was showed him to Heather Down and Heather Down to him.

He moved nearer the window and turned the ring with rigid, steady fingers. Inside the thin circle the initials E. F. stood out, and the date of his marriage.

David's eyes narrowed. The cutting was as sharp and clear as on the day he had first looked at it in the jeweller's shop in Sydney. He said quickly:

"The letters aren't worn. How's that?"

Heather Down's voice rang hard:

"What has there been to wear them? Do you think I've worn the ring?"

"Why haven't you?"

"D'you think I'd wear the ring when the man had gone off and left me without a word? D'you think a girl wants to have anything more to do with a man like that?"

David dropped the ring back on to the table.

"If you didn't want to have anything more to do with me, why are we here?"

"Perhaps I want to punish you," said Heather Down. "You went away and left me. You knew I was ill, and you left me. You knew I hadn't any money, and you left me. I asked you to write and I asked you to come, and you left me without a word."

"I never had the letters."

She threw out the hand from which she had slipped the rings.

"Tell those lies to someone else. The letter said that I was ill. Perhaps that put the idea into your head. You were wishing you hadn't got married—your father had died and you had come in for the property—you hoped I'd die too—you wanted to see if I would. When no more letters came, you thought I was out of your way. When you'd waited a bit longer, you were quite sure that I was dead. Well, I waited too—I wanted to punish you."

A cold, dull pain gripped David. Under the pain a cold, slow anger. He stood separated from her, not only by the years, but by every instinct and feeling of his heart. Yet if she were Erica, he must make amends. He owed a debt, and he must pay it if the price beggared him of all that made life worth living. He constrained himself and said:

"I can't make you believe me. Can you make me believe you? Can you convince me that you are Erica?"

"Don't you know it?"

"I'm not sure." David said the words in a low voice. He did not look at her.

"You're not sure because you don't want to be sure."

"That's not true. I do want to be sure."

She picked up the rings and held them between finger and thumb, turning them this way and that.

"Perhaps I don't want you to be sure," she said. "That would be a good punishment—wouldn't it? Never to be sure—never to know whether you're free or not. I haven't made any claim, have I?"

"No."

"Well, I don't mean to. I don't mean to do anything more. I've done what I came for. I didn't come to make a claim; I came to punish you. You won't see me again; and you'll never, never be sure. You'll never know whether you're free or not—you'll never be able to go to another woman and make her the promises that you made to me. That's your punishment."

She put the wedding ring back on to the third finger of her left hand and slipped the forget-me-not ring after it. All this time she had looked David in the face, and he had met her look. Now, as the blue ring touched the other, she looked down quickly. The look, the shade of triumph that crossed her features; the half-turned head; the black dress that gave her youth and pallor—something in David said "Erica"; something broke—some resistance, some unbelief. He put his hand over his eyes and stood for a moment shaken to the depths.

It was the sound of the closing door that made him lift his head again. The little shabby room was empty. He was alone in it.

He went to the door and opened it. The dark passage was empty too. At the far end of it there was a door. David went to this door and knocked upon it. There was no answer. He opened the door and stood looking into the kitchen. It was nearly dark, but a fire burned in the range. Miss Smith sat over the fire in a wooden chair with her elbows on her knees and her head in her hands; the firelight shone on her grey hair.

"Miss Smith," said David.

She lifted her head with a sort of groaning sound.

"Miss Smith, where is she? I must see her."

"She won't see you—she's gone out."

"How—"

"Oh," said Miss Smith with another groan. "She's gone."

"She can't have gone."

Miss Smith nodded.

"You don't believe me. She took her hat and her coat and she went out by the back door. She's gone."

David could bear no more. He said, "I'll write," and went down the dark passage and out of the house. Outside there was still daylight.

Chapter Thirty-Six

DAVID FOUND HIMSELF in Chieveley Street. He had been walking for an hour, and it was dark. A heavy shower swept up from the northeast. The cold, wet street was empty. He remembered the night he had walked along it with Folly's little shaking hand upon his arm; remembered how he had lighted a fire in Eleanor's room. It was the thought of the fire that made him realize how cold he was. A craving for warmth, and light, and companionship turned him in at the entrance to the block of flats.

He did not ring for the lift, but walked up the stone stair; and again memory showed him Folly standing just above him, Folly catching at his hand and guiding his fingers so that they might feel how her hair had grown. All these memories seemed to belong to another David. The things that they showed him were over long ago.

He found Eleanor alone. She exclaimed at the coldness of his hand, made him sit by the fire, and insisted on sending for fresh hot tea.

David drank the tea and did not talk. If he talked, he would have to think; and he did not want to think. He let Eleanor talk to him, and could not have told what she said. He liked the sound of her voice—gentle, musical, unhurried. He did not know that his silence and his pallor were alarming her more than a little.

A wave of pity and tenderness swept over her as she watched him. What had happened to make him look like this? She wanted to know, but she could not ask him; she could only talk on about meaningless trifles—a book she had read, a play she had seen.

David sat back in the big chair by the fire. The peace, and the firelight, and Eleanor's voice all combined to lull him into a drowsy state between sleeping and waking. It was not sleep, for dreams come in sleep; and if he slept, who knew what dreams might come? It was not waking either, for one is awake, one must think; and above all things in the world he desired the cessation of thought. Where thought leaves off and dreams have not begun there is a resting-place. He saw the room as one sees a scene on the stage; he saw Eleanor, graceful and remote; there was stillness, warmth, and rest.

The peace and the stillness were interrupted by the banging of the outer door. There was a sound of footsteps, a sound of laughter, and the drawing-room door opened to let Folly in. She was all in bright red, with her arms full of the early scarlet tulips. Timmy nestled between her shoulder and the little black curls that almost hid her ear. She came in with a rush.

"Ooh!" she said. "Ooh, how nice and warm!"

The tulips dropped in a heap on Eleanor's lap. She turned and saw David's face.

David had seen her come into the room with a curious sense that, after all, this was a dream—a bright dream that passed before his eyes and would presently be gone; it wasn't real, and he had no control over it.

Folly stood by Eleanor with one hand holding Timmy close against her cheek. The brim of her hat was wet; the glowing cheek was wet. Her eyes were as bright as wildfire.

She said, "David!" in a quick startled way, and then: "What's the matter? David—what's the matter?"

Eleanor put up her hand and laid it on Folly's arm with a warning pressure. Folly moved away from it, moved nearer David, and asked again and insistently what Eleanor had not been able to ask at all:

"What's the matter—*David?*"

David lifted his eyes slowly to hers.

"David—what is it? Tell me."

David said: "I think she is Erica"; and Folly cried out sharply: "She can't be! She can't be!"

"I didn't think so; but I do now."

The hand with which Folly was holding the kitten closed involuntarily. Timmy swore, scratched, and fled, scrambling down until he could jump on to the arm of Eleanor's chair.

"Why?"

David began to wake up. Thought and realization flowed remorselessly in upon him and swept him from his resting-place.

"Why?" said Folly with a little bitter cry that hurt him even through his own pain.

"I think she is Erica. She knows things—" He broke off. "She told me that Erica had written to me, and she told me what was in the letters. They never reached me till to-day. I went to Ford and—found them." His voice failed before the last two words and he recovered it with an effort.

"Betty kept them back," said Folly quickly.

David made no answer.

"The letters are just what she said. And she has Erica's rings—the wedding ring with her initials, and the other ring I gave her. I think she is Erica."

He got up as he spoke, slowly and as if he were lifting something heavy. He said: "I must go." And he said it to Folly, not to Eleanor.

Folly came a step nearer.

"What will you do?"

"I must do what I can. She thought I had deserted her."

"David—what are you going to do?"

"That's for her to say."

"No!" said Folly. "No!"

He stared at her.

"What can I do? If she's Erica, she's my wife—she must come to Ford."

The colour rushed, brilliant, to Folly's cheeks.

"You can't!"

"I can."

"You can't! David—you can get a divorce."

David's voice rang hard.

"Desert her first and throw mud at her afterwards! Is that what you suggest?"

"No—*no*—I didn't mean that. I meant—David, she could divorce you. People do—"

"I'm to cheat my way out of a promise I made of my own free will? I don't see much difference between that and any other form of cheating."

Folly's colour did not fade, but it became fixed, like a bright stain on the white skin. It gave her a strange anguished look.

"People do it."

"People cheat."

She caught her breath.

"No—no—you *could* do it—you could!"

"I won't."

The scarlet stain died slowly from her cheeks.

"Floss did it. You could."

David was silent, and his silence struck at her.

"My mother did it. You've forgotten that. I hate you. Oh, how I hate you!"

Their looks clashed for a moment, and a rage that answered hers sprang up in him so suddenly that it swept him off his balance. He took a step towards her with his hands clenched, and Eleanor cried out and got up, scattering all the scarlet tulips.

He said, "I beg your pardon," and went blunderingly out of the room, walking like a man who does not see where he is going. He had to grope for the handle, and his shoulder struck the doorpost as he flung out. The outer door shut heavily.

Eleanor stood among the scattered tulips. The strange intimacy of the scene left her dazed and trembling. If she had been a hundred miles away, if she had belonged to another century, they could not have regarded her less. From the moment that Folly had come into the room, she and David had been as much alone together as if Eleanor had never existed; to them, for those brief passionate moments, she was not there at all. The shock of this realization made her incapable of speech or action.

She watched Folly go out of the room and shut the door, and she watched Timmy playing at being a tiger in a fallen jungle of scarlet tulips. He played this game with little fierce growls, swift rushes, and wary retreats.

Eleanor sat down suddenly and covered her face with her hands.

David went down the stairs and out into the street. It was not raining any more, but the northeast wind had an edge on it like fine sharp ice. It was very dark; a dozen yards from the lamp that marked the entrance to the flats there was no light at all; the next lamp looked like a faint, far star. The pavement was wet and slippery, as if the rain that had fallen had begun to freeze.

David walked slowly. Thought was awake again and deafening him with echoes. "I hate you." That was Folly—words flung at him as an angry child might fling a stone. But the real hatred had been in Erica's eyes and in Erica's voice when she said: "You'll never be able to go to any other woman and make her the promises you made to me. You'll never be *sure*." Erica looking like that, speaking like that—Was she Erica—could she be Erica? The answer came from the echo of her own words: "You'll never be sure—you'll never be sure."

Behind him on the pavement he heard quick, running footsteps. Then in the darkness someone brushed by him and, turning, stopped right in his path with a little choked cry:

"David!"

David set his teeth.

"Folly, go home!"

"Ooh! I was afraid it was someone else." She came against his shoulder with a snuggling movement.

"Go home!" said David harshly.

"I can't. You're angry with me."

Her hand went up and caught his arm.

He said, "Angry?" in a voice she did not know.

"I can't bear it—it tears me. I *can't* bear it. It makes me want to kill you, and it makes me want to say I'm *sorry*, and—it hurts—it hurts *too much*." She was trembling and taking quick, crying breaths.

"Folly, go home!"

"I can't."

"You must."

She pressed against him in the dark.

"David—David—why does it hurt like this? It *hurts. David!*"

His arms came round her, suddenly and hard. He did not speak; a frightful anguish held him dumb. Once they had kissed carelessly on the brink of this deep place of pain; now they did not kiss at all. They held one another in the darkness, and the long minutes passed them by.

It was Folly who pulled herself away with a sob.

"You're not angry—now?"

"No—I'm not angry. Folly, go home!"

"You won't be angry again?"

He put out his hand to push her away, and felt it caught, held, and pressed for a moment to her cheek.

"I *can't* bear it when you're angry," she said. And then, as suddenly as she had come, she was gone again.

Chapter Thirty-Seven

DAVID WROTE NEXT DAY a letter which he addressed to Miss Down at 16, Martagon Crescent. It had no formal beginning.

"If you are Erica, I beg you to believe me when I say that my one desire is to do all I can to make up to you for the last five years. If you are Erica, you are my wife, and Ford is your home. I beg you to believe that I made every effort to trace you, and that all the evidence available seemed to prove your death. Your letters were suppressed. You have a right to an explanation, which shall be given you. But I would prefer not to write about it. Your resentment makes everything very difficult. If you could put it on one side and meet me in a different spirit, it would make it easier for us both. All that is in my power to do I will do. I only ask that you will cease to believe me capable of having deserted you. We had not known each other very long, but I think that what you knew of me could not lead you to suppose that I would do such a thing."

The letter ended abruptly with no more than initials. David sent it off and sat for an hour looking down the road which he must travel.

Presently the telephone bell rang, and he heard Folly's voice. It was so unexpected that he could hardly steady his own.

"David—is that you?"

"Yes."

"There's something I was going to tell you, only I forgot." The last word shook a little.

"What is it?"

"I meant to tell you. It's about the letters—*her* letters."

"Yes?"

"Betty kept them back—didn't she?"

David did not answer.

"David, don't be tiresome! I do hate people being discreet! I know she kept them back, so what's the sense in not saying so?"

Silence.

A sort of exasperated rattle came along the line; he imagined that the receiver was being shaken. Then Folly's *"Ooh!"* and "David, are you there? You're *not* to go away. I want to tell you about Francis."

"What about him?"

"Francis Lester—Betty's husband. I told you I'd met him—Floss and he are great friends—but I didn't tell you the odd sort of things he said."

"What sort of things?"

"About you."

David gave an odd laugh.

"I don't think I really very much care what Lester says about me."

"Ooh! Don't be stupid. I didn't mean that sort of thing. David, you're being *stupid*."

"Well, what did you mean?"

I'll tell you. Francis had had about fifty cocktails, I should think—he does, you know, and then he talks. He talked about Ford—he talked about it rather as if it belonged to him. So I said, 'I didn't know it *belonged* to you'"—her voice lifted impudently—"and he got cross, and he said if it didn't now, it was all the same as if it did, because you couldn't get married unless he gave you leave, and as long as you didn't marry, Ford was bound to come to Betty."

David considered this. It was what Betty had admitted; but there was something more. If Francis had really said, "He can't get married without my leave," it might mean a very great deal more than Betty had admitted. If there were a legal impediment to his marriage, it could not in any sense of the word be considered to depend upon Francis either giving or withholding his consent. If there were no legal impediment—

David thought about this until Folly's voice broke in:

"Are you there? Don't go away—I haven't finished."

"I'm not going away. I was thinking. Folly, are you sure Francis used those words—I couldn't get married without his leave?"

"'M—that's what he said."

"Did he say anything more?"

"No—not about you. He talked about Betty and said she didn't send him nearly enough money. When I think about being married to Francis I'm quite sorry for Betty."

"So am I," said David.

Folly laughed a little gurgling laugh.

"Ooh! Your voice sounded like swearing."

"I feel like swearing."

"Poor Francis! Because, you know, when I think about being married to Betty, I feel sorry for him. David—"

"What?"

"David, I'm going away."

"When?"

"To-day. I'm going to Floss. I thought I'd tell you. Good-bye." The receiver went on with a click.

An hour later Eleanor rang up.

"David, I'm frightfully distressed. Folly's gone to her mother. I couldn't stop her. Did you hear anything about it?"

"She told me an hour ago on the telephone."

"What am I to do? I don't even know George March's address. He's on his honeymoon somewhere in Italy."

"You can't do anything."

"I want to see you. Will you come and see me? I want to talk to you."

"What's the use?" said David.

"David, don't talk like that. Will you come? I *must* see you."

"All right, I'll come round."

"Thank you," said Eleanor, and rang off.

David found her standing by the fire, and he had the impression that she had been walking up and down waiting for him. She looked pale and troubled.

"David, I'm so glad you've come." She gave him a hand that was cold in spite of the fire.

"I'm afraid I can't do anything to help you," said David.

He looked about the room. It was empty without Folly. Her scarlet tulips stood in a burning sheaf on the piano; Eleanor had picked up the scattered flowers. But there are things that you can't pick up again.

Eleanor took her courage in both hands.

"David, won't you tell me what has happened? I'm all in the dark."

David stood by the mantelpiece and leaned his arms upon it. He looked down into the fire and saw Folly's face there. The room was empty; and the room was full of her. He said in a slow, dull voice:

"I don't know what you know. There's a girl called Heather Down. I think she's Erica. She hates me. She's only come here because she hates me. She says she wants to punish me. I think she is my wife."

"David!" Eleanor's voice shook with her horror of what he was saying. She moved nearer to him and put a hand on his arm.

He lifted his head and gave her a strange, boyish look.

"Beastly—isn't it?"

"My poor David!" Then after a silence: "David—you and Folly—it's better for me to know. You care for each other?"

David went on looking at her, still with that young look of puzzl-ed distress.

"I suppose we do. I hadn't thought of it like that—at least not till yesterday."

Her hand pressed his arm. The old sense of close, strong kinship was between them—stronger, closer, kinder than it had ever been.

"I don't think she knows," said David. "I was angry with her. She asked why it hurt so much." His heart broke in him with tenderness for Folly. "She doesn't know—I don't believe she knows."

"David, *dear*."

Eleanor's eyes clouded with tears. She was so near him that her nearness and her sympathy shook his self-control, and for a moment he put his head down on her shoulder and she felt him tremble.

It was at this moment that the door opened. It was Aunt Editha who had opened it. She said: "My dear girl! My dear boy!" And as David stepped back and Eleanor turned, they beheld not only Aunt Editha, but Aunt Mary, and between these two faithful supporters the portentous figure of Grandmamma.

Grandmamma was a very imposing sight in a cloak of black plush heavily bordered with fur and a truly wonderful bonnet. The edge was incrusted with flowers worked in jet, and it bore three ostrich-feathers sable rampant on a field of beaded net. The weight of the feathers had tipped her wig over her left eye. She leaned upon a tall ebony stick with a silver handle, and she surveyed David and Eleanor with a glance of ancestral disfavour.

David had never admired Eleanor so much in his life. There was a lovely carnation colour in her cheeks; but she went to meet Grandmamma with unfaltering sweetness and dignity, kissed an averted cheek, embraced two fluttered aunts, and provided everyone with chairs. Aunt Editha then loosened Grandmamma's cloak, and Aunt Mary opened a beaded bag and supplied her with a lace-edged handkerchief.

All this time Mrs. Fordyce's hard, bright blue eyes were taking in the room, the flowers upon the piano, Eleanor's heightened colour, and David's pallor. She folded her hands over the lace-edged handkerchief and opened fire.

"I came," she said, addressing Eleanor, "I came to hear for myself the truth about Flora."

The shot was unexpected. Folly having only left the flat an hour or two before, it was certainly surprising to find that the Family was already upon the warpath. Eleanor's surprise showed so plainly that Grandmamma proceeded to majestic explanation.

"I wish to hear the truth from your own lips. I told Milly that I would inquire into the matter personally. I see that you are wondering how it is that I am already informed of the disastrous step that Flora has taken. It happened, *providentially*, that Milly had been to see Euphemia Castleton this morning. On her way to lunch with me she was obliged to pass the lower end of Chieveley Street, and at the moment she turned the corner she saw Flora in a cab with luggage— with *luggage*. Milly was very much surprised, and as the cab was obliged to wait at the corner owing to a block in the traffic beyond, she ran across the road and inquired where Flora was going. I am still hoping that she heard the answer incorrectly. Milly arrived at my house in a state of the most painful agitation and informed us that Flora had left you and gone to her mother." At this point Grandmamma lifted the lace handkerchief and rubbed the end of her nose with it. Then in a different and much brisker voice she continued: "We will talk of this presently. I have told you why I *came*. There is no need, I imagine, for me to tell you what I saw when your Aunt Editha opened the door of this room. I merely ask what conclusion I am to draw from it."

David had retired to his old place by the hearth, where he remained standing because decency forbade him to run away and leave Eleanor to face the Family alone.

She flushed a little more brightly than before and replied:

"I don't think there are any conclusions to be drawn,"

"Dear girl—" murmured Miss Editha. Miss Mary fidgeted with her bead bag.

"H'm!" said Grandmamma. She fixed Eleanor with a hard, bright eye. "H'm! My dear Eleanor, am I to conclude that you are so much in the habit of embracing young men as to consider that what we saw requires no explanation? Or am I to understand that a former foolish flirtation between you and David has been revived?"

David came forward.

"Look here, Grandmamma—"

"I was not speaking to you, David," said Grandmamma stiffly; "I was asking Eleanor whether she considered herself engaged to you?"

Eleanor's colour had faded. David had never seen her angry like this before. She was very angry. She spoke very gently and distinctly:

"I am not engaged to David. I think you forget how many years we have known each other and what close friends we are. There is really nothing to explain."

Mrs. Fordyce rubbed the bridge of her nose. Then she folded her hands again.

"I disapprove entirely of marriages between cousins," she said. "I will never consent to your marrying David."

"Oh, dear girl—" moaned Miss Editha.

Eleanor got up.

"There's not the slightest question of my marrying David." She slipped her hand inside his arm and held it tightly. "We're just the very, very best friends in the world. I—I'm going to marry Tommy Wingate."

The moment she had said it, Eleanor let go of David's arm and sat down again. She was perfectly calm, but very cold. She had not known that she was going to say it; she had not even known that she was going to do it; she had heard her own voice saying the words, and that was all. She had burned her boats with a vengeance.

Ten minutes later David disentangled himself from the Family and took his leave. Eleanor had been cried over, fussed over, warned, lectured, and, finally, blessed. It had been established that Tommy had been known and approved by her late parents; it had also transpired that he possessed an income independent of his profession. It was at this point that Grandmamma thawed. She had a very sincere respect for young men of independent means, and remarked with decision that there did not seem to be as many of them as there used to be.

"And now, my dear, we will return to the subject of Flora."

David departed.

He rang up Eleanor an hour later.

"Have they gone?"

"Yes. Wasn't it awful?" Eleanor sounded a little tremulous.

"Some day," said David, "I shall let Grandmamma have it in the neck. It's what she's wanted all her life."

"David, you can't!"

"I shall," said David. "I was just going to when you cast your bomb. I say, my dear, I'm most awfully glad."

"Oh," said Eleanor, "oh, I don't know what made me say it. I didn't mean to—I didn't know I was going to."

"But you are going to?"

She gave a little shaky laugh.

"I—I suppose so."

David laughed too.

Does Tommy know?" he asked.

"No, he *doesn't*," said Eleanor, and fled.

Chapter Thirty-Eight

DAVID RECEIVED NO ANSWER to the letter which he had written to Heather Down. The hours of the morning dragged interminably.

In the afternoon he went to Martagon Crescent. The little maid opened the door.

"Miss Down's out," she said.

David derived a momentary sense of relief from the fact that she said "out," and not "gone away." All day he had been remembering that Heather Down had said: "You won't see me again." That and her "You'll never be sure" rang dreary changes in his ears.

He asked, "Is Miss Smith in?" and the girl left him standing at the door with an awkward "I dunno. I'll go and see."

She came back in a minute.

"She can't see you," she announced; and she had hardly said the words before Miss Smith came running after her.

"Come in, Mr. Fordyce. Come into my room."

She made him go before her, and shut the door. It was about four o'clock; the light slanting in across dingy roofs and grimy walls was cold and thankless. It served to show that the carpet was darned and the paper stained, but it did not light or cheer the room at all. The gloomy texts frowned from shadowed walls. There was no fire.

Miss Smith, in her black dress with the mourning brooch at her throat, was as sad as the room. She had on a grey checked apron, which she took off and folded with trembling fingers. When she had laid it on a chair, she said in an anxious voice:

"Why did you come?"

David tried to speak reasonably and calmly:

"Did you really expect me to stay away? I wrote to her. Has she had my letter?"

"I can't tell you anything," said Miss Smith. "I can't really."

"Miss Smith—"

"I oughtn't to have seen you. I said I wouldn't see you."

"Why shouldn't you see me?" asked David.

Miss Smith did not answer. She had never come very far into the room, and as he spoke, she went back against the door and made an ineffective movement towards the handle.

"Why shouldn't you see me?" said David gently. "Why are you afraid of me?"

Miss Smith leaned against the door and blinked at him.

"What did you say to her—in the letter? She didn't show it to me. I want to know what you said." She spoke as if she had very little breath, and as if each panting sentence exhausted the small supply.

"I told her—" David broke off short. "It was after I'd seen her here. I went away not knowing what to think. I—I want to do the right thing. If she's Erica, she's my wife; and I want to do what's right to my wife. I had every reason to think she was dead. If she's alive—" He broke off again.

Miss Smith put both hands to her breast; the long, thin fingers with their rough, work-reddened knuckles crossed on the black stuff and pressed it with a certain rigid force against the bony chest below.

"If she's alive—what will you do if Erica is alive?"

"Anything I can—anything she wants me to."

"You'd give out your marriage?"

"Of course."

"You'd do what was right by her—give her her place?"

He said "Of course" again.

Miss Smith put her head back against the door for a moment and shut her eyes. When she opened them they were dry and bright.

"She's not a lady born."

He made a movement of impatience.

"I don't ask about what is past and gone," said Miss Smith; "but I want to know whether you'll do right by her now. I want to know what's in your mind, Mr. Fordyce. She's got her marriage lines, and I want to know whether you're going to treat her as your wife fair and open, or whether it's in your mind to hush things up and pay her to keep out of the way."

David flushed.

"Good Lord!" he said. "What do you take me for?"

"Don't take the Lord's name in vain," said Miss Smith, panting for breath. "How do you mean by her, Mr. Fordyce?"

"I've told you," said David.

"No, you haven't—and I want to know. Is Erica to keep out of the way? Or is she to be your wife and the mistress of your house?"

"Miss Smith," said David earnestly, "I don't know how to convince you. If Erica's alive, I only want to make amends to her for what she must have suffered. There's no question of concealment—there's no question of any of the things you've been asking me. If she's Erica, she's my wife, and Ford is her home."

He was using the words he had used to Folly, and they brought her up before him—vivid, anguished. For an instant it was her face he saw; and his own changed so suddenly that Miss Smith gave a startled cry:

"What is it—Mr. Fordyce?"

"It's nothing."

David recovered himself with an effort. Folly was gone.

Miss Smith came forward slowly. She came right up to him and laid a hand on his arm.

"You mean what you say?" There was something strained about the intensity of her look. David met it very steadily.

"Why won't you believe me?"

"Oh," said Miss Smith a little wildly, "perhaps I don't want to believe you. Mr. Fordyce, are you honest? Will you put your hand on the Bible and swear that you're honest?"

"I will if you want me to," said David. He did not know what was behind all this, but the feeling that there was something behind it gained upon him.

Miss Smith went over to the rose-wood table. She lifted the heavy Bible from the pink and green wool mat on which it lay. With trembling hands she brought it to the edge of the table and rested it there.

"Put your hand on it and swear that you mean honestly by Erica. I don't ask anything about the past; but can you swear that you mean honestly and openly by her now?"

"Yes, I can," said David. He put his hand on the worn, black cover and said: "I swear that I mean honestly by her."

Miss Smith's eyes wavered and fell. She let go of the Bible and stepped back.

"You mean honestly," she said. "I think—I think you're honest. I think—oh, I think I'm a very wicked woman." She clutched at a chair and sat down on the edge of the black horse-hair seat; her hands fell into her lap as if she could not hold them up any longer.

David was appalled at her look. He said very gently:

"Why are you wicked?"

"I didn't think you were honest—and I've not been honest myself. I rebuked you for taking the Lord's name in vain, but I've taken it in vain myself getting on for three years, for I've called myself a Christian, and I've been living a lie. Only at first I wasn't sure, and it's hard—oh, it's hard to go to the workhouse." Her voice trembled lower and lower till the last word was just a horrified breath.

David took a chair, pulled it up close to her, and sat down. Betty's tears had never accustomed him to seeing a woman weep, and the slow, cold drops that were rolling down Miss Smith's lined cheeks touched his pity to the quick. She looked the frailest and forlornest thing on earth.

"Won't you tell me about it?" he said. "You're very unhappy. Won't you tell me why?"

Miss Smith looked down at her hands. Those slow tears went on falling.

"I was too ill at first," she said. "It's not wicked to make a mistake. The wickedness came in when I began to think it might be a mistake and I wouldn't face it. That was when I began to be wicked."

"What did you make a mistake about?"

"About her," said Miss Smith. "If you're honest, I can't go on with it. I didn't think you were honest; but two wrongs don't make a right."

He put his hand over one of hers.

"Miss Smith—what was the mistake you made?"

She lifted her drowned, desolate eyes to his.

"I thought she was Erica," she said in a whispering voice; the words only just reached him though he was so near.

He said: "You thought—don't you think so now?"

Miss Smith shook her head.

"Who is she?"

"I don't know."

She drew away her hand, took out a handkerchief, and dried her eyes. A little strength returned to her voice.

"Erica wrote to me after her father died. She said she was going to her aunt in Sydney. Then I didn't hear any more. I wrote, and my letters came back. It troubled me very much, but I kept on thinking that I should hear from her, or that she would come. I got to think that I didn't hear because she was coming home. I thought about it a lot, because things were going very badly for me. There's a mortgage on the house, and it was getting more and more difficult to keep up the payments. I thought if Erica came home she'd help me."

"I'm sure she would have helped you," said David.

"I thought she would. Then I got ill. It was just after Colonel March and his daughter were here. I was very ill, and they told me I talked about Erica all the time—they said I seemed to be looking for her." She paused, and added in a lower voice: "Then *she* came."

"Heather Down?"

"Yes," said Miss Smith, wiping her eyes again. "She came, and I thought she was Erica—oh, I did think so. And I began to get well."

"Did she say she was Erica?" asked David.

"I don't know." Miss Smith looked bewildered. "It's all so confused. She called me Aunt Nellie and she paid for everything. Of course I could never have let her do that unless—unless she was my own niece."

"What happened when you got better?"

"She told me—not all at once, you know, but a bit at a time—that she'd been married, and that her husband had deserted her, and that she'd come home to find him, and that she wasn't using her own name till the right time came. She said she was calling herself Heather Down. She said Erica was a foreign name for heather—and of course Moor and Down are pretty much the same thing. She was very bitter about men, and about her husband, and marriage, and being deserted. She wanted to punish you, Mr. Fordyce."

"Yes, she told me so. When did you begin to think she wasn't Erica?"

"I don't know," said Miss Smith weakly. "It just came to me. There was a photograph of her father, and she didn't know who it was. It wasn't a good one, but I thought she would have known it. And there were things she didn't remember, and—and it began to come to me. Only I wouldn't let it come, because if she wasn't Erica, I couldn't let her pay for things like she was doing." She laid her wet handkerchief on her lap and plucked at the edge. "It's her money that keeps me going; and if she's not my niece I can't take it, and then—there's only—the workhouse. I've been living a lie because I didn't dare to face it. She's not Erica, Mr. Fordyce, and I can't take her money any more."

There was a quick step in the passage and the door was flung open. Heather Down came in.

Chapter Thirty-Nine

SHE STOPPED in the middle of the room. Miss Smith put a shaking hand on the back of the chair and stood up.

"I had to do it," she said. "I couldn't go on—I had to do it."

"What have you done?" said Heather Down.

"I had to," said Miss Smith. She went to the door and opened it. "I had to do it," she said again. "And may the Lord forgive me for not having done it before."

She went out of the room and shut the door.

"What has she done?" said Heather Down sharply. "Look here, David Fordyce—"

"She's upset," said David. "Let her alone. I want to talk to you."

He thought she hesitated. Then she said, rather defiantly:

"Well, we can't talk in the dark. This blindman's holiday sort of business is enough to upset anyone. Pull those curtains over while I light the gas."

The yellow light flared out and showed him Miss Down in her red coat and bright pink hat.

"Now," she said. "What have you been saying to upset Aunt Nellie? I told her not to see you. I tell you I won't have her upset like this."

"Miss Smith is upset," said David, "because she does not believe that you are her niece. She has just told me so."

"That's not true."

"It is perfectly true."

"She does believe it."

"No, she does not. She only really believed it whilst she was ill. Ever since she has pretended to herself and to you because, she says, she can't go on taking money from you if you're not really her niece, and she's horribly afraid of the workhouse."

Heather Down cried out and clapped her hands together:

"Oh, if I didn't hate you before, I'd hate you for this!"

"Don't be silly!" said David. It was easy enough to talk to Heather Down if she were Heather Down and not Erica. "Why do you talk like that? I shan't let her go to the workhouse—you might know that. I think I could persuade her that there's no reason why I shouldn't help her a bit. You see, I really am a nephew by marriage. I think I shall be able to get over her conscience all right with that. And now let's have things out. Why do you say you hate me? What have you got to hate me for? You're not Erica."

Heather Down stood under the gas-light. Her hands were clenched at her sides. The left hand was ringless. She said vehemently:

"I never said I was."

"Didn't you? You went pretty near it, I think. You tried your level best to make me believe that you were Erica. You wanted me to believe that I was bound to you. You said you wanted to punish me. Why?"

"Because you deserted Erica."

"Do you really believe that? Come, Miss Down, won't you tell me the whole thing? I think you knew Erica—I think you must have cared for her."

"Yes, I did."

"Won't you tell me about it? I don't know anything except that, somehow, she survived the wreck. I don't know how. I don't know anything except—You'll tell me now, won't you, whether she's alive?"

"She died more than four years ago," said Heather Down in a dull, sullen voice.

David turned away and walked to the window. He pulled back one of the bright, flimsy curtains and looked out into the dusk. Vague outlines of dark houses; lighted squares which were windows; a misty, darkening sky. He turned back again. Heather Down saw how pale he was.

"Will you tell me how it all happened?" he said. "I put her in the second boat, and it was never heard of again. How did she escape?"

"She didn't stay in it. You never thought of that, I suppose. She was awfully frightened, and she wanted to stay with you. The first boat upset whilst they were lowering it, and when she saw that, she climbed down on to the deck again. She was going to look for you, but it was all dark and she got very frightened. One of the officers came up to her, and he said, 'You're Miss Baker? There's a place for you here.' He took her by the arm, and she said, 'No—no.' Eva Baker was the girl who was in her cabin. She was little and slight like Erica. The officer got Erica half across the deck, and then she fainted. When she came to she was in a boat with a lot of other people. I think something had hit her head—she said she felt all queer and didn't know who she was or where she'd got to. She remembered taking her rings and hanging them on the little chain that she wore round her neck. She thought she did it partly because of not getting the turquoises in her engagement ring spoilt with the sea-water, and partly because people round her called her Miss Baker, and she said she thought she oughtn't to be wearing a wedding ring. She was all confused and light-headed, poor kid. And that was the last thing she remembered. The boat was picked up by the *Lennox*. Erica was still unconscious when she was landed at Cape Town. Everyone thought she was Eva Baker."

"Who was Eva Baker?" said David. He remembered her vaguely. Erica had not liked her very much.

"Eva Baker was my uncle's granddaughter. He hadn't ever seen her, because she'd always lived in Australia, and she was coming to make her home with him after her mother died. Erica came to his house as Eva Baker, and for six months no one thought anything else. Then Erica began to come to herself, and she told us who she was."

"Six months?" said David.

"Yes, she was queer in her head, you know. I was nursing her most of the time. I took away the rings so that no one should see them. She used to talk a lot—conversations with you, and with that woman she stayed with in Sydney. She used to say the things over and over like a gramophone record till I got to know them by heart. I thought some man had got her into trouble, poor kid, and I wouldn't let anyone else hear her. Then she came to, and she told us she wasn't Eva at all. She told us she was Mrs. David Fordyce."

She looked at him accusingly.

"My uncle didn't believe her at first—I'd a work to make him. But after a bit we could all see she was quite sensible in her mind. She wrote to you—I helped her with the letter. That's how I knew what was in it. And uncle wrote. That was the first letter. It was posted the first week in September."

David nodded.

"Well, then, we waited for you to answer—and you didn't answer."

"Why didn't you cable?"

"Uncle wouldn't. He was old fashioned and had a horror of telegrams and things like that. I very nearly sent one on my own, but by the time I'd worked myself up to it, it was getting on for time for your answer to come; so I waited."

"Why didn't you cable when the answer didn't come?"

"She wrote the second letter," said Heather Down. "I helped her with it, and I registered it for her. And she died two days afterwards—just slipped away in her sleep."

She began to cry and to rub away the tears with the back of her hand. Then all at once she threw back her head.

"I promised myself then that I'd punish you, and when you didn't answer the second letter, I hated you so that I could hardly bear it. I'd not much use for men anyway—I'd been let down myself when I was no older than Erica; and I thought to myself, 'I can't punish *him*'—he'd gone away and I didn't even know his right name—'but if I ever get a chance of punishing David Fordyce, I'll do it, and I'll reckon I'm paying my own account as well as Erica's.'"

"I see," said David. "Why did you wait so long?"

"I waited because I had to. Needs must when necessity drives. I was in a manicure business—partner with the woman who started it, and I couldn't leave her in the lurch. And I couldn't leave uncle. I was very fond of him, and he was all broken up about Eva and about Erica. When he died, I sold my share of the business and came over here. I hadn't got any plan in my head. I came to look for Erica's Aunt Nellie, and I found her ill and down to her last penny. And she took me for Erica because her head was full of Erica. Well, I didn't mean to deceive her—I wasn't brought up to tell lies, whatever you may think—but I just hadn't the heart to tell her Erica was dead. I thought it would kill her, so I made up my mind I'd let her go on thinking I was her niece until she was a bit stronger. Well, I never did tell her. I nursed her, and I got fond of her. You get awfully fond of people when they've got nobody but you. I got to know pretty soon that she wouldn't let me help her unless she thought I was Erica, and after a bit I just let it go at that. She hadn't anyone, and I hadn't either, so where was the harm?" She looked defiantly at David. "I wasn't thinking about you at all—not till afterwards. I went on hating you like poison, and one day it came to me that I'd got a way to punish you all ready to my hand, because if Aunt Nellie could take me for Erica, I could play it up on you enough to get you all upset. I went over everything Erica had told me and everything I'd heard her say those nights when she'd go over and over all the things she'd ever said to you, or you to her; and I felt certain I could get you so that you wouldn't know what to believe." She gave a little hard laugh. "I did it too—didn't I? You thought I was Erica. You weren't sure; but you did think so."

David regarded her with some pity.

"What made you ring me up when you did?"

"I'd been finding out about you—I'd been down to Ford two or three times. The last time I went, everyone in the village was talking about you and Mrs. Rayne. They said she was an old sweetheart, and they were all hoping you'd marry her. It made me wild to hear them. And then, on the top of that, I saw your advertisement asking for news of Erica, and I thought to myself, 'Now I'll let you have it.'"

She had been flushed and excited, but suddenly the flush died, her voice went flat.

"Funny—isn't it, the way things turn out? I'd thought about punishing you for years, and it came off better than I ever thought it could. I'd lain awake nights and nights planning what I'd say. And when I'd done it all, I just didn't care a bit. I thought if I could pay you out, that I should feel as if I'd got rid of something. But I didn't—I just felt as if the bottom had dropped out of everything and there wasn't anything left for me to do. That's what I felt like. And then I got your letter, and it made me think perhaps I'd made a mistake. I didn't want to believe it."

"Look here," said David, "can't we be friends? I'd like to be because of what you did for Erica. Why can't you believe I'm honest? I'd like to be friends with you, and then we could join forces and see what can be done for Miss Smith. Can't we be friends?"

"No, we can't," said Heather Down. The high, hard colour came back to her cheeks. "And if you're going to come between me and Aunt Nellie—"

"Miss Down!"

"My name's Ida Baker. And what's the good of your talking about being friends? If Aunt Nellie lets you help her when she won't let me, isn't that coming between us? Do you expect me to stop hating you? If you had come out to Cape Town, Erica would have gone away with you and wouldn't have cared if she never saw me again. I used to hate you when I thought about it. And now you want to take Aunt Nellie from me. And you talk about being friends—*friends!*" Her voice rose sharply. "You'd better let me alone, David Fordyce, or I'll do you a mischief yet."

She stared at him for a moment, and then went out of the room, slamming the door behind her.

Chapter Forty

DAVID WENT BACK to his rooms. The certainty that Heather Down was not Erica had released him from the intolerable burden which he had been carrying. It had been very horrible to think of Erica changed into this bitter, twisted creature; and horrible to feel himself bound by an intimate tie to a woman whose hatred and resentment spoke in every word and look. He had again his gentle, pitiful memories of the child who had been his wife for a fortnight.

He wrote a long letter to the solicitor who had acted for him in Cape Town, repeating Heather Down's statement and asking him to verify it. He wrote also to Miss Smith.

All this time he kept himself from thinking about Folly; and yet all the time it was just as if she were there at the door, clamouring to be let in, calling to him. A sense of uneasiness which was past his own control gained upon him.

He rang up Eleanor, and was told that she was dining out and had just started. Somehow this piece of news immensely increased his uneasiness. At the back of his mind there had been the feeling that Eleanor was there to turn to. Now Eleanor was not there any more.

He walked up and down the room calling himself every sort of fool, but unable to rid himself of the insistent sense that Folly was calling to him. He had been engaged to dine with Frank and Julie, but had put them off. Now he would have been glad to go. Anything was better than to stay here alone, a prey to overstrained imaginings.

The telephone bell rang, and his mood underwent a change. It might be Frank Alderey; and suddenly he felt an extreme disinclination to go out. He took up the receiver impatiently, and heard the voice that had been crying in his ears for an hour—Folly's voice, quick and unsteady.

"David!" The name came to him, and then a confusion of sound and a click.

He called, and got no answer. After several efforts, he got the exchange.

"I've been cut off."

"What number?"

"I don't know the number. They rang me up."

After a second attempt he got a short "No reply from the number."

He left the telephone with his mind clearly made up. It was not for nothing that he had thought he heard Folly calling him; his dislike and distrust of Floss Miller came up like a tide. Folly had called to him, and nothing should keep him from going to her. He blessed the memory that never forgot an address as he hailed a taxi and gave the man the direction which Floss Miller had given him the night they had met at The Luxe.

At the entrance to the block of flats he told the driver to wait and took the lift to the fifth floor. As he stepped out of it, the door in front of him opened. Mrs. Miller in a black and silver coat with a very handsome grey fox collar stood on the threshold.

As he came towards her, she exclaimed and took a half involuntary step backwards, and at the same moment David, with every sense strained to the utmost, heard distinctly the sound of a turning key. He reached the doorway as Mrs. Miller, recovering herself, came forward.

"I'm just going out," she said.

"So I see," said David.

He was most keenly aware of everything—the dark cage of the lift behind him on the left; the lighted hall of Mrs. Miller's flat with its pink-shaded drop-light; and away on the right the closed door from which had come the click of the turning key.

He said: "Is Folly in? I wanted to see her."

Mrs. Miller made another step forward. She was heavily powdered and, under the powder, very heavily flushed; her eyes were rather vacant; the step she had just taken was unsteady. He realized with disgust that she was half drunk already.

He repeated his question sharply:

"Is Folly in? I want to see her."

"Well, you can't," said Mrs. Miller. She leaned against the door-post. "You can't see her to-night. And I'm going out. Tell you what, you come along with me and we'll be a nice little family party. I'm dining with Francis Lester—he's a very great friend of mine. You come along with me and we'll be a nice little family party." Her voice slid thickly over the consonants. She put a hand on David's sleeve and smiled at him. It was a horrible ghost of what had once been an enchanting smile. "Come along," she said.

"Where's Folly?" said David.

Mrs. Miller stepped out into the hall and pulled at his arm.

"Other fish to fry. You come along with me."

Then she came back and took hold of the handle to close the door. David stood his ground, half in, half out of the flat.

"I'd like to see her if she's in," he said. Then he raised his voice and called, "Folly!"

His ear had been straining for any sound from behind the door on the right. Now a sound came in answer to his call, a desperate, broken little sound. He turned his back on Floss Miller, walked to the door, tried the handle, and spoke through the panel:

"Folly, are you there?"

There was no answer.

"Open the door or I shall break the lock! Open it at once!"

Floss Miller's voice called his name:

"Look here, David Fordyce—"

"Open this door!" said David.

The key turned in the lock, and with a wrench David opened the door and took a step into the room.

It was the drawing-room of the flat. There was an overwhelming impression of pink lights, pink cushions, scent, and cigarette smoke. Mr. St. Inigo leaned against a rose-coloured sofa with his hands in his pockets, and on the far side of the room David saw Folly. She was up against the wall with a tall chair in front of her; her hands were clenched on the top of the chair; her face was of an agonized, terrified pallor.

"Don't you know when you're not wanted?" said Mr. St. Inigo.

David took no notice of him. He went to Folly and touched her arm. It was quite rigid. He said, so low that only she could catch the words:

"Has he hurt you?"

She moved her head a very little. The movement said "No."

David crossed the room again. He addressed St. Inigo:

"Get out of this at once!"

There was something about the pale lounging figure that made David hope that he would not go; he wanted to hit St. Inigo; he wanted to kill him. He held himself in and said:

"Get out!"

St. Inigo began to say something, but before the half of it was said, David's fist took him on the mouth and he went down sprawling.

Mrs. Miller screamed. She stood back against the wall and watched St. Inigo being run out of the flat. The door shut upon him.

"You're strong!" said Floss Miller, as David came back. She spoke in an admiring tone.

"I'm taking Folly away," said David.

Mrs. Miller shrugged her shoulders.

"What a fuss about nothing!"

David went back into the drawing-room. The room filled him with disgust—the whole place filled him with disgust—Mrs. Miller made him feel physically sick. His mind was bent on getting Folly out of this beastly place. He went over to her and told her so.

"I'm going to take you away. You'd no business to have come here. I'm going to take you back to Eleanor."

Folly had not moved. Her hands still gripped the back of the chair with so much force that the knuckles showed white on the little straining hands. David unclasped the hands.

"Pull yourself together. Where's your room—where are your things? Can you get them?"

She made again the movement that said "No."

David's voice hardened.

"You must pull yourself together. I want to get you away. Where's your room?"

She moved then in the direction of the hall; with David's hand on her shoulder they came past Floss Miller to a door at the far end. David opened it—Folly's room; her hat thrown down on the bed; an evening dress across the pillow; trifles scattered everywhere. He left the door open. Folly sat down on the edge of the bed and stared in front of her.

"Can't you pack?" He spoke sharply and felt desperate. What on earth would he do if she fainted? She looked ghastly. Every moment that they stayed here added to his impatience. To get her away, to get her out of this horrible place, was all that mattered.

Folly shook her head. She could not tell David that the room was full of mist—thick, white, baffling mist; and on the mist, like a picture on a screen, Floss Miller's face, smiling. She could not tell David this; she could only sit still and hold on desperately to the fact that he was here.

After one glance at her, David let her alone. He pulled out the trunk which stood in the corner of the room and put into it everything that he could find. Then he strapped the box, took it through the hall, and put it outside the door of the flat. The hall was empty.

He went back for Folly. She was still sitting on the edge of the bed, still looking into the mists in which she saw Floss Miller's face, Floss Miller's smile. He put her hat on her head and pushed her arms into her fur coat as if she had been a child. Then he put his arm round her and set her on her feet. She was quite passive, but to his relief she was able to stand. He took her through the hall, and, as they reached the door, Floss Miller came out of the dining-room, and the smell of brandy came with her. She spoke, and at the sound of the thick voice Folly gave a sort of shaken sigh.

"Well," said Mrs. Miller, "I don't care which of you gets her. Always back the strongest—that's a good plan, isn't it? That's my plan, anyway." She came a step nearer and dropped her voice a little. "I say, David Fordyce, Stingo said he'd pay my debts. I suppose you'll do as much?"

He felt Folly quiver. She pressed against him. Her voice came back in a dreadful gasping whisper:

"Don't listen to her—David—don't—she's my mother!"

All of a sudden David understood. It was not St. Inigo but Floss Miller who had brought that look of dazed agony to Folly's face. It was a betrayal of the most intimate sanctities and loyalties of a very loyal heart. It was the betrayal of woman by woman that had left Folly so helpless before St. Inigo. He felt the greatest passion of anger of which a man is capable, and another deeper, stronger passion of protecting love. His arm closed hard about Folly. There was nothing to be said. It was finished.

He lifted her over the threshold and shut the door on Floss Miller and her flat.

Chapter Forty-One

DURING THE DRIVE to Chieveley Street, David did not speak at all. They went up in the lift and rang the bell of Eleanor's flat. No one came. David rang again, and the sound of the faint, shrill ringing died away. He spoke then, almost angrily:

"Eleanor's dining out, but there ought to be someone in the flat. What's happened to them?"

Folly answered.

"Not if she's dining out. She lets them go to the pictures." She spoke in a small weak voice, but it had lost the hoarse, unnatural quality which had frightened him; it was her own voice again, small and faint.

"Oh, Lord!" said David. "What are we going to do?"

"I've got my key." Then, after a pause and a long sigh: "It was in my bag."

"Your red bag? I shoved it in the top of the box."

"Yes, it's there."

He got out the bag, found the key, and opened the door. It was like the first time he had brought her here—like and yet different. He had been angry with her then; now he knew that he loved her utterly, and that to meet her need he must be mother, brother, friend, and lover all in one.

He put on the lights, and they came into the drawing-room. It was warm, and the fire not yet out. In the lap of the largest chair lay Timmy very fast asleep.

When he had revived the fire, David went and foraged in the kitchen. He came back presently with eggs, hot soup, and coffee, to find Folly sitting forward on the sofa with her elbows on her knees and her chin in her hands, staring at the fire.

He made her eat, and when she had finished he heaped cushions behind her.

"I shall stay till Eleanor gets back."

"'M—" said Folly. Then, after a pause: "You're kind."

David's eyes stung; the words were said so childishly.

She had taken off her fur coat. Her dress was the pink one she had worn at Ford when she had first tied on the little black curls and asked him if he liked them. She had short curls of her own now, which only covered her ears halfway. Her small black head lay back against a pale blue cushion. The colour had come to her lips again, but her cheeks were pitifully white, and there were blue smudges under her eyes.

David put his hand on hers and held it in a warm, gentle clasp. After a long time she lifted her lashes.

"Why are you kind?"

"I'll tell you presently."

She sighed deeply.

"I tried to call you."

"I heard you."

"Did you? I didn't think you could. I only had time to call once."

"You'd been calling me for an hour before the telephone bell rang at all."

"Had I? I didn't know. They came—I couldn't go on."

David's hand tightened on hers.

"Don't talk about it."

Her eyelids closed.

"I can't—ever."

"I don't want you to."

He got up, because, just for the moment, he couldn't bear to be so near her and not take her in his arms. But she looked up at once with a little cry:

"Where are you going?"

"Only to put some coal on the fire."

When he came back she sat up a little and stretched out her hands towards him.

"You won't go till Eleanor comes?"

He shook his head. Then, as he took the cold hands in his, she gave a little sob.

"Don't go! I'm frightened."

David went down on his knees and put his arms round her.

"My darling little thing—my darling, darling little thing!" he said.

There was just a moment when she clung to him, trembling. Then he felt her draw back; her hands pushed him from her.

"Folly—my little darling!"

She shrank into the far corner of the sofa.

"No—I'm not."

"Didn't you know it? Didn't you know how much I cared?"

She shook her head; her eyes were wide and blank.

"I couldn't tell you, because I didn't know if I was free. I saw Heather Down this afternoon, and she told me that she wasn't Erica. She told me Erica died in Cape Town more than four years ago."

Folly's eyes lost their unseeing look. She said:

"I'm glad you know. It's dreadful not to be sure—it's dreadful to feel you have to love someone whom you *can't*. Sometimes you *can't*."

He knew she was thinking of Floss Miller.

He said: "I didn't mean to tell you that I cared. I meant to wait. But I can't see you like this and not comfort you with all the love I've got."

Folly gave a little cry. She caught at the arm of the sofa and stood up.

"No—no—*no!*" she said. "No—no, it's not true. *Oh, it isn't!*" She spoke in a horrified whisper.

"Folly!"

"No, it isn't true. David—it isn't. *David!*"

"Of course it's true," said David. "My little darling!"

"Oh!" said Folly. It was a bitter little cry that wrung his heart.

"Folly, what is it? I love you with all my heart."

She said "No" on a quick, shuddering breath, and then: "Did you think I would? Did you think I'd take you from Eleanor? Oh *no!*"

"Folly, darling—what nonsense!"

She came up to him and caught his arm.

"It's not nonsense. You're hers—you're not mine. I always thought you were hers, and I flirted with you. Yes, I know I flirted, but I wanted to see if you were a beast like Stingo—I wanted to see if you were good enough for Eleanor—I wanted to be sure she was going to have a real chance of being happy. She wasn't happy with Cosmo Rayne— nobody could have been happy with him. I *want* her to be happy. You mustn't love me." She shook the arm that she was holding; the vehement colour came up in her cheeks like a flame. "You mustn't— you *mustn't!* You must love Eleanor."

David put his other arm round her.

"Then Tommy Wingate'll break my head," he said gravely.

"Why will he?"

"Because Eleanor's going to marry him."

Folly stared with all her eyes.

"Who said so?"

"Eleanor did."

"Ooh! David—she *didn't!*"

"Folly, she did." He laughed a little unsteadily. "She said it in front of Grandmamma, and Aunt Editha, and Aunt Mary, and Timothy and me."

"Ooh!" said Folly again. "You're sure?"

"Ask Timothy—or Grandmamma. Now am I allowed to love you? Or must I have a hopeless passion for Mrs. Tommy Wingate?"

Folly flung her arms round his neck.

"David—no, David, I want to say something. No, David, I want to say it in your ear."

"What is it, you silly little thing?"

"David—are you *sure* you don't love her?"

"I'm quite sure. I love you. I love you so much that I don't know how to say it. Do you love me?"

"I don't know. Do I?"

"I think you do."

"I don't know," said Folly in a troubled voice. She put up her face to be kissed like a child. "It's been hurting so. Why did it hurt?"

The tears were running down her cheeks.

"David—will it go on hurting like that? I didn't ever mean to be in love with anyone—I didn't. I hate men, really; only I like to flirt. I don't know why, but I do. I loved flirting with you, but I never, never, *never* meant to fall in love."

She slipped out of his arms with a quick shrinking movement and stood away from him with her hands at her breast; her colour came and went.

"If you *love* people—it hurts. They—let you down." She took a long sighing breath. "Eleanor—Eleanor and Cosmo—she got hurt—he let her down."

She paused again, then said in a trembling whisper:

"Floss."

David did not move or touch her. He looked into her eyes, and he saw things that he never forgot—a child's gay bravado shocked into terror, a child's loyalty and trust betrayed.

She met his look. There was silence between them, a long, long silence; her eyes looked into his. Then he saw something rise up, clear and shining. It was something new. It was Folly's love for him.

He spoke to her very gently.

"Do you think I would hurt you? Do you think I would let you down?"

That shining love looked out of Folly's eyes.

"No, David," she said.

Suddenly she ran into his arms.

"Ooh!" she said. "You *wouldn't*."

THE END

Printed in Great Britain
by Amazon

29580774R00119